A Mistletoe Vow to Lord Lovell is dedicated to
everyone who helped, supported, listened to me and
walked with me through the difficult times this year.

To my husband, parents, family, friends: thanks.
I couldn't have done it without you.

Chapter One

❧❧❧

1817

There was someone in the house.

Even in the frozen darkness of a December night Honora Blake could sense it. A thrill of instinctive caution had roused her from her sleep, but she was not afraid.

She possessed courage to match any man's—as well as a flintlock pistol on her bedside table, and she was an excellent shot. A childhood spent in the shadow of Virginia's Blue Ridge Mountains under her father's tutelage had seen to that. Felling a bear at twenty paces did wonders for a girl's confidence.

Honora lay perfectly still, ears straining to catch another tell-tale creak of uneven floorboards. Usually the tired old house of which she despaired gave her nothing but trouble, with its leaking roof and draughty doors, but tonight its groans were allies, helping her track the steps of whoever was moving about downstairs.

They weren't even bothering to try to keep quiet, she thought with a flicker of irritation. Would they have been so brazen if she still had a husband? Did they imagine a woman on her own was too weak to challenge them?

If that's what they're thinking, they're due a surprise. Whoever it is creeping around my parlour will soon wish they hadn't.

The mournful keening of the wind outside her window covered the sound of Honora's light step as she slipped from her bed and threw a shawl over her nightgown. Her hand was steady as she retrieved the flintlock and checked the muzzle, holding it up in the dim moonlight filtering through ill-fitting shutters.

Since her husband had vanished into thin air she'd had to fend for herself, the wretch having disappeared without a backward glance when the money he'd been counting on showed no signs of appearing.

She cursed herself daily now for allowing him to turn her head, travelling with him to England and actually thinking herself lucky to be his bride. Frank Blake was so *handsome*, so dazzling with his charm and wit and way of making a person feel they were the only one in the room and he'd come along just as Honora was beginning to believe nobody would ever place a ring on her finger. Ma and Pa had tried to reason with her, sensing he was not all he seemed, but Honora had loved Frank so hopelessly that their pleas only made her more determined to prove them wrong and nothing would satisfy her but crossing the churning Atlantic to become Mrs Blake.

The wedge that Honora's stubbornness had driven between her and her parents only increased over time, that final bitter argument on the day she'd boarded the boat and sailed away from them more painful than ever now that Honora had to admit they'd been right. How could she ever face them again, knowing how poorly she had repaid their concern—with angry words and defiance, wounding the two people who loved her more than anything else in the world? How could she return to them, knowing how little she deserved the heartfelt welcome they would give her?

I can't, that's how—which is why I still find myself here. Thousands of miles from home, the mistress of a house crumbling all around me and a good-for-nothing husband I haven't seen in three years. If only I'd listened, hadn't thought I knew best, I could have saved myself this misery—a naive bride at twenty-something, now a worn-out cynic of thirty-five. And now there's an intruder in my parlour. That's all I need.

Steeling herself against the cruel chill of the night, she crossed the room and pressed an ear against the bedroom door. From the other side of it came the vague sounds of someone blundering in the darkness. With her full lips pressed into a tight line, Honora eased open the door, wincing at the squeak of its hinges. Whoever was below evidently didn't hear, however, and she slid from the room without a further sound, one hand holding her shawl close to her chest and the other firmly grasping the flintlock's wooden grip.

Careful now. Go slowly.

She crept down the landing towards the stairs and peered through the banisters. The hall below was shrouded in darkness and for the first time Honora felt a shiver of apprehension prickle up her spine. Brave or not, she was still entirely alone at Wycliff Lodge, half a mile of Somerset countryside lying between her and her nearest neighbour. Her maid, Mary, had gone back to her cottage for the night and wouldn't return until the next day, the only help Honora could still afford and, after years of service, now more a friend than a servant—which was just as well, for nobody else seemed particularly interested in getting to know her.

Perhaps it was the colour of Honora's skin that troubled those living nearby, a soft tawny bronze courtesy of her father's African heritage, or the fact she'd survived alone in the crumbling old house ever since Frank abandoned her. Only her presence stopped it from falling down completely, the sole reason Frank allowed her to stay on in a property he had no intention of revisiting. Hadn't the doctor's wife even caught her chopping firewood once, a strange display from the equally strange young woman Mr Blake had brought home from the Americas? Whatever stopped her neighbours from coming to take tea was nothing she could change and as the years went by Honora found herself growing accustomed to solitude, her independence blooming with her fierce vow never to depend on a man again…

Another bump, louder this time, came from downstairs and Honora swallowed a jolt of unease. Beneath the thin linen of her nightgown her heart began to jump, the pistol's grip sliding a little as her palm grew damp with sweat. Searching through the gloom, she clamped her fingers tighter around her shawl and descended the stairs, hardly daring to breathe in the now silent night.

Have courage. Think what Ma would do.

As always, even after five years, the thought of her mother gave Honora a pang of homesickness and longing for the woman she missed more than any other. Pa might have taught her to shoot, but surely much of her natural spirit came from Cicily Jackson. It had been the stuff of scandal, a white plantation owner's daughter wedding a freedman, and Honora's grandfather had cut the couple off without a cent. He'd mellowed a little when his granddaughter was born and tried to make amends, but by then the damage had been done. Ma wanted no part in a family that wouldn't welcome her husband, so blinded by their prejudice they would cast out their own flesh and blood.

She and Pa had made their way alone, opposite in so many ways and yet coming together to create Honora, who bridged the gap between them. Her mass of curling black hair and tapered chin came from her father while Ma had contributed wide-set hazel eyes, the best parts of both parents combining to make a striking face not soon forgotten. Mr and Mrs Jackson had hoped their cherished daughter would find a man deserving of her when she came to wed, their pride and joy sure to attract the very best of husbands...but instead it had been Frank Blake who came to call, damn him, his lies and false promises blinding Honora to all good sense and tearing the family apart.

She reached the hall and stood for a moment to collect herself. The parlour lay to her left, the door slightly ajar and footsteps muffled by tattered carpet just audible above the rapid beat of her heart. If it pounded any harder she feared the trespasser might hear it, the hand that clutched her shawl to her chest feeling how it railed against her ribs. On the other side of that door lurked who knew what, perhaps a thief or perhaps something altogether more frightening, and the only way to know for sure was to push it open and look inside—

The first glimmer of light took her by surprise, flaring round the edge of the door frame and faintly illuminating the chilly hall. Surely nobody could be so brazen as to break into the Lodge and then *light a fire*, making themselves quite at home—could they? Hardly able to believe her eyes, Honora stiffened as the light grew stronger, the only explanation one she could hardly credit.

They've lit the candles? They've come into my house in the middle of the night, made a fire and lit my good candles? The ones I have to ration to last out the winter? How dare they!

A spark of temper erupted in her chest, warming her despite the cold draught that crept beneath the front door. Whoever this person was had gone too far in their arrogance and, with anger masking the fear of moments before, Honora gathered her courage and burst into the room.

'You can stay *exactly* where you are!'

Honora held the pistol so firmly her knuckles stood out beneath the skin, aiming the muzzle squarely at the strange man kneeling before her fireplace. He started at her sudden appearance and made as if to stand, evidently reconsidering when she waved the flintlock threateningly.

'One more step and it might be your last. You'll tell me who you are and what you mean by skulking around here at this hour.'

The intruder settled slowly back down again on his haunches, never taking his eyes from Honora's rigid face. His own features were difficult to read, although in the light of the dancing flames he didn't look the least bit afraid, instead a decided jaw and straight chestnut brows set in an expression of complete composure. Honora might as well have been holding a bouquet of flowers for all his lack of concern and she felt a gleam of irritation that he was so unmoved. Did he think she was to be trifled with? That because he was handsome she would hesitate to run him off? She had to admit that particular fact, sour though it tasted.

The stranger's dark eyes shone like deep pools in the firelight and his hair, scattered with sparse grey at the temples, was interestingly disordered. It was impossible to tell how tall he was as he crouched on the ground, but he looked around her age, perhaps a few years off forty, with a lean physique beneath expensive clothes that a much younger man would have been proud of. If Honora had seen him five years previously, she couldn't deny he was the kind of man she might have slid a smile, but that was before Frank had taught her the error of her ways, and now she glared at the trespasser so coldly it was a wonder he didn't turn to ice.

'Well?'

'I beg your pardon, ma'am.' The man inclined his head in a gesture that Honora might have found apologetic if she'd been in a more forgiving mood. 'I didn't know you were here. When I saw the state of the place I thought for certain any inhabitants must have shut it up and moved on. I've travelled a long way and thought I'd pass the night here before continuing my search for the mistress in the morning.'

His gaze flickered towards the dingy curtains and a spreading patch of damp that left an ugly stain on the ceiling, and Honora felt herself prickle with sudden shame. It wasn't out of any sort of kindness that Frank had allowed her to carry on living at Wycliff. In fact, quite the opposite. He just didn't care. His complete indifference to her was present in every faded tapestry and broken pane as if he had forgotten she even existed, his apathy the only reason Honora hadn't been thrown out like a pan of ash. Frank had better things to do, other places to live, and Honora doubted he ever spent as much as a moment considering the comfort of the unwanted wife he had left behind.

'Of course I still live here. But who sent you? And you've yet to tell me your name.'

She redoubled her grip on the pistol, bringing her other hand up to cover the first. Even with the muzzle still pointed firmly in his direction the handsome man seemed quite at ease in a way that some part of her could have admired—a dangerous thought she dismissed without hesitation.

Don't be ridiculous. As if arrogance and a half-decent face make the slightest bit of difference to this absurd situation.

'My name is Lord Lovell, Mrs Blake. You *are* Mrs Honora Blake, I presume?'

At Honora's curt nod he began to rise carefully to his feet, holding a steadying hand out towards her when she stiffened. 'It's on account of your husband that I visit you. We met at a card party about eighteen months ago, although it was only *very* recently I learned he was married.'

A swift punch of shock knocked some of the wind from Honora's sails and she leaned back against the door frame, still holding the flintlock, but with suddenly less focus. The mention caught her entirely off guard, so unexpected she only half noticed her mysterious guest take a cautious step forward.

Frank had sent him?

He hadn't bothered to contact her in three years, she thought now with one eye making sure the intruder—*Lord Lovell? How fine Frank's taste in friends has become!*—didn't come any closer. Ever since she'd answered Ma's strained letter those three years previously Frank had been a ghost, disappearing as soon as he learned she had rejected the inheritance her grandfather had left her at his passing. She wanted nothing to do with that money, made on his tobacco plantations by the toil and suffering of slaves. Honora would rather be poor as a church mouse than accept wealth tainted by such cruelty, but Frank had disagreed. He'd been waiting for it to come to her and then to him by law—and when it didn't there was nothing to keep him by his wife's side, only the prospect of a hefty inheritance making it worth his while to stay in a marriage to a woman he had fooled into loving him with no hope of return.

Honora gritted her teeth, her jaw hardening in distaste. Of course Frank and this lord were friends. They were quite similar in a way, she saw now. Both so self-assured and comely enough to catch any woman's eye. No doubt the man in front of her was just as good for nothing as her husband and she felt a sharp stab of dislike lance through her at the thought.

The last thing I want is a friend of Frank's spending another moment in this house. Like attracts like, after all—no man of honour would pursue an acquaintance with my husband, no matter how high and mighty he might be.

'If you expect me to be impressed by your title, I'm afraid you'll be disappointed. Peer or not, you can't go about breaking into other people's homes, even if you do know the owner.'

Lord Lovell shrugged with the perfect confidence of a man accustomed to doing exactly as he liked, when he liked. 'The garden door only needed the slightest persuasion. I said in the darkness this house looked uninhabited. You'll have to forgive my mistake. I'm not sure it's one I could be blamed for making.'

Fresh annoyance coursed through Honora. It was true Wycliff Lodge had seen better days, its decline starting long before Frank brought his heiress bride to England to be its mistress. By the time he left her Honora could do nothing to halt its sorry sinking, the once fine rooms growing dreary and cracks appearing in the outside walls. Only by renting out the handful of fields around the Lodge could she keep the wolf from the door, able to afford essentials but little else.

Ma and Pa would have sent money had she asked, but Honora never would. It would humble her to dust to admit how wrong she'd been about Frank, her stilted and infrequent letters home to Virginia skating over the details of a life she was now ashamed to own. The estrangement between her and her parents was an open wound that hurt her every day, but there was no way of healing it now without the miracle of turning back time.

'That's very well, but it doesn't explain *why* you're here. So, go on. Tell me.' She knew her voice was hard, but she couldn't seem to soften it. Between this aggravating stranger and memories of Frank her chest felt clamped in a vice and cold anger flowed through her like a stream. Hadn't she been imposed upon enough by men who thought charm a fit substitute for morals? Frank hadn't even bothered to come to see her himself, instead sending this man to scare her in the night and then insult her home. Surely Lord Lovell deserved no politeness, tainted by his association with one who had ruined Honora's life.

'What does my fool of a husband want so badly he dispatched you to seek me out? Is it money? He's finally gambled away all of his and now he demands mine? I would hope not, for he knows full well I have none.'

Her unwanted visitor hesitated, for the first time looking unsure, and Honora could have found a grim smile that she had finally discomforted him. No doubt he was more used to women simpering and throwing him admiring glances, his title and admittedly engaging face finding favour wherever he went.

Well, not here and not from me. If Frank sent him, thinking I'd fall prey to his charms, he'll be most put out to find me entirely immune—

Lord Lovell took another step towards her and Honora pulled back, all of a sudden wary at the new seriousness in his face. His brow was creased soberly and his already deep voice lowered when he replied, his words reaching Honora's ears and yet hardly making any sense at all.

'He'd have no need of money, ma'am. I'm sorry to tell you—your husband is dead.'

Isaac watched her fold slowly down on to a threadbare sofa near the door, all the bluster of seconds previous bleeding out, and he hardened his heart against a distant pang of sympathy. The pistol fell from her fingers to land with a soft thud on the floor, but she didn't seem to notice, her now empty hand coming up to cover her mouth.

'Frank? Dead?'

She stared up at him as though half suspecting he was lying, eyes wide and lips parted likewise with disbelief. In her anger she'd been impressive, but now in shock she looked almost vulnerable—although neither state one Isaac had any intention of admiring, under these circumstances or any other.

So. I've done as I determined I would and that's as far as it goes.

A murmur of guilt nagged at him and he turned his face away, determined as ever not to consider it. He had no reason to feel that way and yet still it whispered to him as it had ever since that fateful night one week ago, its voice only intensified by the sight of Frank's striking widow mere feet away from where he stood.

Damn you, Blake. Only revealing the fact you were wed as you lay dying? Leaving me the burden of locating and telling your wife? Perhaps you thought I'd show pity to a married man, but you left me with no choice but to act after what you did to Charlotte, whether you pleaded to be spared or not.

The wife in question sat quite still, sleep-tousled black curls shining in the dancing light of the fire that threw undulating shadows across her amber skin. She was far more attractive than he had expected and briefly Isaac wondered how Frank could have neglected such a unique beauty. His first glimpse of her had been unexpected to say the least. What kind of woman came flying into a room in her nightgown waving a pistol around? She'd been like a Valkyrie swooping down to challenge him, hardly seeming to feel any fear at all. Perhaps it was no wonder Frank had fled from her, that face beguiling but fire lurking behind its angelic façade. He hadn't been a brave man, Isaac thought with a flit of contempt—probably his wife had been too much for him to handle, leading his attention to stray where it never should have...

The thought of poor Charlotte's tear-stained

face made his insides twist and he bit down on a growl as he recalled that terrible night. His young ward was so naive, far too sweet and guileless to have been exposed to a man like Frank Blake…but hadn't Isaac believed Blake to be a friend to him, someone who could be depended on not to treat Charlotte as Isaac had to admit he himself had once treated other women?

Perhaps his conduct hadn't been *quite a*s bad as Frank's, but the fact their friendship had begun with a chance meeting over a rowdy game of cards in some shadowy den, the wine flowing thick and fast and more than one pretty girl catching Lord Lovell's approving eye, didn't reflect well on either man. He couldn't deny Frank had made him laugh with his quick wit and willingness to up the stakes of every game, sometimes playing until the sun rose, and that he'd been pleased to find a friend with whom it seemed he had so much in common…until the truth came out and with it a sense of shame for his rakish actions that Isaac had never felt before.

Charlotte was barely sixteen, damn it, scarcely more than a girl, and by who knew what coaxing Frank had got her with child, then had the gall when confronted to deny it was his. She hadn't even known what was happening when she began to show, hiding her condition beneath loose-fitting gowns and fearing she was grievously ill until finally seeking Isaac's help. What other choice had Isaac had when he discovered the truth but to chase the blackguard down, Frank running for his life but his weak heart close to bursting with every step? Only when he keeled over on the frosty lawn of Lovell's estate, Marlow Manor, did he seem to realise his time had come, with his last breath pleading his married state as though Isaac might show him mercy on account of whatever wretched woman he'd wed.

But he deserved none. It's only as a kind of penance for my own sins that I came to find this Mrs Blake, in some way to make amends for how I behaved before Charlotte was dishonoured by a man who held a mirror up to my own dealings. I see now how actions have consequences I should have considered. For Charlotte's sake from now on I shall strive to do better.

He glanced at Honora, once again trying to take her measure. He'd been anticipating more of a scene and had steeled himself to weather whatever storm of weeping Mrs Blake might rage over his head. Surely most women would have fallen to pieces, he thought as he observed her narrowly, but no such emotion seemed forthcoming, her long lashes bone-dry and, now the first sharp shock had passed, her face settling into determined composure.

Very carefully he moved a little closer, expensive boots scuffing worn carpet. She glanced up at him, a swift suspicious thing that did nothing to dim the pretty hazel of her eyes, and not for the first time Isaac felt an unwelcome glimmer of appreciation for the elegant tilt of her chin.

Attractive. Unusually so. But enough to overcome all good sense? For a moment Isaac's thoughts swerved in the direction of his late father and gave the answer he already knew without a shadow of a doubt.

Absolutely not.

If the previous Lord Lovell had taught his son anything it was the danger of getting too attached, a lesson Isaac had learned well—or too well, given how lightly he had always treated women, now to his lasting shame. Father had married again after the untimely passing of Isaac's mother in childbed, when she had traded her life for that of her wailing son. The new marriage hadn't been a joyful one and as he had grown it pained Isaac to see two lives so ruined by their ill-advised binding together, his childhood marred by shouting and sulks, arguments and bitter tears on both sides. As far as he could tell marriage was a recipe for disaster—sooner or later the arrangement would sour to indifference or rage, leaving behind sorrow that could have been avoided with the absence of a ring.

A wife would only tie him down, an unwanted responsibility likely to make him miserable in the end—he enjoyed female attention on his own terms, and there had never been any shortage of *that*. Only for the begetting of legal heirs was there much of a case for matrimony, but the knowledge he had caused his own mother's death haunted Isaac like an unescapable spectre and always gave him pause whenever the dull matter of progeny crossed his mind. It was better to spare some poor creature the pain and danger of childbirth, he'd resolved years before—something he wished now he might guard Charlotte against, the idea of her sharing the fate of his mother making his blood run cold.

She was the only person in his life he truly cherished, after all, the only family he had left. The orphaned daughter of his late cousin, Charlotte had come to live with him as a sad child of just nine years old and he had grown to love her as if she were his own daughter, making her his sole heir and hiding from her the less admirable side of his character. Just as, he realised now with hideous hindsight, he should have concealed his choice of friends. The poor

motherless girl would become a mother herself
soon enough, with no idea how to go about it
and nobody to guide her, and Isaac had nobody
to blame but himself for allowing that to happen—apart, of course, from Frank Blake, whose
name he had forbidden Charlotte from ever uttering again in his hearing or out and certainly
never beneath the roof of Marlow Manor.

So, no. Honora's loveliness would not be allowed to interest him and was *certainly not*
enhanced by her connection to Frank. Association with such a character did nothing to prompt
fondness, Frank's conduct towards Charlotte
souring any sympathy Isaac might have had for
the wife left behind.

Still. Perhaps I ought to offer some consola-
tion, no matter if I feel the world has suffered
no great loss. It's what she'll be expecting, I
suppose.

'I'm very sorry to bring you such news. Do
you want a glass of something to ease the shock?'

He caught the minute shake of Honora's head,
although whether it was to refuse his sympathy
or the drink he couldn't tell. She still held herself warily, mistrust clear in her every movement and her whole air entirely opposite to that
of most ladies he met. Usually they warmed to
him at once, his face and effortless charm draw-

ing them in—although admittedly he wouldn't often meet one for the first time in the middle of the night after walking uninvited into her house, then proceed to declare the death of her husband.

'You needn't attempt to remain stoic on my account, ma'am. I would not intrude upon your grief.'

The fact she hadn't cried yet was…disquieting. She merely sat, hands folded neatly in her lap, and the green shawl draped around her shoulders shielding the slim lines of her figure from his reluctant gaze. If she had seemed the type to appreciate it he might have taken her hand and pressed her slender fingers, an action that usually prompted delighted flutters from its object. Instead Isaac swallowed down his unease as she slowly turned her head towards him, high cheekbones catching the light to throw her mouth into shadow.

'You mistake me. It isn't stoicism that renders me so quiet. I simply have no tears left to fall. My husband drained that particular river many years before and I ceased crying for him long ago.'

Isaac blinked, caught entirely off guard by her coldness. She was like a woman of fire and ice by turns. Her anger when she first leapt into the room might have burned another man and now her coolness was disconcerting, a contrast that confused him no end. Which was the real Honora Blake? And why was he suddenly, dangerously, struck by the desire to figure out the answer to that question?

'How did it happen? I'd like to know that at least.'

Honora fixed him with a stare so direct Isaac almost looked away. It was no surprise she asked surely the most obvious of questions. She had the right to know, part of him insisted, but another held back.

Wouldn't telling Honora exactly what had happened that night pour fresh disgrace down upon Charlotte's already bowed head? She was beside herself with shame so deep it was agony for Isaac to witness, both for her pregnancy and for believing Frank's lies that he had loved her, even still without knowing he had a wife tucked away in the south. If Isaac confessed he had chased Frank to his death, Honora would want to know why and nothing could persuade him to expose his ward to her contempt. Charlotte had already hidden herself away for her confinement and the baby would need to be explained somehow. For the sake of her precarious reputation the fewer people who knew the whole truth the better. Honora owed him no allegiance and there was nothing to stop her from spreading the tale far and wide should she wish, out of spite or who knew what other reason she might conjure.

'It was his heart. He was calling on me at my home in Northamptonshire, Marlow Manor, and I'm afraid last week it gave out completely. There was nothing to be done.'

'And the funeral?'

'Small but proper. Only myself in attendance.'

The black curls gleamed again as she nodded, apparently lost in thought. What was running through her mind Isaac couldn't say, although Honora showed no sign of suspicion and he felt an absurd flare of relief she didn't question him further. Discussing the night Frank had died was something he would rather avoid and it felt something of a reprieve when she rose slowly to her feet and regarded him closely.

'I still can't say I'm delighted at your method of introduction, but I suppose I appreciate you coming to tell me in person.'

She glanced towards one curtained window where feeble daylight had yet to struggle through. It was difficult to know what time it was, but the shadows beneath her eyes suggested she slept poorly anyway and for the first time a spark of pity surfaced. Honora must have had a difficult time since her husband left and doubtless before that, too—but that was none of his concern. Whatever befell Frank's discomfiting, unfriendly widow was none of his business, no matter how beguiling her countenance.

'There's a spare bedchamber upstairs, first room on the left. As you're here you may as well make use of it. You'll be more comfortable in there than in my parlour.'

He offered a short bow of thanks and she accepted it with a wordless dip of her chin before turning away, retrieving the pistol from the floor as she went. She moved with such purpose and dignity the idea of feeling sorry for her seemed suddenly misplaced, until she paused at the door and looked back, the tired resignation in her face sending a jolt through Isaac he didn't understand.

'Goodnight, Lord Lovell. I hope you sleep well—and don't forget to extinguish those candles. I need them to last until spring.'

Chapter Two

'Who's that man on the landing?'

At Mary's hissed question Honora turned from her bedroom window, still worrying at a cuticle with her teeth. She'd barely slept a wink and had risen early, staring out at the frost-laden trees since dawn and long before her friend arrived to slip through the bedroom door, now hastily closing it behind her as if concerned the strange man might try to follow her inside.

'I didn't dream him, then?'

'I'm afraid not. Would you rather you had?'

Awkwardly the maid set the laden tea tray she bore down on Honora's barely disturbed sheets, cradling her swelling midsection with one hand. She was big with her third child, her two young sons already busy shadowing their father in his work as a carpenter. Honora knew Mary hoped for a girl this time, but whatever baby was born to her would be very much loved, an emotion that with a sharp pang Honora now wished, not for the first time, she had been able to experience for herself.

And now I suppose I never will. While Frank lived there was the smallest chance he might have returned one day and given me a child— now I don't even have that.

For two long years Honora had prayed each month might be the one she missed her course and knew a life had begun inside her, only giving up her hopes when Frank disappeared without trace. He'd claimed his marital rights until the very end, she thought bitterly, all the while feeling nothing for her. Doting on Mary's two boys and the new baby yet to arrive was her only consolation, all possibility of a son or daughter of her own now gone along with the loss of her husband.

Is it a loss? Is that how I feel? I can still hardly tell.

Despite lying all night staring up at the darkened ceiling she was no closer to working through her complicated emotions. She hadn't been able to stop a few quiet tears from creeping beneath her lashes to run down on to the pillow, far more than Frank deserved, but Honora wasn't entirely made of ice as she'd wanted Lord Lovell to believe. The man who had once held her heart in his hand was dead, although the fact that he had gone on to crush it so completely couldn't be denied and the most painful confusion wrestled within her. Once upon a time Frank had been all she had wanted in the entire world, even at the expense of her poor parents, but for three years he had been only an unhappy memory— and now, on top of everything else, she had to face the prospect of one of his cronies loitering around her house.

At the thought of Lord Lovell's handsome face Honora's lip twisted and she waved Mary towards a chair.

'If I *had* dreamed him, I think it would have been more of a nightmare. Sit down before you fall down and I'll tell you.'

With uncharacteristic obedience the maid dropped heavily into the plump old armchair and waited with clear curiosity as Honora settled her shawl more warmly around thin shoulders. Now the time had come to put Lord Lovell's news into words she hardly knew where to begin, her jumbled emotions and the bizarre events of the night making it a difficult task.

'Surely it's far too early for paying calls. You didn't say you were expecting company today.'

'I wasn't. I'd never seen him—Lord Lovell—

before he arrived a few hours ago. He just appeared out of nowhere in the middle of the night. By the time I'd discovered what he wanted it was so late I offered him a bed, although why he's now lurking about on the landing I can't tell you.'

Mary leaned forward sharply. 'He's been here all night? A strange man, who appeared unannounced out of the dark?'

'Unfortunately so.'

Honora saw Mary's shoulders tense with horror. 'You offered him a bed while you were all alone? But he could have been anyone! Not to mention the scandal if folk were to learn a married woman let a man who isn't her husband sleep here with nobody else in the house…what can you have been thinking?'

'I had other things to occupy my mind last night than what the neighbours might think—not that my name is particularly revered by them anyway. And you're wrong, you know.'

'About what?'

'My being a married woman. Our unexpected guest came to deliver a message that caught me rather by surprise. Frank… Frank is dead.'

There. I said it out loud. That means it must be true.

Honora watched as several different expressions fled one after the other across Mary's face, finally coming to a halt on stunned silence. It must have been the same look she herself had worn last night when Lord Lovell had told her the news, his annoyingly handsome face clouding with what a more naive woman might take for concern. She wouldn't be taken in by *that*, however—no friend of Frank's would be that kind, more likely to fake sympathy than truly feel it.

Birds of a feather...if Frank was a rogue it stands to reason this lord is, too.

'How? What happened to him?'

Mary still looked as though she couldn't quite believe it, following with wide eyes as Honora moved the tea tray from her bed and sank down on to it with a sigh.

'His heart, apparently. Gave out at Lord Lovell's grand estate somewhere in Northamptonshire. He must have been living nearby, although how or when that came about I've no idea.'

'Well. God rest him, I suppose.' The laces on Mary's white cap bobbed as she slowly shook her head. 'He was a poor husband to you, but it's still a waste to be taken so young. How do you feel? Will you grieve for him?'

'I hardly know. I loved him once and still might now if he hadn't shown me how little he cared for anything but my inheritance. Any passing is a sad event, but I don't think I've many tears left to cry. Does that make me sound cold?'

The cap swayed again, this time more vigorously. 'How many women could weep for a man who treated them as cruelly as he did you? I've been in service since I was eight and only when I came to wait on you did I know what it was to have a mistress who was a friend as well as an employer. I'm afraid I came to dislike Mr Blake for how he made you so unhappy and I can't pretend some part of me isn't glad you're free.'

Honora couldn't help a grim laugh as the vaguest flicker of warmth unfurled in her otherwise chilly chest. Mary was a good friend, the only one Honora had, and more dear to her than anybody else in all of frostbitten England. 'Free? To do what?'

'You could marry again. To a good man this time who would treat you properly.'

Honora had taken up the cracked teapot with the idea of pouring, although she stopped short to flick Mary a glance.

'Could I indeed? Will you allow me to draw breath before you scheme to have me take some other man's name?'

'In time, I mean. A kind man who might… might give you the child I know you long for.'

Honora didn't look up. Instead she dropped some milk into her cup and stirred it, vaguely dismayed to see her hand quaked a little. For all her bravado the reality of her situation was beginning to set in and an unfightable feeling of sadness crept outwards from her heart until it invaded every sinew.

I had my try at marriage and it slipped through my fingers—alongside the one chance I had of ever being a mother. Neither is something I can now hope for and it would be foolish of me to think otherwise.

'We both know that won't happen. Who would take me? A penniless widow with a reputation that's uncertain to say the least. You've heard how people have whispered since Frank left. Half the men for miles around think there must be something wrong with me to drive my husband away and the other half are horrified my father is a freedman. There will never be a crowd of suitors for my hand, no matter how hard you might wish it, and for my part I never wish to be beholden to a man ever again. I'm afraid my hopes of a child—a family of my own—are well and truly over.'

The creep of that icy despair renewed its vigour and Honora suppressed a shiver of sorrow. With his death Frank had taken more from her than he would ever know—but that assumed he had ever paused to think of her and his silence for three long years left no doubt that he had not. She would never be a mother now aside from in her dreams, a deep-rooted unhappiness she had no option but to live with for the rest of her life. The old words of her parents echoed through her mind once more, their desperation and fear turned to anger at her blind stupidity. Frank had ruined her, just as they'd warned her he would, and the hopeless rift between Honora and those that truly loved her had all been for naught.

With another sigh that felt as though it came up from her soul Honora twisted her unruly curls back from her forehead and attempted a wry smile despite how little she felt like trying.

'I suppose I ought to attend to my guest. Even if he wasn't invited I imagine it's still bad manners to leave him languishing in the corridor outside. If you'd fetch out my black bombazine, I think I'll dress.'

Mary got to her feet with surprising agility and bustled for the armoire, drawing out the gown with as much care as if it was made of the finest silk. She brought it towards Honora, wrinkling her nose slightly at the drab colour that still enhanced the soft fawn of Honora's skin.

'It seems a shame you'll have to wear mourning now. Especially with such a handsome man close by. Your rose muslin is so much more becoming…'

Half off the bed, Honora shot Mary a brief frown. 'What? Do you mean Lord Lovell?'

'Is there another handsome man in the house?'

Honora gave an unladylike snort Lord Lovell would have been surprised to know she could make. The idea of dressing with the irritating man out on the landing in mind was absurd. It didn't matter one single straw what he thought of her *or* whatever gown she chose to wear and he needn't think otherwise for a moment. If the chestnut gleam of his hair had struck her as fine the night before, it meant nothing and neither did her fleeting appreciation for the lithe shape of him beneath an expensive shirt. Perhaps some women might fall prey to his charms, but she was not one of their number—even if the thought of Lord Lovell waiting outside her bedroom door *did* make her pulse skip a fraction faster, a reaction she shied away from in alarm.

Oh, I think not. Birds of a feather flock together, don't forget, and that particular bird is no doubt the same as the one I lost.

'I couldn't care less what he makes of my appearance. As soon as I've dressed I'll be sending him on his way—handsome face included.'

* * *

Isaac drummed his fingers on the banister as he looked down from the landing into the hall below. By daylight Wycliff Lodge seemed even more dishevelled than it had the night before, clean and tidy enough, but still giving off an unmistakable air of fatigue. The wallpaper was faded and the rugs worn, some of the paintwork flaking off a little from a few of the walls and the windows well washed, but allowing freezing winter air to seep in. The bed he'd slept in had been comfortable enough, but he'd woken with his nose cold at the tip and now he rubbed his hands together as he waited, with rising impatience, for Honora to emerge.

She must know I'm out here. Her maid will have told her. The sooner she appears the sooner I can take my leave, then I'll never have to think of her again.

Despite all his efforts to the contrary, his unwilling hostess had somehow managed to elbow her way into his mind as he'd lain in the chilly bedchamber opposite hers. It was by no means the first time he'd found himself in a bed that wasn't his own—*when I was a poor excuse for a man and should have known better*—but this time was different. Try as he might, he couldn't quite set aside the image of her wan face as she'd looked back at him from the parlour doorway, her eyes holding a world of unspoken thoughts he had no way of deciphering. He knew he shouldn't waste a single second trying to puzzle her out, yet he couldn't deny Frank's widow was almost as intriguing as she was vexing.

She was sharp tempered, blunt and had completely dismissed him *and* his title—in a way that secretly rankled, *not* that Isaac wanted to admit it. Honora Blake seemed completely immune to the good looks and easy charm that found so much success elsewhere, his peerage the icing on the top of a usually eagerly nibbled cake. If he'd been the kind of man who valued female approval, he *might* have been offended. As it was he tried to ignore the little voice at the back of his mind that wondered what it was about him Honora evidently found so lacking, his new determination to improve himself for Charlotte's sake murmuring in his ear.

I don't truly care what she thinks of me. Just idle curiosity I won't indulge.

Finally the sound of a door creaking open behind him made him turn. The same maid he'd seen scurry past earlier emerged, followed close behind by a tall figure decked all in black—and to his dismay his heart turned over before he could halt its ungainly leap, a disturbing reaction he cursed as soon as it occurred.

There were dark shadows beneath Honora's wide-set eyes as she dipped him a short curtsy, sparing him only the barest minimum of civility and once again making him wonder *why* she was quite so hostile. The black gown contrasted with the warm hue of her skin and toned with the ebony curls piled high on her head, a cluster at each ear highlighting the angles of her face like a frame around a work of art. Her gaze was steady and lips set in a firm line, and with a flicker of alarm Isaac swallowed down an aggravating flit of admiration at her composure.

Enough nonsense. I've better things to be doing than standing around in this hovel all day.

He tossed Honora a shallow bow, determined not to afford her any more courtesy than she'd shown him. If she wanted to be standoffish and cool, so be it. He had no desire to court her friendship, after all.

'Good morning, Lord Lovell. I hope you slept well. Was there something you needed so urgently you had to wait outside my bedroom?'

Isaac felt his jaw tighten at her tone, her sunlit drawl of an accent unfamiliar yet the undercurrent of distaste abundantly clear. She wanted him gone and to *that* he could find no objection. Charlotte's time could come any day in the next few weeks, her innocence making it impossible to reckon for sure, and he wouldn't take the chance of not being there when she needed him—especially not on account of *Honora Blake*. She clearly didn't like him and his rational side didn't like her either, only that damnable corner of his mind that insisted on being swayed by her striking presence rebelling against every sensible thought.

I shan't waste another moment on her. She doesn't want me here and I have no reason to stay any longer.

'Needed? No. I just thought I should do you the courtesy of saying goodbye before I left and to thank you for your...*warm* hospitality.'

She narrowed her—vexingly pretty—eyes at the edge in his voice, her hazel meeting his brown in matching aversion.

'You're welcome, I'm sure. I'm so glad my poor, unlived-in-looking home suited your needs.'

'Perfectly. I won't trespass on your kindness a moment longer.'

With another bow that was little more than a nod he turned away, striding from the aggravating woman towards the stairs. He felt her eyes on him all the way down the landing and paused just before he dipped out of sight, looking back at her with his foot on the first step. She hadn't moved, standing among the shadows and seeming almost like one herself in her black gown that with a sudden prickle of guilt Isaac knew he had played a part in making necessary. If he hadn't chased Frank down like a dog, Honora wouldn't be cloaked in mourning now—but had there been a choice? He was the closest thing poor Charlotte had to a father and he would protect her until his dying breath, even if it meant concealing the full truth from the woman who stared back at him now and caused such unwanted confusion. She disturbed him, provoking yet fascinating in equal measure, and he wanted nothing more than to escape and forget she—and her damnably fine countenance—even existed.

'I doubt we shall meet when you come up to Northamptonshire so I'll leave you with my condolences for your loss. Goodbye, Mrs Blake.'

He descended the stairs, reaching the hall below and was almost at the front door when a voice from above came to make him pause.

'Wait. What do you mean?' Honora frowned down at him, both hands resting on the landing banister. 'Why would I travel to Northamptonshire? There's nothing for me there other than a grave and I can't afford to be sentimental. I don't have that luxury.'

Isaac's own forehead creased with the lifting of one eyebrow. *A woman of ice and fire indeed. Cold yet scathing all in the same breath.*

'For the reading of Frank's will. I'd have thought that was obvious.'

She blinked, momentarily off guard until she shook her head. 'Frank always conducted his business affairs with Laurel and Sons in Weston. They've been his solicitors for years.'

'Perhaps once, but no longer.' Isaac shrugged. Didn't she know anything about the man she'd married? 'About six months ago he sought my advice on finding representation closer to his lodgings in Northampton. I recommended my own man to him and he made the exchange soon after. Mr Drew of Filliol, Ellis and Drew, based in the town of Carey not far from my home.'

He saw her shoulders slump, a small movement that nevertheless drew his eye like an arrow to a target.

'No. I wasn't aware. How could I be? I'd had no word from Frank in above three years.' Her fingers tightened on the wooden rail, short nails gripping polished oak. 'So now I'm to find my way from Somerset to this *Carey*? A distance of what—a hundred miles? More?'

'Closer to a hundred and twenty. It's no small undertaking, believe me.'

Time consuming *and* expensive—a double blow Isaac would have avoided if he could. It had taken almost two days to travel to Wycliff Lodge, getting down from the coach halfway with his bones aching from constant jostling and glad to spend the night at an inn. He'd have to make the same tedious journey again now and the thought did nothing to lift his spirits, although Honora looked more troubled by the prospect than he might have expected.

'One hundred and twenty miles by coach and then the same back again. The expense…and I'll have to break the journey overnight in some tavern or inn…'

Still craning his neck to look up at her, Isaac saw the pinch of her straight black brows, cinched together in uneasy thought as she spoke more to herself than to him. For the first time that morning she looked vulnerable, some glimmer of uncertainty showing beneath her icy mask, and the same pang of *something* he'd felt as she left him the night before pricked him like a handful of pins.

She's a woman alone, even if she is also one of the most unfriendly I've met. It'll be a hard road to travel on her own, especially if she plans to stop at an inn on the way. They can be rough, not to mention expensive.

A horrible suspicion began to unfurl in the depths of Isaac's stomach—slowly at first, but growing gradually until it coiled there like a snake. If he didn't know better he might suspect some part of him felt *sorry* for Honora in the task ahead of her, a daunting venture even he would rather not undertake...

Absurd. He rejected the idea at once. *She's done nothing to gain my sympathies. I'm sure she can fend for herself perfectly well—especially if she keeps that pistol in her reticule.*

Still... Some part of him, some glimmer of the better man he had resolved to become since Charlotte's predicament, baulked at the notion of her setting forth alone. Cold and independent she might be, but she was still a new widow, with evidently precious little money to spare for such an arduous and unexpected journey. Wycliff Lodge was fairly crumbling around her ears as it was. Where would she find the funds to hire a stagecoach, pay tips to the guards and lodgings for herself overnight? Aside from anything else her unusual, striking looks might well garner attention no woman travelling alone was likely to enjoy— a fact Isaac couldn't deny no matter how hard he might endeavour to ignore her unconscious allure.

'Do you have the money to afford such a trip? A manservant to travel with you, perhaps?'

The shiny black curls at her ears swayed a little with the reluctant shake of her head. 'The only servant I keep is Mary. Under other circumstances I might ask her husband to accompany me, but I've no wish to take him away while she's so near her time. A safe delivery and healthy baby are far more important than my comfort in a coach, no matter how others might whisper.'

She'd avoided the question about money, Isaac noted, although a large part of him registered nothing but surprise at her answer to the other. Her concern for her maid was the first gleam of warmth he'd seen in Honora's set face, the smallest hint of softness that might lie within and echoing his own sentiments about Charlotte so closely it was unnerving. Why she was so determined he didn't see her kindness he couldn't quite grasp, but his confusion was enough to allow his lips to speak before he could curb them—and damn him with a betrayal that should *never* have been uttered.

'I see. In that case it seems you have no alternative. With no other choice available to you— you'll have to travel with me.'

Peering down from the landing, Honora felt the tick of her pulse beneath the thin skin of her throat and hoped fervently Lord Lovell couldn't see how quickly it skipped. He was just as handsome in the daylight as he had been at night, possibly more so, with flecks of silver scattered among his warm brown hair and a jawline that looked chiselled from stone. In the weak December sunshine trickling into the hall she saw his forehead was crossed with the lines of a deep thinker and his mobile mouth could probably lift into a heart-stopping smile if he chose—not that there was much chance of that at present, so firmly did he wear an expression of long-suffering patience that made her bristle in spite of the rapid patter of her pulse.

'I beg your pardon?'

'You will have to travel with me.' He spoke as if spelling something out to a particularly confused child. 'I'll pay for you. I don't see how else you could proceed.'

She drew herself up to her full height. Of all the patronising, self-important… No wonder he and Frank had been friends. They were both so sure of themselves, so maddeningly certain they knew best. It was nothing but sheer bad luck the face that made her want to stare belonged to Lord Lovell, as irritating as he was pleasant to look upon. Frank had been just the same, a comely man far too secure in his appeal and abilities—

and more dangerous than she ever could have known.

I've no desire to find myself mixed up with another of those. Frank took a wrecking ball to my life and now his friend seems set to try taking over where he left off.

'I'm quite capable of organising myself, Lord Lovell,' she snapped—perhaps a little too sharply. 'I don't require your charity.'

She rather suspected he fought the urge to roll his eyes and felt her jaw tense in reply. 'Perish the thought, madam. You have an idea, then, of how to pay for yourself? The funds to make such a long journey lying around somewhere?'

Damn.

Honora knew her face had scrunched into a scowl, but for the life of her she couldn't seem to iron it out. The insufferable man standing below was right. She barely had enough to pay Mary and buy some little Christmas fairings for the children, let alone afford to cover her travel. Her money was stretched to breaking point already and she had no savings, the small sum from the sale of her wedding ring dwindling rapidly. Stuck between a rock and hard place she didn't have much choice—something the infuriating lift of Lord Lovell's eyebrow indicated he knew all too well.

'I didn't think so. Take my offer. A favour is different to charity after all.'

Even a favour is more than I want from him, she thought bitterly.

It would tie her to him and complicate matters more than her bizarre reaction to him already had, but there was no other option and her practicality would have to triumph over her hesitation.

'In the absence of any other way I suppose I'll have to accept—on the basis you understand it's a loan only. I was present when Frank made his will, only days after our marriage and when he still cared to make a favourable impression on me, and unless he thought to alter it after our estrangement I ought to have some provision. Once my widow's jointure is settled I shall repay every penny I owe.'

'There's no need. The amount involved will be inconsequential to me.'

It was Honora's turn to control the wayward roll of her eyes.

Does he think to impress me with his wealth?

'There's every need. The only person a woman should be obligated to is herself. Will you shake on our agreement? If you're willing to enter into it, of course.'

Still looking up at her, Lord Lovell gave a short laugh. It was brief, over and gone the very next second, but something in the low note sent an inexplicable flutter through Honora's stomach. 'Shake on it? Are you a merchant?'

Setting the disquieting feeling aside, she pursed her lips. 'I intend to keep my word. A handshake will make it binding.'

'Very well. If you insist.'

Lord Lovell lifted a nonchalant shoulder and watched as she descended the stairs, her fingers gripping the wooden rail as if it could help stem the tide of unease swirling within her. Each step brought Honora nearer to him until she stood close enough to extend one hand, determined to hold it steady as Lord Lovell took it in his firm grip.

Her arm lit up as though tamed fire streaked under her skin the very instant he touched her.

Flaring out from her hand, the sensation skittered higher until it invaded the secret hollow beneath the bodice of her gown, a shock that made her snatch an unwilling breath. Once there the feeling rebounded, arcing to light a bonfire in her lungs and send her heart galloping like a wild horse over the Virginian mountains. It was the most delightful, tingling commotion in every nerve—and almost brought Honora to her knees.

No. It can't be. Not again.

Time reeled backwards as she stood and stared

up into Lord Lovell's face, feeling the warmth of his skin and taking in the play of coffee and amber that made up each iris. For one hammer-stroke of her heart she was a girl again, standing in front of Frank Blake, the handsome adventurer from England, and wondering at how the mere touch of his hand made her feel as though she was walking on air. It was the exact same sensation that coursed through her now like a merciless river, unrelenting, savage and a warning she couldn't ignore.

Perhaps some of what twisted through her horrified mind showed on her face. Lord Lovell forced a dry swallow, the smooth line of his neck convulsing with the effort, and he dropped her hand as though it were a snake to turn and walk away.

'You should go to pack. I want to leave as soon as possible.'

Chapter Three

Isaac had read and reread the same paragraph of his newspaper three times. Out of the corner of his eye he could see the lithe form of Honora, soberly wrapped in a black coat, swaying with the motion of the coach in a movement he found unutterably hypnotic. She'd already almost caught him staring twice, once more would be difficult to explain away, both to her and to himself.

He frowned down at the page. Ever since he had taken her hand and felt a wild swell beneath the expensive linen of his shirt he hadn't been able to get the uncanny sensation, or her, out of his mind. How many women's hands had he held in his lifetime, perhaps gently tracing the line of an elegant knuckle to hear its owner sigh? *Countless dozens*, he thought irritably, yet none of them had sent a rush through him he could only compare to the thrill of placing a risky bet in a game of cards. It was the same pulse of excitement of taking a chance and not knowing whether it would be a prize he won or the taste of defeat—and it didn't please him one little bit.

We've only been on the road an hour and already I fear I made a mistake in offering to bring her with me. This journey is tedious enough without her presence making it worse.

With a brisk snap of paper he turned the page, determined not to glance over the top of it in the direction of his companion—once again. Honora had barely spoken a word since they'd left Wycliff Lodge, and the silence between them seemed in little danger of being broken as she gazed out at the passing fields of the West Country.

Fine by me. Hearing the thoughts of Frank Blake's widow on any subject couldn't be of less significance.

Each time she caught his eye he felt the same, a flicker of unwanted interest bookended on either side by loathing of the husband she had once chosen. If he had never befriended Frank, falling for the façade of roguish charm he'd thought they shared, Charlotte's life wouldn't have been ruined—or teetering on the brink of being so, the risk of her sharing his mother's fate never far from his mind—and Honora was a reminder to Isaac of how he had failed to protect the one person he loved…

'Is there something you want?'

The voice from the corner came crisp and curt and when Isaac looked up he saw Honora watched him with as much enthusiasm as she might regard a wasps' nest.

'Pardon?'

'I said, is there something you want? You keep glancing at me as if there's something you wanted to say.'

'Of course not. You're mistaken.'

'Am I? How strange. I could have sworn I saw you peering at me from over the top of your newssheet.'

She turned her attention back to the window and Isaac glared down at his page with small hope now of continuing to read. Annoyance with both himself and the provoking woman opposite him made the words blur before his eyes and he set it aside with a bad-tempered rustle of crumpled paper.

Anyone would think I'd dragged her along with me against her will rather than doing her a favour. She certainly hasn't thanked me as much as one might expect.

Perhaps she wanted him to ask what was bothering her, he mused as he stretched his legs out more comfortably into the space between the seats. There was nobody else in the coach aside from Honora and himself and he saw her bristle slightly, as straight-backed and unfriendly as a feral cat. She pulled her pelisse a little tighter about her body and gave a sniff of disapproval, although whether it was the proximity of his boot or his general existence that riled her he couldn't say. No doubt she'd jump at the chance to tell him *exactly* what it was about him she disliked, sure to seize the chance to take him down a peg or two if only he'd ask.

But he wouldn't.

He'd rather sit in silence for the rest of the journey than deign to ask what bothered her so much to force her cool displeasure. He wouldn't give her the satisfaction. She could stew on her discontent for the next hundred miles, Isaac thought resolutely, no matter how much she huffed and sighed. He *would not* allow her to draw him out—even if both his curiosity and, frustratingly, pride was roused by her determination to dislike him, the complete opposite to his usual reception. Didn't she know how eligible he was considered? Was she unaware he could charm whatever society woman he chose, their smiles following handsome Lord Lovell wherever he went and falling into his arms if he invited them—which he no longer would, it was true, now Charlotte's fate had opened his eyes to the ruin a man's feckless behaviour could wreak.

I'm not asking her.

No matter how she pursed her pretty lips and looked away.

I'm not asking her.

Even if she ignored him for the next day and a half.

I'm not asking her.

He sat forward. 'Mrs Blake. Perhaps you might tell me what it is I've done to offend you.'

Damnation.

'Whatever do you mean?' Honora allowed him one sidelong look that set his teeth on edge, suspicious and faux innocent all at once. 'I don't understand you.'

Ignoring the obvious lie—and the feeling of wanting to kick himself for his lapse of control—Isaac pressed on. 'Ever since I arrived at Wycliff Lodge—'

'—uninvited and unannounced—'

'—you've seemed displeased by almost everything I've said and done. Why is that?'

Honora's lip twisted. 'You've hardly been a model of charm yourself.'

'Based entirely on your frosty reception.'

'What else did you expect? A friend of Frank's appearing out of nowhere and invading my home?'

'Invading your home?' Isaac felt his face crease in annoyance. 'I explained the mistake that led me to go inside and don't forget—it was for your husband's sake that I was there in the first place!'

'Exactly so!' Now Honora sat forward triumphantly. 'For my *husband's* sake. You and he were obviously good friends. Can you blame me for not wanting any acquaintance of his lingering about?'

'You dislike me because of my choice of friends?'

She shot him a look that suggested he was the biggest simpleton alive, asking a question with so clear an answer it was beneath her to reply. He stared back, the steady tick of his temper growing quicker beneath her silent scorn.

'But what does that say about you, following that logic? Aren't you just as bad? Worse, even—I may have been his friend once, but you *married* him!'

'And see where it got me!' Honora's eyes flashed, fire melting her glacial contempt. 'Frank held my life in his hands and crumbled it as though it was nothing to him. He pretended to love me when he thought I was to inherit a fortune, but when I rejected it he left me alone and penniless. He caused me to break with my own parents, to be so shamefully stubborn and stupid I can never go back! To have been on intimate terms it stands to reason you're cut from the same cloth. Nobody would blame me for not welcoming you with open arms, given your similarity to one who treated me so badly.'

Isaac stilled. 'Frank and I were not so alike.'

'No? And yet you were close enough he died in your arms?'

A denial sprang to the tip of Isaac's tongue and almost fled his lips before he wrestled it back.

Wait a moment. Be careful.

If he corrected her assumption, it would lead a direct path to Charlotte and her pitiable situation. How could it be otherwise, after explaining to Honora the reason Frank died in Isaac's arms was not out of friendship, but because he had been hunted past the brink of exhaustion for seducing an innocent girl? That far from being friends, Isaac now loathed Frank with every sinew of his entire body for lying to Charlotte, concealing from her his marriage and leaving her with a child to remind her of her shame for ever? If Isaac told Honora how wrong she was, she would demand answers and that would put Charlotte at risk of a scandal he would shield her from at all costs.

And yet, despite your indignation...were you truly so different? Can you really deny your conduct was sometimes less honourable than it should have been, towards women especially?

It was an unpleasant question, but one that none the less he had to face. He hadn't always been a paragon of virtue, his disregard for marriage and commitment stemming from childhood and directly influencing his behaviour as a grown man. Only now that Charlotte was suffering had the scales fallen from him and it was difficult to look his reflection in the eye—especially now it was Honora Blake holding up the mirror, another who had known torment at the hands of an unthinking man.

'I can't answer for that,' he ground out between gritted teeth, wishing more than ever he had left Honora in that tumbledown old house to make her own way north. 'He must have trusted me. Perhaps I made it easier for him to be a friend than you did to be a husband.'

Her face tightened and Isaac knew at once he had been cruel. Irritating as she was, he shouldn't have insulted her and felt a glint of guilt for allowing his temper to carry him too far, his worry for Charlotte clouding his judgement and sharpening his tongue.

He sighed.

I ought to apologise. Not that I think for a moment she'll accept it.

'Mrs Blake—'

Honora cut him off with a resolute turn of her head back to the coach's filmy window. The driver was drawing the horses to a gentle halt as they neared an inn at the side of the road and a glance outside showed Isaac a couple of passengers waiting to board. 'You're right, Lord Lovell. At first I did dislike you for being Frank's friend, but now...' Her face was obscured by the brim of her bonnet, but Isaac didn't need to see her expression to understand her tone as the coach rolled to a stop. 'Now, however, it's more because I find you one of the most unpleasant men I have ever had the misfortune to meet. I think perhaps we had better not speak any further.'

Honora kept her eyes firmly on the scene outside her window although she barely saw the trees and fields skipping by. The jolt of the coach made her teeth feel as though they were rattling in her head and she longed to be able to get down, even if only for a moment, and take a deep breath of biting December air.

Not only to settle my stomach. To escape from Lord Unlovable would be just wonderful.

How *dare* he imply she was to blame for Frank's abandonment? Out of the corner of her eye she could see him scouring his newssheet once again, entirely ignoring both her and the young couple who had embarked when the coach stopped to change horses. The woman sat next to Honora now and her escort had drawn the short straw of Lord Lovell for a companion, although neither of them seemed to have eyes for anyone but the other.

Just as well they don't try to speak to him. I doubt they'd hear anything agreeable if they did.

At least she had the satisfaction of knowing she'd been right all along, Honora thought acidly. Lord Lovell was just as unlikable as she'd suspected, every bit as unkind as she had predicted given his friendship with Frank. Now she knew for certain what type of man she was bound to for the next hundred miles she could go about treating him with the distant disdain he deserved. All there was left to do was make her disloyal senses fall into line with her rational thinking—starting with preventing her eyes from sliding in his direction more often than she liked.

Whatever had passed between them at the foot

of Wycliff Lodge's sweeping stairs had been a mistake. She knew that for certain. It was a momentary lapse, nothing more, and she should put it from her mind before she risked giving it more importance than it deserved. Of course touching a handsome man had given her a short, sharp thrill. Wasn't it more contact with an attractive male than she'd had in above three years? Any woman might experience a moment of weakness if she'd lived as a nun for such a long time and Lord Lovell was tempting enough to make any female with a pulse sit up and take notice.

And that's as far as it goes. I noticed and now I will stop noticing, easy as that. Even if I do like a man with salt-and-pepper hair.

Honora gave herself a little shake.

Did. Did like, I mean. Not any longer. And that's that.

The woman sitting beside her leaned forward a little to whisper something to her husband, who looked across at Honora apologetically.

'I beg your pardon, madam. I wonder…my wife gets so bilious when we travel by coach. Would it be too much to ask if I might switch seats with you? I'd like to sit beside her if I may.'

'Oh.' Honora felt herself tense, the desire to refuse flaring immediately. As it was she had tucked herself neatly into a corner as far away from Lord Lovell as possible within the cramped cabin, able to disregard him completely as long as she kept her face turned to the window.

'I wouldn't ask, only she's…in delicate health, at present.'

One swift look down was enough to show Honora what he meant. The young woman's warm cloak covered most of her gown, but a slight bump was just discernible beneath it and her face was nauseously pale.

As always the sight of another with child skewered Honora with a lance of pain so sharp it might have made her gasp if she hadn't grown accustomed to it over years of suffering. It was the same bittersweet mixture of happiness for the mother-to-be and agony for herself that always flowed over her with no mercy and this time was no exception. Every time it brought home to her in brutal clarity everything she would never have for herself—and now Frank was in the ground any chance at all lay with him in the silence of the grave.

Three pairs of eyes were fixed on her, waiting for her to speak. Even Lord Lovell had glanced up from his paper, although she didn't look at him as she tried to arrange her face into a pleasant smile despite the chill wending its way through her innards.

'Of course. Of course I'll swap.'

She exchanged places with the man and settled into his vacated seat, acknowledging the couple's thanks with another painful smile. They had no way of knowing what it cost her to curve stiff lips, although an unwelcome murmur from beside her suggested she hadn't been entirely successful.

'Are you unwell?'

She gave Lord Lovell a sideways glare. At the sound of his quiet voice so close to her a curious tingle threaded up the back of her neck, but she stubbornly ignored its delightful stirring of the hairs at her nape. 'No.'

'You look troubled.'

'Is that any wonder?' she hissed, one eye on the couple opposite who had thankfully retreated back into their own world. 'Now I have to sit next to you for the next who knows how many hours?'

Lord Lovell made a sound that might have been a humourless laugh. 'Ah. Is that what it is?'

Honora gathered her pelisse about her, tucking it in fastidiously to avoid having to reply. As if she would ever tell Lord Lovell, of all people, of her secret sorrows. She wouldn't even tell him her shopping list for market, let alone the sadness that lived inside her and would never go away, how she missed the parents from whom her shame held her back and the desire for a family that gnawed at her bones. He wouldn't understand and he certainly wouldn't care, probably too preoccupied with counting his money and searching for mirrors to look in to bother with anyone's feelings but his own.

'I thought we agreed not to speak any further.'

'We did, didn't we? Forgive the intrusion.'

He disappeared again behind that damned newspaper and Honora took the opportunity to surreptitiously run a hand down the back of her neck. Sitting so near to Lord Lovell seemed to have lit a taper beneath her skin, the sensation at her nape triggered by his murmur alarming in the extreme. At this distance she could just catch the scent of his shaving soap—*expensive, no doubt*—and hear the steady rhythm of his breathing that made her own want to match its slow march. Secreted beneath layers of black bombazine she felt suddenly hot despite the December chill and with a frown angled her body as far away from Lord Lovell's broad form as the small seat allowed.

I won't regard this. Any of it. I know better and I'll do better.

Her eyes were growing heavy. A combination of the coach's rocking motion and having lain awake for hours the previous night made it tempting to close them for a moment and surrender to the sweet call of sleep that sang her name. It would mean an escape from the sight of the pregnant woman in front of her with a new life growing and a husband who loved her—and a temporary reprieve from Lord Lovell, rude and handsome and dangerously close.

I shouldn't. It's probably impolite. Most things seem to be.

Unaware Honora watched them, the husband tenderly stroked a damp curl back from his wife's forehead and squeezed her hand, receiving a shaky smile in reply. It was such a picturesque scene Honora almost smiled herself, before the ice in her belly won out. She would never have a man care for her like that, comforting his beloved as she carried his child. Even in the first days of their marriage when she thought Frank meant the pretty words he spoke they had been lies. She had never been loved like that and never would be, too poor and unusual for most men to consider. Back in Somerset her reputation was questionable to say the least and no man was brave enough to see past it to the woman within—even if she had wanted one to. The knowledge clamped her in a tight fist of unhappiness and she looked away, seeking distraction in the world trundling past outside the coach window.

Perhaps a few minutes won't hurt. I'd rather be asleep than trapped in this life anyway.

The bed Honora lay in was warm and soft and she rubbed her cheek against the smooth silk of her pillow. Perhaps it was odd that the spacious four-poster stood among the spruce forest of her childhood, songbirds hopping through the branches and even a whitetail deer tripping past, but Honora couldn't seem to mind. The sights and sounds of wild Virginia surrounded her on every side, even the smell of fir coming back to greet her like an old friend. She hadn't been back in five years aside from in her lonely memories and yet now it was as though she'd never been away, lying comfortably and taking in the beloved sights of home. She felt so safe, so perfectly at ease, and it seemed the most natural thing in the world to stay just where she was and enjoy the sunlit peace.

Someone was approaching through the trees. Honora watched the indistinct shape come closer, completely unafraid and only mildly curious. Whoever it was wouldn't hurt her. She hadn't been hurt in Virginia. That had come later, when

Frank had spirited her away to freezing England and crushed her heart beneath his boot—but here she had nothing to fear. Frank couldn't touch her in the safety of this wonderful forest bed and she smiled to know she was protected by something he would never understand.

'Honora.'

Her smile widened. Was that Ma calling her name, the one she missed and loved so dearly? Summoning her back to their wooden house, made by Pa's own capable hands?

'Honora.'

No. The voice was too deep to be her mother's. Perhaps it was her father instead? Her kind old Pa, wanting her to come and practise her letters as she had as a child?

'Honora!'

The silky pillow beneath her head moved and she moved with it, trying to cling on even as it shifted under her. Whoever was calling her from among the trees was louder now, their vaguely familiar voice too close to her ear...

Her eyes snapped open.

It took a moment for her to gather her wits and for an unpleasant second Honora had no idea where she was. The place was shrouded in darkness, pale faces staring like uncanny moons and her cheek pressed against something that was definitely the wrong shape for a pillow. From somewhere nearby came the whinny of horses and sounds of heavy loads being dragged across cobbles, of footsteps and men shouting to each other in the frosted night.

'Good. You're awake.'

The voice from her dream came again—and this time there was no mistaking its owner.

Honora lurched upright like a puppet on a string, horror flooding every vein. She turned to Lord Lovell with eyes wide, her mortified gaze switching from his face to the padded shoulder of his silken coat and back again.

Heaven save me. I fell asleep on him!

Her heart skittered horribly and a wild surge of heat roared up to consume her rigid face. Lord Lovell looked back at her with the most unreadable expression on his dimly lit features, perhaps a combination of strained endurance and—somehow *so much* worse—dry amusement that only made her cheeks flare hotter.

Why didn't he wake me before? How could he let me embarrass myself like that!

She was still very close to him—close enough to feel the warmth that radiated from his body and the knowledge she had strayed even nearer still while sleeping was almost too much to bear. Her head had rested on that pleasingly solid shoulder, only a few thin layers of linen and silk separating his skin from hers, and she must have curved against him while she dreamed. In all it was the most discomfiting thing imaginable— and the most appealing, a fact that sent her shuffling away in alarm.

'We've gone as far as I had planned for today. We'll stay at this inn and then continue on in the morning.'

She nodded, refusing to meet Lord Lovell's eye. Shame and anger swirled inside her, but she would *not* give the infuriating Lord Lovell the pleasure of seeing her unease. No doubt he thought it entertaining to allow her to make such a spectacle of herself, but he wouldn't get the better of her *that* easily.

The young couple stepped down from the carriage first and then Lord Lovell followed, straightening his back with a contented sigh. He turned and held out a hand to Honora, offering to help her down to stand beside him in the moonlit night, but she stubbornly waved him away.

'I can manage, thank you.'

'Very well. If you're sure.'

I'm very sure. The last thing she would do was to give him another chance to make an exhibition of her, Honora resolved grimly. If she behaved with icy disdain, he wouldn't get the opportunity, her dignity shaken a little now but perfectly able to be hitched back into place. She was a strong woman, after all, self-assured, confident, poised...

Lord Lovell had moved away a pace or two and was peering up at the stone façade of the inn, but he looked over his shoulder to call back, 'Oh, Honora?'

'Yes?'

'Your bonnet's askew from your nap.'

The candles flickered in a cruel draught that followed Isaac through the inn's front door, but a fire leaping in the hall grate soon chased it away. Stepping fully inside, he chafed his hands together, cold despite his fine woollen gloves, and glanced about for Honora. She glided in behind him, head held high, her bonnet now perfectly straight, and he stifled a reluctant smile.

You're not giving her any reason to like you better, teasing her like that. Then again, she's hardly trying much herself.

A cold flicker of alarm had swum through his nerves at the first touch of her head on his shoulder, each one already heightened in sensitivity from her sitting so near. When she had relaxed against him further, nestling closer and turning her head so her cheek might rest on the smooth fabric of his coat he had frozen entirely, unable to stop a rapid—and unwelcome—thrill from searing into his chest. The young couple opposite had smiled, evidently assuming Honora was his exhausted wife, so he'd had no choice but to smile back and endure the torture of that warm body pressed against his own, part of him hardly able to stand it—and another vexing, cursedly *disobedient* part enjoying every moment.

Enough of that. Isaac peered down at his pocket watch, determined not to glance across to where Honora stood before the fire. Out of the corner of his eye he could see how the flames played over her face, her clear skin amber-gold in the soft light and the fine shape of her profile silhouetted against the leaping orange tongues. What he needed was to get away from her. That was all it would take to collect himself, a glass of something and a goodnight's sleep in a comfortable bed, sequestered away from his irritating companion behind a locked bedroom door.

She isn't the only one who's tired, after all. I haven't slept properly since I learned of Charlotte's condition and after today I don't know what I want more than to close my eyes.

Tensing his jaw on a yawn, Isaac looked about

for the landlord. The man in question was talking to another traveller, but he broke off at Isaac's approach, the tall, fair-haired traveller moving off in a way that struck Isaac as oddly furtive.

'Can I help you, sir?'

'I was hoping to secure lodgings for the night. For myself and the lady at the fireplace.'

Isaac gestured towards Honora, noticing the fair-haired stranger had drifted closer to where she stood. He seemed to be watching her, something Honora appeared to notice, too, as she subtly shifted position so all the man could see was the back of her black coat.

The landlord nodded. 'Of course, sir. You're just in time. It's been a busy evening, but fortunately we have one room left for you and your wife.'

Isaac stared at him. 'Only *one* room? For me and my—?'

'Your wife. That's right. I'm very sorry, sir.'

'But—'

The rest of Isaac's sentence tailed off as he felt a shower of cold water drench him from head to toe, absolute dismay and alarm coming together to drag pure frustration up from his soul.

No. Surely not...he must be joking.

He couldn't even escape Honora in sleep? Isaac's eyes darted toward her of their own volition, taking in her rigid back and the man that loitered a little too close to her—a sight that set him oddly on edge. What he wanted was to forget all about her for a few blessed hours, not be forced into even greater proximity with her and the bizarre reaction she provoked with no effort at all.

'Are you quite sure there are no other rooms available?'

'I'm afraid so. Not to worry though, sir.' The landlord smiled encouragingly. 'It's a very comfortable room, well appointed.'

With the muscles of his face feeling like granite Isaac mustered a nod. *No joke after all, then.*

Honora would be horrified beyond measure when she learned they would have to share, no doubt disgusted and appalled and all manner of other unflattering adjectives to describe her feelings. For himself there was more annoyance than anything else, unable to snatch a moment alone and made to endure yet more time spent with a breathing reminder of Frank Blake.

But what choice do we have? There's no other inn for miles and even if there was I doubt we'd find it in the dark. She'll have to put up with it—as will I.

Isaac's teeth were gritted so hard they almost squeaked as he stepped to Honora's side. She looked up at him, suspicion growing in her hazel eyes as she took in the stiffness of his mouth.

'What is it?'

He bent his head a little to speak into her ear, aware the blond man still hovered nearby. She had delicate, well-shaped ears, he noticed for the first time…before shying away in vexation. 'We will have to share a room tonight. All the others are taken.'

Honora started back as if he'd struck her, glaring up into his face in clear affront. 'What are you talking about? This is no time for stupid jokes. I'm tired and I want to go to bed.'

'As do I. Unfortunately, I'm in earnest.'

She stared at him for a long moment, searching his features for the truth. He gazed back grimly, his irritation growing with each breath.

'Absolutely not!'

'Keep your voice down.' Isaac stepped nearer still, turning a shoulder to the stranger who watched them from his place on the other side of the fire. Why the man didn't look away Isaac didn't know, but with his temper rising he had half a mind to stride over and ask him. 'You'll have a very cold and uncomfortable night on a hard stone floor otherwise. There are no other rooms.'

'There must be.'

'No. Believe me, I asked. Do you think I'd insist on it if there was any other choice?'

'I don't know what you'd *insist* upon.'

The upward turn of Honora's chin was even more irritating than her words and Isaac couldn't help but bite back. 'Don't flatter yourself,' he almost growled. 'The landlord thinks you're my wife. It will raise far less suspicion and cast no aspersions on your honour if we just quietly go along with it. It's one night. Surely even you can manage that.'

Honora bristled slightly, but there were shadows beneath her eyes and finally her exhaustion won out. 'Fine. But remember—I have a pistol in my luggage.'

'*You* remember—don't flatter yourself.'

Hitching a smile back on his face, Isaac gestured to the landlord waiting at the foot of a staircase leading up to the rooms above.

'Come along. It's been a long day. I'd like to retire now.'

The look Honora shot him contained such venom Isaac was briefly grateful he was still alive, but she turned for the stairs and accepted the landlord's hand to climb the uneven wooden steps. Isaac followed behind her, the hem of her black coat disappearing into the shadows of a night neither one of them had expected.

* * *

Unseen by either of them the fair-haired man watched them go, a look of unpleasant contemplation creeping across his face as he took Honora's place beside the fire.

Chapter Four

Curled on her side Honora screwed her eyes closed, determined to ignore the flickering light that peeped through a gap in the tightly drawn bed hangings. How long she'd lain there waiting for sleep to claim her she wasn't quite sure, the minutes marked by the ticking of an unfamiliar clock somewhere nearby.

Is he asleep? Surely he must be by now.

She couldn't hear any sound other than the clock and the soft shifting of burning logs in the fireplace on the other side of the room. Orange light slanted across her covers in a thin skewer, the only interruption of the midnight darkness, and if she hadn't known Lord Lovell sat in an armchair pulled up to the hearth she might have thought herself alone in the December night.

She listened intently. It was the second night in a row she'd kept perfectly still, trying to catch a hint of what Lord Lovell was doing out of her sight, and the notion made her frown. Was it really only twenty-four hours since he had appeared in her parlour, a stranger in the darkness with news she hadn't expected? In the space of a single day she had found herself widowed and hurtling north with a man she barely knew—but who still affected her in a way so unnerving it put her on her guard. She'd fallen for the charms of a handsome man once before and it had been her downfall—she'd never stumble into the same trap twice.

Not that he's been especially charming. It seems he dislikes me as much as I dislike him.

There was still no sound from the other side of the bed curtains and, despite her efforts to the contrary, Honora couldn't help a glimmer of curiosity. It had been an unspoken agreement that she would have the bed, consigning him to sleep in the squashy armchair by the fire. When was the last time she'd been on such intimate terms with a man? she wondered reluctantly as a treacherous tingle crept over her skin. Certainly not since Frank had simply walked out the door and closed it behind him with such finality she should have known he wasn't coming back. Now only a blanket and a thin nightgown guarded her from Lord Lovell's dark gaze, eyes so direct and uninhibited it made her shudder with delicious unease…

It was no use.

Honora sat up. She would never be able to sleep while Lord Lovell sat mere feet away doing who knew what, a silent presence that somehow made itself known to her without as much as a word.

I'll just take one little look and then I'll go to sleep. One peep through the curtains is nothing. He'll be asleep, like as not, and will never know I did it.

Moving slowly, Honora peeled back her covers, wincing slightly as the night's chill attacked her bared skin. Moving like a fox stalking a rabbit, she crawled to the end of the bed and tried to look through the gap in the hangings, pursing her lips when it gave her nothing but an eyeful of fireplace. After a moment's hesitation she twitched the curtains a little further apart, gingerly craning her neck to catch a glimpse of her perturbing companion and satisfy the insistent beat of her curiosity.

He wasn't sleeping. Instead Honora felt her throat suddenly clench as she took in the sculpted line of his profile, a straight nose and well-shaped chin showcased against a backdrop of flame as if to deliberately highlight

their handsome contours. Lord Lovell sat mo-
tionless in the chair with his eyes fixed on the
fire and both hands clasped before him as though
in prayer—although what a man like Lord Lovell
might pray for Honora couldn't begin to guess.
His brow was creased with deep thought and
a tightness about his lips suggested whatever
played on his mind was no trivial matter, staring into the flames and in his seriousness looking every one of his almost forty years.

Honora knew she shouldn't continue to watch
him although she couldn't quite tear her eyes
away. Lord Lovell was still cloaked in mystery,
but in one respect she *knew* she was right. Seated
by the fire he was wretched, lost in thought about
something that brought him no joy. Honora could
tell from his face and felt her dry throat give
another convulsive swallow as a strange trickle
of pity welled up inside her at the thought. She
shouldn't care if he was unhappy. He'd done
nothing to deserve her sympathy. But it gleamed
within her all the same, a quick flit of softness
she had long since thought buried beneath suffering of her own.

'You can't sleep either, then.'

His voice made her jump and when he turned
his head in her direction Honora saw the complex expression replaced by one of wry under-

standing. 'Or is it you just wanted to check I'd kept my distance?'

Caught in the act, Honora felt her face flush hot. Had he known she was watching the whole time? It seemed suddenly silly to be lurking behind the curtains and pulling a blanket up to cover her modesty Honora opened the gap a little wider, still safe within the shadowy sanctuary of the four-poster bed.

'Of course not. I'd hope you would keep to your word without needing to be reminded.'

Lord Lovell laughed shortly, another of those deep notes that reverberated through Honora's chest. 'You needn't worry. I'm a reformed character these days.'

When she didn't reply he unclasped his hands and waved towards a table set out to one side of the fire. 'I was contemplating a glass of wine to help me drift off. Would you like one? You never know, it might put you more at ease.'

Making fun at my expense yet again.

Honora gave Lord Lovell a narrow look, but he didn't seem to notice—or perhaps he just didn't care. She watched as he got to his feet and crossed the room, tall and proud in the firelight and moving—as ever—with the confidence of a man born into wealth and title. Any trace of the emotion Honora thought she'd seen in his face was long gone when he turned to her, bottle in hand, and raised a questioning brow.

'Very well. A small one.'

With all the caution Pa had taught her when hunting in the Virginian forests, Honora gathered the blanket more tightly around her and stepped off the bed, her awareness of every move Lord Lovell made heightened by suspicious interest. He had his back to her as he poured and for a moment she admired the clean shape of his dark hair at the nape of his neck, his shoulders pleasantly wide beneath a costly waistcoat, before snatching her eyes away. Another chair stood close to the one Lord Lovell had vacated and, with a breath of hesitation, she folded into it, tucking the blanket around her so not even a sliver of nightgown showed.

She took the glass held out to her with a word of thanks, one hand sneaking from beneath her wrappings. A small sip did indeed help her to relax, although she would have bitten her own tongue than admit it to the man who took his seat next to her.

For a while neither of them broke the silence that descended. Honora drank her wine slowly and Lord Lovell seemed to relish his likewise, a stark difference from the way Frank had used to gulp down a glass and then pour out another.

Drink and gambling had always been his vices—
as well as pretty women, a lesson Honora hadn't
learned until it was far too late.

'It's a shame we have no spices or we could
have mulled the wine. It's getting close to Christmas, after all—less than a fortnight.'

Honora nodded, welcoming the distraction
from her unhappy thoughts of the past. 'It is. In
the chaos of the past day I'd almost forgotten.'

Lord Lovell huffed. 'No hope of that for me.
It's my ward's favourite time of the year and she
begins talking about it about halfway through
July.'

Honora couldn't help the upward flicker of
her eyebrows. 'You have a ward?'

The idea of Lord Lovell in charge of a young
girl seemed so unlikely it took her entirely by
surprise. *That* was something she never would
have imagined. Wasn't he too dismissive and
self-satisfied to concern himself with anyone
else, let alone assume the role of a guardian? To
be entrusted with a ward implied somebody had
a good deal of faith in him, a prospect Honora
couldn't quite believe.

Lord Lovell's face tightened at once and for a
moment he was silent. Perhaps he'd spoken before he'd thought the better of it, Honora won-

dered at the sudden tension in his face, although why he might wish he hadn't she couldn't say.

'Yes. Her name is Charlotte.'

His lips barely moved and his eyes were trained now on the fireplace, deliberately avoiding Honora's curious gaze.

'Somehow I wouldn't have guessed you were a guardian. Has she been with you long?'

She watched his curt nod, his chestnut hair gleaming in the warm glow, but that warmth not quite reaching his eyes.

'Ever since her parents died seven years ago, when she was just turned nine. Her mother was my only cousin so Charlotte came to me. She's the only family I have left and I love her now as if she was my own child.'

Honora swallowed. A piercing shard of yearning lodged between her ribs and the only reply she could find was nod of her own.

How lucky he is to have that love, even if he isn't her real father. I think I would give anything to experience that for myself.

To find Lord Lovell capable of such feelings was disturbing, she had to admit. Before he had seemed so proud, so arrogant in his confidence and so like Frank it had roused her distrust at once. Another handsome, false man come barrelling into her life to stamp all over it with expensive boots.

And yet...

With his sorrowful gaze into the fire Lord Lovell shook that belief, making her question that first impression. Now, with real affection for his ward coming from his own tongue, Honora had to wonder—

Could there be more to Lord Lovell than I first imagined?

He felt Honora's eyes on him, but Isaac affected not to notice, instead keeping his focus firmly on the glowing hearth.

You idiot. Why did you mention Charlotte?

He had been thinking about her—or perhaps brooding was more the word—when he'd become aware Honora watched him from the bed, her secretive observation sending a ripple through him and startling him into unnecessary candour. There was no reason for Honora to even know Charlotte existed and now surely her curiosity would be roused, leaving him to field questions that might stray too close to uncovering the truth.

What possessed you? Have you lost all control, so bewitched by a pretty face?

Still avoiding Honora's study, he took a sip of

his wine, feeling its warmth run down his throat, but doing nothing to chase away the chill in his stomach. Somehow, sitting before the tumbling flames in a comfortable chair with Honora at his side, he had allowed himself to stray too far, her presence an aggravation and a pleasure that had loosened his disloyal tongue. A few more words and he might have betrayed Charlotte's secret, and for what? To make conversation with Honora Blake, the admittedly striking wife of the very man who had thrown Charlotte into the deepest pit of shame?

Look where Father's weakness for a comely woman got him. A miserable second marriage and years of unhappiness—all for nothing. The feelings he allowed to develop for my stepmother led to nothing good and I'll be damned if I let myself fall as he did. It would hurt far more than myself, after all.

Once they arrived in Northamptonshire he would be free of her, Isaac reminded himself as he rolled the stem of his wineglass between two fingers. They would go directly to Carey without stopping at Marlow Manor and from there Honora would be on her own. No doubt Frank's solicitors would advance her some little money from the jointure she'd spoken of, enabling her to engage a manservant and get herself home again, and then Isaac's obligation towards her would be at an end. She would never set foot in Marlow Manor, never lay eyes on Charlotte and never know her husband had left a part of himself behind in the baby almost ready to enter the world.

And she need never know. It's Charlotte's life and reputation on the line and I doubt Honora would be filled with delight either.

Nobody could have missed the twist of her lips on seeing the young wife on the coach. Even Isaac could tell there had been more to Honora's sudden stiffening than she'd wanted to let on—but that wasn't something he should consider. The most pressing concern was to change the subject before she could focus any more time on Charlotte and he grasped at the first idea that came into his mind.

'We could still warm this wine even if we have no spices to mull it. A poker would do the job if you don't mind a little soot in your glass.'

'If you like.'

Isaac needed no more encouragement than that to escape from Honora's scrutiny. He got up immediately to kneel before the fire, taking the poker from the stand beside the hearth and plunging it into the flames. Sparks leapt all around it and the metal handle grew warm, but still Isaac stayed where he was, dragging out the task for some minutes until Honora might have forgotten what they'd been talking of before.

Only when he heard her shift restlessly behind him did he turn back. She was still watching him, but curiosity had faded to simple fatigue and Isaac had to stop himself from allowing a small smile.

She looks as tired as I feel. Hopefully soon both of us will be able to get some sleep, even if only to escape the other.

'Hold out your glass.'

Honora did as he asked without a murmur—*surely proof she's exhausted indeed*—and carefully, taking great pains not to knock the sides of the tumbler, Isaac touched the poker to the wine inside. It sizzled at once, a lovely sound that at any other time he would have enjoyed, had his attention not been abruptly wrested away by something entirely different.

In leaning forward to offer the glass, Honora brought her face closer to his than it had ever been before, even when the soft weight of her had settled on his shoulder in the swaying coach. Then she had been somewhat shielded from him by the brim of her bonnet, but now there was nothing between them but a few scant inches of empty space, the black curls that framed her face falling in gentle corkscrews to almost tickle his nose. Her eyes were on her glass and the downward sweep of her lashes was suddenly the most intriguing thing Isaac had ever seen, hiding the pretty hazel of each iris, but that secrecy only enhancing their allure. At this distance he could see every hair of her dark brows in perfect detail and appreciate the smooth amber of her skin, following the line of her cheekbones down towards full, well-shaped lips…

He was aware his heart had begun to beat more quickly and tried at once to halt its mindless charge, but it was too late. His pulse leapt now like a startled cat, fast and erratic and with a life of its own, and he was powerless to stop the chaos unfolding inside him. Honora was just so close, so *warm*. If he just reached out a hand he could touch her with no effort at all, his fingers brushing soft skin and perhaps even dragging a sigh from that *fascinating* mouth—

Honora jerked back with a yelp, clutching her hand to her chest, and the spell shattered alongside the sound of breaking glass.

'My hand!'

Still a few beats behind reality, it took Isaac a moment to understand—the remnants of the tumbler lying in shards on the floor, a pool of claret surrounding it, the poker still in his fist—

but then his mind caught up with the present and he tossed the poker back into its stand.

'Damn it, Honora, I'm sorry. I must have slipped and touched the glass—did the wine scald you?'

'It certainly feels like it!' She sucked a breath in between her teeth, cupping her fist against the pit of her stomach, and Isaac felt a wave of guilt and alarm rise up inside.

See what happens when you get carried away?

His throat had dried with Honora's cry and now regret for his lapse of control made it even tighter.

If you'd been concentrating instead of mooning about you'd be drinking now, not throwing it all over the carpet. Take a hold of yourself!

'Stay there. I'll get a compress.'

A handkerchief steeped in cold water would have to do and as Isaac poured some into the wash bowl he attempted to steady his whirling thoughts. That flash of yearning for Honora was the absolute last thing he wanted to entertain. It was dangerous, worrying and not to be repeated. She was *Frank Blake's wife*, albeit now widow, and Isaac felt a glimmer of loathing for the man who had died in his arms. Not content with ruining Honora's life Frank had tainted Charlotte's, too, a fact he couldn't escape—Honora was a reminder of how he had failed to keep poor Charlotte safe from harm and any entanglement was far too complicated to even entertain. Honora might be intriguing in her lightning flit between fire and ice, but there could be no more to it than that. Even if his father's example hadn't taught him the folly of seriously pursuing a woman, his own good sense *must* tell him this absurd interest would lead to nothing good.

One more day.

Isaac wrung the handkerchief out, feeling a little as though he had been wrung out himself.

One more day and then I'll never have to see her again. If I want to look at a pretty face I'll go to a card party or a ball—plenty to see there and none of them a risk to Charlotte or myself.

He returned to the fire. Honora's lips were set tightly and she gripped her hand with the other, casting Isaac a suspicious look when he knelt at her side.

'Let me see.'

'I'm not sure that's wise.'

'I need to put this compress on it. Let me see.'

With a low mutter she extended her arm, watching his every move as he reached out to take her hand. His fingers found hers and Isaac saw something flicker over her face—a nameless glimmer that he knew, without knowing quite how, was twin to the expression that streaked over his own.

It was a sensation so similar to the one that had seized him when they shook on their bargain at Wycliff Lodge that Isaac almost choked on his own breath. The very same burst of heat kindled at the feeling of her slender fingers in his, so delicate and yet if he wasn't mistaken slightly calloused by real work. Did she help her maid with household tasks? he wondered distantly without taking his eyes from her face. He'd never felt roughened skin on a lady's hand before, but then there were so many things about Honora he hadn't encountered in his rakish career and as she stared back at him his stomach dropped in dismay.

I must take control of this ridiculous fancy. There must be some way to exorcise this demon before it's too late.

He was still holding her little hand, gripping those slim fingers with hardly a clue now of what he'd intended to do with them, and he only remembered just in time to look down at her knuckles. His thoughts were spinning faster and faster, concern growing with each beat of his leaping heart, and her voice sounded as though it came from far away when Honora spoke.

'Your diagnosis?'

He cleared his dry throat. 'No damage. The compress will be sufficient.'

'Good. As I recall that was my mother's treatment for most things.' Honora shifted a little in her chair, so close to where Isaac knelt she almost brushed him with the blanket around her shoulders. 'That and kissing better whatever mischief I'd done to myself, romping around outside. I was never a very ladylike child.'

Isaac stiffened, his fingers suddenly clumsy in their work of wrapping the damp handkerchief around Honora's fist. That word—*kissing*—sent a spark of static electricity right through to his very centre, bold and brazen and spelling out the very essence of his most secret desire.

In that moment that was *exactly* what he wanted to do: abandon his self-control and indulge the ungovernable part of him that so insistently wanted to taste Honora's lips. Despite every instinct that cried out for him to turn away, some other voice shouted louder, a flicker of insanity that it seemed nothing could quench. Honora had quite innocently hit the target of his shameful feelings as squarely as an arrow, unwittingly adding fuel to the fire that already raged in Isaac's chest.

Or perhaps—not so innocently at all.

Slowly, his throat painfully tight, Isaac allowed his gaze to lift from their study of her hand.

Honora watched him with an undecipherable flicker of something in the very depths of her eyes. It might have been any number of things—some good and some not so—but she hadn't pulled her hand from his grasp and her lips, stained a little from the cheap red wine, were parted as if on a silent question.

Could she be thinking the same? One kiss to perhaps free both of us from this folly?

Isaac could hardly tear his eyes away. Perhaps Honora truly *did* feel the atmosphere, too, charged like the sky before a storm. On the coach she had been so insistent in her dislike of him, but heaven knew how desire laughed in the face of logic. Her rational mind might have spoken, but surely there was no way her instinct could have missed the tension stretched out between them now, tightly wound and aching to be severed. Forbidden fruit always looked sweeter, after all, and what could be more forbidden than a friend of the husband who had turned her heart to ice?

Isaac made up his mind with the feeling of throwing himself to the wolves.

I said I needed to exorcise this demon—this

may be my only chance. One leap to break this strain and then I can put it from my mind for good.

Usually when Isaac kissed a woman it began in the same way. A curl would be brushed gently away from a glowing cheek and then his hand would cup that soft curve before slowly, tenderly, bringing his lady forward until her lips met his and the same old dance could begin, his mouth moving and hers following his lead, making sure not to startle her while confidently taking charge. It was the same routine he always used and he trusted in its success, a coolly orchestrated thing that allowed him to act without thinking or feeling anything more—

This time, however, everything changed.

When he brought his lips down on Honora's there was no familiar choreography, no usual sense of being in complete control. Instead every sinew in his body cried out at a wave that swept through him like lava down a mountainside, torching everything in its path with molten heat and leaving him breathless.

She tasted just as he'd thought she would, of wine and warmth, and her lips were so soft it was frightening. There was nothing for him to cling to, none of his old indifference holding out a guiding hand and instead he was set adrift to be swept out on a strange and unnamed tide. He felt her breath on his face, her hand still in his and he was on his knees, both literally and figuratively, helpless to stop the wild pounding of his heart or his enjoyment of that sharp-tongued mouth turned gentle under his own.

It was the itching of his hands to draw her closer that broke Isaac's trance. He wanted to hold her, perhaps slip a palm round to fit against her back, and he broke away as the temptation to obey that urge bloomed like a flower. That was too far, too much—and by the look on Honora's flushed, flame-lit face he'd gone quite far enough already.

She stared at him, apparently too shocked to even be offended. Her eyes were round, all suggestion of tiredness gone, and she seemed so much younger with her usual composure stolen by wordless disbelief.

Isaac rose to his feet as quickly as he could and backed away, a cold finger of dread beginning to snake down his spine. She didn't look angry, but then she didn't look pleased, exactly, either, and his cursed decision had done *nothing* to quell the torment raging in his innards.

'Forgive me. I thought—' He ran a hand through already disordered hair. What *had* he thought? It seemed so stupid now to think Honora might have been hinting for him to act, clearly a figment of his imagination run wild by a foolish desire he struggled to tame. Of course she hadn't felt the same draw he had. He'd made a catastrophic error, making himself look a fool, and, worse than that, his weakness for Honora hadn't diminished one iota, instead the touch of her lips against his something he wanted more than anything to feel again. 'I made a mistake. I shouldn't have done that.'

An understatement if ever there was one.

Honora opened her mouth to speak, but nothing came out, only a parting of those wine-red lips Isaac looked away from hastily. When she managed to find a reply it was hoarse, the voice of a woman confused or horrified—or perhaps both, Isaac thought with bitter regret.

'*What* did you think? That I'd finally succumbed to your charms?' She clutched her blankets to her tighter than ever before and from somewhere deep inside seemed to dredge up some flicker of her usual spirit, momentarily suspended by shock. 'You thought I'd finally seen reason and would fall swooning into your arms like everybody else?'

'No. Of course not. You made your feelings for me perfectly clear today.' Isaac leaned against the fireplace, resisting the urge to place his head in it as Honora's voice rang in his ears. *You complete oaf. Far from saving yourself you've just made things a hundred times worse.*

'You can't go about kissing whomever you please, Lord Lovell! Or perhaps you think a man of your stature can do as he likes?'

Isaac closed his eyes briefly. Honora was entitled to be piqued, of course, but each sharp word stoked the embers of his temper and he took a moment to ensure it remained under his control. 'It was a lapse of judgement and I apologise. The strain of the last week... I'm not myself. Please forgive me.'

He saw Honora swallow, a quick movement of her slender throat that captured his attention with no effort at all. She still seemed ruffled, her feathers stirred like an indignant hen, but she allowed him a short nod, an acceptance of his pitiful explanation Isaac knew he didn't deserve.

'Well. As you apologised, I suppose so. This once.' She glanced up at him, the briefest flash of hazel set against cheeks that with a start of confusion Isaac could have sworn glowed brighter than before despite her apparent disapproval. She looked flushed, so startlingly similar to a shy girl rather than a grown woman it made him blink. 'You were Frank's friend and I was his wife. That can't be forgotten.'

'Of course.' Isaac found his jaw was set, teeth pressed together as if to guard his tongue. If his stupidity of the night was anything to go by that was a wise precaution—who knew what might slip out if he wasn't careful? With one rash act he'd opened himself up to more aggravation from Honora, more risk he needn't have courted, and that danger was something he could do without. Frank had brought Isaac's world crashing down and now with Honora before him he feared things might get even worse.

'I'd never be able to forget that. You can take that for a promise.'

Chapter Five

Lord Lovell was nowhere to be seen when Honora woke from a fitful doze to greet another freezing morning and she washed and dressed with swift unease, fearing his reappearance any moment. The absolute last thing she wanted was for him to catch her about her toilette—although modesty wasn't the only reason she dreaded his footstep outside their chamber door.

You sly, dissembling thing. Your performance last night was one Sarah Siddons would have admired. What was it Ma always said? A man will do whatever you want him to as long as he thinks it's his idea?

Feigning surprise was all she'd been able to do when Lord Lovell had leaned down to cover her disloyal lips. She could hardly admit to having been the one to sow the seed in the first place, talk of kissing springing from her tongue before she could stop it. With Lord Lovell kneeling so close to her with the firelight playing across his proud features, that whisper of new, unexpected sentiment for his ward warming her despite her resistance... What chance had Honora had of controlling the wayward swerve of her thoughts into places they shouldn't have strayed, the desire to taste Lord Lovell's sometimes cruel lips leaping inside her like an animal in a trap? She'd spoken too soon, uttered that magic word—*kissing*—and lit the fuse on a trail of gunpowder, leading to an explosion she'd been a fool to allow.

And so you denied you meant anything of the sort and allowed him to think he'd come up with it himself, offending you in the process. Safer than the truth, definitely, but cowardly all the same.

Carefully avoiding the disapproving gaze of her reflection Honora stood before the cracked mirror mounted above the washstand, twisting and pinning her hair into place. A glance down into her own eyes was out of the question, the idea of what she might see there something Honora didn't want to dwell on. She'd all but lured Lord Lovell into kissing her with her well-timed hint, for goodness sake—a friend of Frank's and doubtless just as dangerous to her well-being as her husband had been all those years ago.

That she could have sworn she saw real emotion on his face as he'd gazed unseen into the fire meant nothing. Neither did the gleam of warmth she'd heard in his tone when he spoke of his Charlotte, surely both hazy mirages that would trick her into thinking him something more than a charming rake. His kiss had certainly been skilled enough to imply he'd had ample practice, the soft brush of his mouth over Honora's *just* the right pressure and speed and more enjoyable than any she'd experienced before...

Honora's face grew hot just *thinking* about it and she turned hastily away from the mirror before she could see her own blush. The events of the night should be forgotten as soon as possible for both their sakes. Fewer than fifty miles now lay between her and Frank's lawyers in Carey— less than a day's travelling and then she would never need lay eyes on Lord Lovell ever again. She could send the money she owed to him by letter and that would be that. A strange, disturbing interlude in a life that would soon hopefully go back to being entirely unremarkable, not to be troubled any more by any handsome, hazardous men.

A brisk tap at the door made her jump.

'Are you almost ready? The coach will be leaving soon.'

Lord Lovell's disembodied voice crept up to caress her ear and Honora felt her cheeks flare once again. Was she going to turn the colour of a radish every time he spoke to her from now on? she wondered, ramming one final pin into her curls with more force than necessary. She could curse aloud for letting her weakness get the better of her the previous night and even more so now she would have to sit beside Lord Lovell for hours, jolting along next to him and feeling the firm breadth of his shoulder against hers. Perhaps if she was lucky there would be no other passengers in the coach and she could take refuge on the seat opposite, reclaiming her corner and trying to stop her mind from revisiting how every nerve had lit up like a firework at the touch of his hand, the fine hairs on her nape arching up to celebrate his lips moving with such purpose across her own—

'Honora? Did you hear me?'

'Yes, I heard you,' she managed to croak. 'I'll meet you downstairs.'

This time she heard the tread of heavy boots as they retreated and she ran a hand across her brow. Putting off the inevitable wouldn't make it go away. The best she could do was face Lord Lovell head on and try to maintain the icy façade that she hoped would be her saviour. He *couldn't* know how much she had enjoyed their encounter, or how rapidly the mere sound of his voice sent her heart skittering. He'd be too pleased by half and if there was something Lord Lovell needed no more of it was self-confidence…just the same as comely, charming, *devastating* Frank.

With one final glance around the room Honora opened the door and stepped on to the tavern's narrow landing. It was an old building and the boards creaked beneath her boots, voices coming from below and a harassed-looking maid bustling up the stairs with an armful of laundry. Honora drew to one side to let her pass—and heard a grunt as her foot came down smartly on that of a man standing at her back. He must have come out of a room further down the corridor and walked up behind her, Honora thought as she turned to apologise, and when she saw his face she couldn't help a strange flicker of unease.

'I beg your pardon, sir. I didn't realise you were there.'

The blond man who had approached her near the fire the previous evening smiled back. His cheeks lifted, but there was no change to the shape of his eyes and with another uncomfortable flicker Honora realised how much she wanted to move away. He wasn't just looking at her—it was more like a hunter singling out its prey, as if she was a helpless creature he wanted to tear at with sharp teeth.

'Not at all. My fault entirely. I was standing too close.'

He gestured apologetically—and then Honora's stomach dropped as she felt his cold hand lightly graze her arm, so intimate and unwanted she froze perfectly still.

'In truth I was hoping to meet you here. I saw you arrive last night and will admit your beauty captured my attention at once. Won't you stay and talk a while?'

The maid had disappeared and for a moment all Honora could think was how much she wished somebody would come out of one of the other rooms. The fair-haired stranger was close, much too close, and she took a step out of his reach.

'Thank you, but, no. My coach will be leaving soon and I've no intention of missing it.'

'Ah.' The traveller's smile hadn't faltered, still hanging from his lips like a cobweb at a broken window. 'There's no way I could persuade you?'

'I'm afraid not.'

'On account of your husband?'

For the briefest of seconds Frank's face flashed through Honora's mind and she faltered, confused. Did this man know him? Were they in some way acquainted? Then she realised her mistake. It was Lord Lovell the stranger was referring to, not Frank, and he laughed at her hesitation.

'That was a joke. From what I overheard last night I know you're not married to your companion—yet you still spent the night in his room...'

Honora felt her lips part as she looked up into his face, unable to fully comprehend the sudden turn the conversation had taken. What had she stumbled into? And what *exactly* was he implying? It certainly sounded as though he was making a distasteful insinuation about her morals and with her spine feeling like a block of ice Honora backed away.

'I'm not sure what you can mean, but you'll excuse me all the same. My *companion* is waiting for me and I don't feel inclined to speak with you any longer.'

Perhaps the stranger didn't see the warning in Honora's eyes or perhaps he thought it insincere. Either way he merely smiled more widely—and coldly—and reached out once again for her arm. 'Don't go so soon. I'm sure he can spare you a few moments.' His fingers brushed her sleeve, but Honora jerked away just in time, prompting a cloud to pass over the unfamiliar face. 'You're a good deal too proud for a woman who's just

spent the night with a man who isn't her husband. I'd have thought the time for airs and
graces has long since passed.'

Without a word Honora turned away. The
hairs at the back of her neck were raised just
as they had been by Lord Lovell's kiss, but that
had been with delight, not disgust, and now as
she hurried for the stairs she was aware how
every breath came sharp and fast. It wasn't the
first time a man had shown too much interest
in her and, knowing her luck, it wouldn't be the
last, but she couldn't remember one so frankly
predatory before and the thought of what he'd
been suggesting made her stomach churn. *She*
knew only circumstance had thrown her and
Lord Lovell together, but evidently the stranger
had come to a different conclusion—one he'd
thought to turn to his own advantage, casting
aspersions on her honour she wouldn't soon forgive.

'Honora? Are you well?'

Reaching the bottom step, she saw Lord
Lovell's quick look, a narrow scan that must
have taken in her flushed cheeks and breathing
heightened with what she realised—with a pang
of displeasure—was fright. It rankled to know
she had been afraid, yet the blond stranger had

put her so on edge, something so unnerving in his air her usual self-assuredness had failed her.

'Perfectly.'

'You look ruffled.'

Out of the corner of her eye she saw a figure descending the stairs behind her and stiffened as the fair-haired man passed by. He threw her a bright smile that she didn't return and nodded at Lord Lovell, who followed the man's leisurely retreat with a pinch of dark brows.

Honora looked at the worn carpet beneath her boots, feeling Lord Lovell's questioning gaze on her downturned face. She had no intention of telling him what had just transpired or how a gleam of aggravating fear had bled under her skin, but all the same she couldn't ignore an inexplicable sense of relief in his presence. He didn't need to know how her heart had leaped to see him appear, frowning but at least familiar and the perfect defence against the stranger's designs. No doubt Lord Lovell would crow to know he'd been of use to her and she couldn't allow that—even if it was the truth. After the events of the night things were confused enough between them and nothing else should add to the already disturbed waters.

'Not at all, I assure you. I imagine the driver will be ready to leave by now. Shall we go down?'

* * *

The coach was in fact still being loaded as Isaac stepped from the inn's friendly warmth into the winter's chill and he hugged himself as a freezing breeze tried to find an unguarded opening beneath his coat. Beside him Honora sucked in a harsh breath, white plumes drifting from her mouth to rise and mingle with those coming from his own—not for the first time turning Isaac's thoughts in the direction of her lips.

Stop that. You learned your lesson last night, or should have if you've a lick of sense.

Gritting his teeth on a grumble, Isaac fixed his eyes on the restless horses, determined not to allow his gaze to stray to where Honora wavered on the very edge of his vision, jigging from foot to foot in an effort to keep warm in the most distracting manner possible. Did she do it on purpose, these things to catch his attention? If he hadn't known better he might have wondered at her knack of drawing his eye, her bobbing up and down now shaking the glossy curls peeping from under her bonnet to shine like a raven's wing in the crisp sunlight.

Apparently she'd decided to pretend the events of the previous night hadn't happened. She hadn't mentioned them at any rate and there was no way on earth Isaac would be the one to raise the subject. As far as he was concerned the sooner they both forgot about his painful lapse in judgement the better—especially considering there were still some miles to go before Carey came near.

Other passengers were waiting to board the carriage into Northamptonshire. There was no sign among them of the fair-haired stranger Isaac had seen on the stairs and he could have sworn he saw Honora glance around as if searching likewise, her shoulders relaxing slightly at the traveller's disappearance. For all her denials she had seemed ill at ease and the man's odd smile as he had passed her, combined with her rigid posture and tense face, didn't help persuade Isaac nothing had happened when his back was turned.

Not that it's any of my business. Nothing to do with Honora Blake is any of my concern.

'It's even more bitter today than yesterday.'

Honora's voice at his shoulder was thin with cold and when he looked down he saw how she was huddled into her cloak like a turtle withdrawn into its shell. She was peering upwards at the gleaming clouds, the huge white heaps lit from behind and threateningly heavy-bellied.

'Back home clouds like those would mean snow. Blizzards, too, sometimes, although I'd never seen a storm as bad as the one during my first winter in England. I recall it made the whole house shake and forced a mountain of soot down the parlour chimney.'

Almost amused, Isaac nodded.

Talking about the weather to steer conversation away from any awkward subjects, whether it be of kissing or discomforting men?

Honora must have been in England too long indeed, although beneath his wry entertainment Isaac felt a flicker of real curiosity. He still knew next to nothing about her, hardly able to glean anything to answer the questions that rose unbidden in his mind. She *was* fascinating, despite his attempts at indifference, and that prickle of curiosity overcame the determination to hold himself aloof that his night-time lapse had made so essential.

'Where exactly is back home? Somewhere in the Americas, I think?'

'That's right. Virginia, just below the Blue Ridge Mountains. Most beautiful place on earth if you want my opinion.' There was the barest suggestion of wistfulness in her tone and it caught Isaac's ear at once.

'You miss it?'

She hesitated, seeming to weigh up whether he deserved a truthful answer. 'Yes. My parents still live there, in the same house I grew up in. My father built it himself and I can still remember every knot in every wooden beam even though I haven't seen it or them in five years.'

'Five years? They haven't come to visit you in all that time?'

Honora shook her head, all at once the wistful edge replaced by vague defensiveness. 'It's a very long and dangerous journey. My father is in poor health and my mother could never leave him to travel alone.'

'But couldn't you have gone to them?'

She flicked him a long, cool glance. Perhaps he was asking too many questions. Certainly his interest was well and truly roused, his desire to learn more about her uncomfortably strong and yet too tempting to be ignored.

'During our marriage Frank wasted all our money on gambling and other vices. I couldn't afford the passage then and once he left... If I'd asked my parents they would have known how Frank had abandoned me and I couldn't bear the shame. They risked everything for their love, faced such hardship for choosing to honour their marriage—how could I admit to them what a mess I'd made of my own? Especially when they'd warned me against marrying him in the first place? We parted on bad terms when I saw them last and I'm heartily ashamed of some things I said. To go back now, to feel their love for me again, would be more than I deserve.'

'You would want to see them again, however? If you had the chance?'

'Of course. We were so close once, before all this began… But I can't forgive myself for choosing Frank over them. Do you see? This is my punishment. This unhappiness is what I deserve.'

Isaac frowned, but Honora didn't see it. She had turned her face away, hiding beneath the brim of her bonnet so he might not see whatever emotion flickered in her eyes. She'd given a far more honest answer than he had anticipated and now he hardly knew how to respond, a shadow of pain underlining each of her words that he suddenly found he wanted to help her forget.

She's estranged from her parents? Because of Frank? Just when I thought he couldn't get any worse.

'I didn't realise.'

'Well. Now you know my situation there's really nothing more to ask.' Still looking towards the coach, Honora held up a hand in response to the driver's gesture for them to board, her back ramrod straight and so tense Isaac felt a gleam of pity surface. 'I have nobody here except for Mary and she has her own family to occupy her, something with which I was never blessed…to my lasting sadness. With my parents the other side of the globe I might as well be entirely alone in the world. It certainly feels that way at times.'

Without waiting for his reply, Honora stepped towards the coach and Isaac watched her go, momentarily thrown by her unexpected candour. There was no bitterness in her words—only the resignation of a woman who had come to terms with her lot in life and accepted it without complaining. Her strength was admirable, some disobedient imp murmured in Isaac's ear, yet more proof of the spirit he already knew she possessed. The longer he spent in her company the greater his appreciation of that mettle grew… and all the more reason for him to deliver her to Carey as soon as humanly possible.

Think of Charlotte. Think how badly wrong things could go if Honora learned she carries Frank's child.

That was what he should focus on, he thought as he followed Honora up the coach step. Charlotte was his first concern in all things, the only woman it was safe for him to love, or had been before the possibility of her following his mother to an early grave rose to beckon her in. Provided she survived the perils of childbirth she would never grow tired of him, or long for another, or cause him the misery his father had known as a result of entering into marriage. She was his responsibility, not Honora—and if he had learned anything about his reluctant companion it was that she was quite capable of looking after herself.

There were already two people seated inside the coach, one on either bench, and Isaac didn't know whether to be disappointed or relieved that he couldn't sit next to Honora. Instead he took his place beside an older gentleman, leaving her to settle into a corner by a woman with a large basket on her knee. The usual polite smiles and murmured greetings were exchanged and then with a clatter of hooves they were off, swaying out of the inn's yard and back on to the road, the coach's wheels bouncing over the pitted ground and the jingle of the horses' tack sounding almost festive in the wintry air.

Isaac peered out at the bare trees sliding past, their branches reaching up to claw at the sky. Honora was right. The clouds certainly threatened snow and he wondered if Marlow Manor would soon be covered with a blanket of soft white. Usually Charlotte would be the first one to pitch a clumsy snowball if that happened, but she stayed in her rooms now, hiding away from any prying eyes that might notice her swollen middle. Her wan little face had grown so thin and pale it pained him to see, her misery palpable, but nothing he could take away. He'd bear it all for her if he could and hated how powerless he was to lift the shame and unhappiness that stalked her, still only half grown and yet soon to have motherhood thrust upon her, a role she'd neither planned nor desired.

Unlike Honora. Judging by what she said it seems a baby was something she longed for. Such cruel irony for Frank to leave Charlotte with a child she didn't want, while Honora's wish for one never came true.

Isaac allowed himself one swift glance in her direction. She had her eyes closed, head moving gently with the rhythm of the coach, and he couldn't suppress a sudden searing memory of that same head resting on his shoulder the evening before. It seemed neither of them had slept much during the previous night with all its strange twists and turns and his eyes felt gritty with tiredness, itching to close likewise and abandon him to blessed unconsciousness. There was too much to think about while he was awake—*Honora, Charlotte, the baby, Frank*—and the yearning to escape was irresistible. Hopefully he wouldn't end up with his own head in the elderly gentleman's lap if he allowed himself to drift away for a while, a prospect mirroring Honora's mortifying lapse closely enough to summon a grim smile.

If I did disgrace myself I'd deserve it. I suppose I ought to be punished in some way, for my behaviour towards Honora last night and for concealing the truth of Frank's death. It might be a necessary evil, but I can't help but feel she should know what really happened—or shake the suspicion I might still get caught out.

It was the movement of the woman next to her gathering up her belongings that woke Honora from her light doze. They were changing horses again. The coach had stopped at another inn and the cabin was empty now apart from Lord Lovell propped up in the opposite corner, his sharp eyes firmly shut and the brim of his hat pulled down low on his brow. Apparently he was too deeply asleep to hear the sounds that echoed around the inn's yard as fresh horses were hitched in place and Honora might have continued her own catnap if a new passenger hadn't clambered inside, closing the door behind him just as the coach began to pull away once more.

Arranging her skirts more warmly around

her ankles Honora looked up, a vague greeting hovering on her lips to offer to the newcomer—which froze the moment she saw his face.

'That was a close-run thing. Very nearly missed my connection…and you. How lucky for me I didn't.'

Any leftover sleepiness evaporated instantly as Honora took in the cold smile of the fair-haired stranger, staring in sudden dread as he dropped into the seat beside her. She could only watch as he glanced across at Lord Lovell, the horrible smile widening as he noted the tightly closed eyes.

'I thought he was asleep—certainly looked it through the window. That gives us an opportunity to get to know each other without any interruptions.'

Honora's throat constricted, her tongue dry.

He must have caught an earlier coach to get ahead of us. Was he waiting for me?

The thought twisted her innards sickeningly. Something in the ominous curve of those lips robbed her of her usual spirit and she could hardly muster a reply, instead only able to mutter as her heart began to pound in her ears.

'It does nothing of the sort. I can wake him up in a matter of moments.'

The blond man chuckled lightly as if she had

said something amusing. He crossed one leg over the other, one arm coming up to rest along the back of Honora's seat and turn her blood to ice. 'But I don't think you will. You could have told him about our encounter at the inn, but you didn't, did you? There must have been a reason you didn't want him involved. To avoid a scene, perhaps? Or more likely…maybe you weren't as offended as you were pretending to be. That alone gave me reason for encouragement.'

Honora pressed herself as far back into her seat as she could, never taking her eyes off the revolting specimen in front of her. Back at the inn there had been at least the possibility she'd misunderstood his intentions, but now there was no doubt what the stranger wanted. Captivated by her striking looks, he thought he could possess her, taking her connection to Lord Lovell for that of a woman of uncertain virtue, and despite the fear prickling up her spine Honora felt her hackles raise.

'I am every bit as offended,' she spat. Her reticule lay on the seat beside her and she wondered distantly if she had time to snatch it up and delve inside for the flintlock. 'Whatever you take me for, you are incorrect. You will remove your arm and keep your distance.'

The smile slid from the fair man's face. His

cheeks darkened a little, growing dusky pink
with what Honora recognised with a thrill of
apprehension was ugly temper.

'You're in no position to issue orders. I have
the winning card, after all.'

When she didn't speak he reached for her
wrist. Cold fingers closed around it and Honora
tried to pull away, pulse leaping, but the stranger
holding firm.

'If you don't oblige me the way you did your
friend over there…' he jerked his head in Lord
Lovell's direction '…I shall return to the inn and
find out your name. I have many friends in many
places. How long do you think it will take for
half of England to learn how you behave with
men who aren't your husband? Is that what you
want?'

Honora swallowed, her throat filled with broken glass.

He wouldn't. A rumour like that would easily
reach back to Somerset, the culmination of the
whispers that already circulated around her. Her
name was already stained by Frank's abandonment. How could she ever show her face again
if she was brought any lower than that?

'That would be a lie. I've done nothing that I
need be ashamed of.'

'But who would believe your word over

mine?' The cruel fingers dug into her skin as the man leaned forward, the jolting of the coach making him sway nauseatingly. 'Who would side with you? Who would take the word of a—'

But Honora would never know what slur he intended to utter next.

'Take your hand off her. Now.'

The blond man jumped, his head snapping round to look at Lord Lovell—who was awake and watching every movement, his face turned to granite and his jaw held so firm Honora couldn't help a tick of admiration despite the snakes coiling in her stomach.

'I was—'

'I know exactly what you were doing and *I'm* doing *you* a favour by intervening. One more moment and she would have taken matters into her own hands— that's a far more frightening prospect than any threat of my own.'

The stranger let go of Honora's wrist and she scrambled away at once, fairly flinging herself into the seat beside Lord Lovell. She barely had time to register his reassuring squeeze of her fingers—or the spark that crackled through her at the contact—before he was on his feet, the other man flinching backwards, but Lord Lovell's fist flying out toward the carriage roof rather than to land a blow.

'Driver, stop a moment. Somebody wishes to get out.'

Lord Lovell's stare never wavered as the coach shuddered to a halt, dark eyes boring into the traveller's watery blue. He seemed to have grown taller still in his anger—on *her* behalf, Honora thought with a jolt of surprise. It was unexpected yet more pleasant than she might have predicted, and when he shoved the other passenger bodily towards the door her amazement only increased.

'This is as far as you wanted to travel by this coach. Get out.'

'How dare—? You can't make me!'

'I can and I am. Unless you'd like to argue with me further?'

Honora watched with shallow breaths as Lord Lovell bent down, his face mere inches from the fair-headed man's. The last time Lord Lovell had been so close to another it had been her on the receiving end, but there was nothing romantic about the working of Lord Lovell's jaw now, or the flexing of fingers into balled fists.

Without another word the stranger ducked his head and slid out of the door, stumbling down the steps to land untidily on the frosted ground. Lord Lovell threw his bag out after him, slamming the door on the man's pitifully angry shout.

'I'll find out her name, and yours, and then everybody will know what kind of woman she is! You might think you can do as you wish, but I'll make you sorry!'

Lord Lovell's lip merely curled. With another sharp rap on the cabin's ceiling he folded back down into his seat, sitting for a moment with his head lowered as the coach lurched forward again. When he looked up there was something in his expression that made Honora pause, some complex mixture of aggravation and—could it be gruff *concern* that touched the soft underbelly of her guarded heart and sent a rush running through her she struggled to name?

'Did he hurt you?'

Honora shook her head, still trying to understand the sequence of events that made it spin. Lord Lovell had defended her and not merely half-heartedly—he had been genuinely angry in his defence of her, with no sign of the offhand indifference she might have expected given their strained relationship. Frank had never intervened on her behalf for anything at any time during their marriage. That Lord Lovell had leapt into the fray with no hesitation was surprising indeed.

'No. I think you awoke just in time, although I never would have anticipated your taking my part so strongly—' She broke off, suddenly unable to look him in the eye. A hundred different feelings and thoughts ran riot through her mind, one chasing after the other in strange half-formed bursts. Lord Lovell had protected her, gone above and beyond what her own husband would have done in his place—and for all her determination never to fall into a man's arms ever again, to never depend on anyone but herself, she couldn't deny a gleam of warmth in her soul.

Lord Lovell frowned, a crisp fold appearing between his eyebrows.

'You may be among the most trying individuals of my acquaintance, but you are still deserving of respect. I won't have you spoken to like that or manhandled by every wretch that thinks he has the right to any woman he pleases. That rarely ends well—I've seen it.'

His voice was low and bitter and Honora felt her own brow crease in reply. When else had Lord Lovell seen the mistreatment of a woman to speak so strongly against it? And who had it ended for so badly? He spoke as though from experience, but the grim set of his expression gave Honora no encouragement to ask.

She looked down at her fingers twisted together on her lap. It was impossible for them to still tingle with the sensation of Lord Lovell's squeeze, yet Honora could have been fooled into thinking she could feel his touch lingering on her skin, delightful and confusing and only adding to the tumult already looping through her gut.

'He said he'd ask for my name at the inn and then tell everybody he knows that my honour is…tainted. Do you think he was in earnest?'

Lord Lovell gave a rough snort. 'He can ask if he likes, but it won't get him very far. I gave the owner false names for both of us—to avoid a situation exactly like this one.'

At Honora's blank look of surprise he clicked his teeth in a tut. 'Did you really think I'd take any chances with your reputation? I know how people like to whisper and I've lately come to be aware of the damage that can do to a respectable woman. I wouldn't want that for you.'

Honora hardly knew how to reply. He'd had the forethought to not only consider her reputation, but to actually take steps to safeguard it? That was a kindness she never would have imagined to occur to a cocky, feckless man—but then hadn't her opinion of Lord Lovell begun to change already, his love for his ward and protection of herself bathing him in a newly positive light? If she wasn't careful she might fall more prey to Lord Lovell's ready charms than she had already, his hidden goodness beginning to peep through and challenge everything she thought she knew.

'Thank you.' She attempted a smile, but her lips refused to co-operate, too stiff to move into anything but a brittle curve. 'For your help today and for acting to save my good name. I'm grateful.'

Lord Lovell shifted in his seat. It seemed he could handle her irritation with him better than her praise, for he nodded shortly at the scenery outside the window without meeting her eye.

'Yes, well, Carey isn't far away now. I'd wager we'll arrive within the hour and then you'll be free of me. I imagine you must be wishing the minutes away until I set you down at Frank's lawyers and leave you alone.'

The white clouds had swollen even more, it seemed to Honora as she gazed out at them, trying to think up a suitable response. Snow would start to fall soon, covering the landscape with pristine white and paving the way for Christmas. By the time the festivities began Honora would be safely back at Wycliff Lodge—far away from Lord Lovell and destined never to set eyes on him again. That was how it should be, of course…and yet some fragment of her, deeply buried and doubtless foolish, wished their parting didn't have to come so soon. She was just getting to know him, catching a glimpse of the real man beneath the title and swagger, and she couldn't deny she liked what she saw.

Which is precisely why it's a good thing you go your separate ways now. Her rational side spoke up firmly, squashing any argument with its cool logic. *You thought you'd found a good man once before and you were sadly mistaken. Best escape now before you make another error that could ruin your life even further.*

Honora swallowed. The little voice was right. She'd already strayed far too close to the edge. Lord Lovell's kiss had threatened to awaken something in her she'd long since thought dead and buried, something she had no use for, and that couldn't be allowed. The longer she stayed in his company the more the risk to her safety grew—the lesson Frank had taught her and one she didn't intend to forget.

'I won't pretend to be sad the journey is over, but as for the rest... I couldn't possibly say.'

Chapter Six

Isaac sank down more comfortably into his favourite chair and thought fleetingly how glad he was to be back in the warmth of Marlow Manor. His prediction had been correct. Snow had begun to fall just as the coach entered the county of Northamptonshire and now it was settling the temperature would only plummet further into a blustery, freezing night.

The tip of Honora's nose had been rosy as she'd bobbed a goodbye curtsy to him outside the rooms of Filliol, Ellis and Drew three hours before, her breath rising in white streams that matched the clouds above. His final glimpse of her was the rippling of her black coat scattered with flecks of white as she climbed the stairs and disappeared inside—bringing their acquaintance to an end, or so Isaac knew he should hope, drawing a line under a complicated encounter he ought to be glad to see the back of.

And yet…

Alone in his study he sat back in his chair, eyes roaming the various portraits that smiled down at him. A particularly fine one of his mother hung in pride of place beside one darkening window—its prime position another bone of contention during his father's disastrous second marriage—and not for the first time Isaac wished the woman contained within it could offer him advice. It was hardly possible to *miss* a person he'd never known, but as always the sight of those painted eyes looking down at him so kindly kindled a spark of regret. She'd died giving birth to him, the long-awaited heir Father had been so keen for, but had it been worth it, in the end? The death of one to bring forth the life of another—a fate he would keep Charlotte from at all costs. *She* was the only person who mattered…or had been, until one other had come crashing into his life to make him suddenly doubt…

Of all the women in the world, why did it have to be Honora *damnation* Blake who had captured his interest? Her meeting with Frank's lawyer would be over by now and she would no doubt be settling into a respectable hotel for the night rather than a rough inn no place for a woman on her own—even one with a pistol in her handbag. Mr Drew would have advanced her the money from Frank's will to engage a man to escort her home the next day, with the promise of a tidy sum ringing in her ears if her hopes were correct, and that was that. Nothing else for Isaac to do but wait for her letter containing the money she insisted she owed him. Their connection was at an end and not a moment too soon, the unsuitability of Honora as an object of interest given her link to Frank something that couldn't be ignored.

So why then did he feel some ghost of regret that she had disappeared from his life just as abruptly as she'd entered it?

Because you're an idiot? A simpleton who learned nothing from the example Father set when it came to the perils of women?

Isaac realised he was clenching his teeth and made a conscious effort to relax his jaw.

He was being ridiculous. Honora was beautiful, that much was true, and dismissive of his face and fortune in a way both piquing and refreshing, but she was gone now and he ought to forget her, just as he had so easily forgotten many other pretty faces attached to far less vexing females. That the stranger on the coach had riled him so was unfortunate, more proof of the dangerous fondness that had begun to unfold in Isaac's chest. He could have merrily thrown the blackguard out of the window for daring to manhandle her, even aside from the predatory advances that reminded him so uncomfortably of Frank's treatment of Charlotte—and his own now regrettable behaviour, if he was truthful, an unwelcome acknowledgement that stung. The fair-haired man had tried to take advantage and it had boiled Isaac's blood, although he had to admit the idea of *anyone* pursuing Honora wasn't one he relished.

Just trying to untangle the various threads of his emotions made his head ache and it was a relief when a gentle tap at the study door heralded one of the maids with a laden tray.

'Some tea for you, sir. You must want some after such a long, cold day.'

'Thank you, Clara. I think you must have read my mind.'

She carefully deposited the tray on the desk in front of him and with a swift bob made as if to leave, turning politely when Isaac called her back.

'Yes, sir?'

'Is Miss Charlotte up now? She wasn't when I arrived.'

Clara nipped at her lower lip and Isaac knew at once she was wondering how to word a delicate reply. She was a loyal servant with a kind heart and if she'd noticed Charlotte's condition— still for the most part hidden beneath ever more voluminous gowns—she could be trusted not to spread gossip outside the Manor.

Isaac sighed. 'She keeps to her rooms still?'

'I'm afraid so, sir. I don't think she emerged the whole time you were away, not even to eat. I took her up a tray, but it always came back untouched. Even when it was her favourites.'

'I see. Thank you for trying.'

With another dip Clara slipped from the room and for a moment Isaac closed his eyes, screwing them shut as if it could help him block out the misery of reality. Honora should be the absolute *last* thing on his mind given the circumstances and a wave of guilt swept over him that he'd allowed anything to divert his full attention from Charlotte. She was starving herself, wasting away before his very eyes, and if he didn't manage to get through to her quickly there was no telling where her unhappiness would take her.

He dropped his head into the cradle of his palms. If only his mother was still alive, hadn't succumbed to the tragic fate he feared Charlotte could so easily share. She'd know what to do with a young girl forced to grow up too fast, her future all but ruined and lying in tatters at her feet. What Charlotte needed was female guidance, a good-hearted woman with a gentle hand to help steer her through the rough waters to come. Her own mother had died when Charlotte was nine, but some older maternal figure was *just* what the situation demanded, someone who knew better than him and his blind groping for an answer that evaded him at every turn...

He didn't look up when another tap sounded at the door. No doubt it was Clara returning with a forgotten milk jug or something similar—so a sharp pang of surprise tore through him when instead an entirely different voice murmured hesitantly from the threshold,

'May I come in?'

Isaac jerked his head up so quickly his neck clicked, but he was too distracted by the figure in the doorway to notice.

'Honora?'

He couldn't help but stare, his pulse rocketing skywards at her sudden appearance. Shock coursed through him, followed so closely behind by an instinctive thrill it took him a moment to notice the state she was in.

'What are you doing here? And—what *happened* to you?'

She gazed back at him, one hand gripping the study door handle as if clinging on for dear life. The maid who let her into the Manor must have taken her coat and bonnet so there was nothing to hide the filthy, sodden hem of her dress or how her hair had tumbled halfway down from its crown of curls. Honora's mouth was pressed into a tight line and her shoulders were rigid...until with a start of concern Isaac saw them slump hopelessly, the shabby bag she held thumping down on to the floor.

'I'm sorry to intrude. I know I've no right to come here after everything you've already done for me. It's just... I didn't know what else to do.' She took a deep breath, still lingering in the doorway like a spectre in the night. Isaac knew he ought to insist she come inside and sit down, but he was transfixed by confusion, only able to break his trance when he noticed how her free hand shook as it hung down limply at her side.

'Honora, come in here. Sit down and tell me... what's happened?'

Finally regaining control of his limbs, Isaac strode to the door, taking her elbow and firmly directing her to his own vacated chair. She sank into it, wrapping her arms around herself as if to ward off whatever was causing the desolate look in her eye.

'Well?'

Honora stared into the depths of the hearth and Isaac had to lean forward to catch her reply, low and dull as an empty cask. 'The will was read this afternoon, as we thought it would be, and Frank's solicitor told me everything. It seems my dear husband had debts from here to the moon and to pay them off he instructed Mr Drew to sell Wycliff Lodge—despite it being my home. A buyer has been found and I am to vacate the house immediately.' She stopped to hug herself tighter and Isaac, perched next to her on a chair of his own, had to steel himself against the urge to take her in his arms and attempt to stem her obvious unhappiness.

'But that isn't even the worst of it. At least with my widow's jointure I could have found some small place, even if just a handful of rooms of my own...if Frank had left provision for one as he once promised. The will I witnessed him draw up was changed only days after he first made it, as Mr Drew was clearly ashamed to tell me, and the money Frank swore so faithfully I would have, when he still pretended to love me, was never to be paid.'

Isaac stiffened. 'Do you mean to say—?'

'That I'm destitute? Without even enough money to return to Wycliff Lodge, which isn't my home any longer? Or to repay my debt to you for the journey here? Yes. That's precisely the predicament *that man* left me in. But why should I be surprised? Lies were all he ever gave me. It was foolish of me to think he might keep any promise he made.'

She hunched further in her chair, curled over on herself as if in pain. The difference between when he had last seen her and the present moment was dramatic and Isaac felt the desire to comfort her roar up inside him once again, fingers itching to catch up one small hand and feel Honora's warmth mingle with his own. How could Frank treat his own wife so abominably? And not just any wife—one so vibrant and interesting as Honora, who he had never even slightly deserved? Isaac had thought his contempt for his former friend couldn't grow any more venomous, but with Honora before him Isaac found himself plumbing new depths of revulsion for the man who had died in his arms.

'I left the solicitors' rooms in a daze with no idea of where to go, or indeed any money to take myself there. In the absence of a better plan I asked the way to Marlow Manor and walked here…to throw myself on your mercy, I suppose.'

Isaac ran a hand through his hair, the cogs in his mind beginning to turn in sluggish thought.

She'd walked almost four miles through the snowy darkness to arrive at his door, all alone and fighting against the wind and freezing cold? No wonder she was soaked to the bone and her hair disordered, although the haphazard arrangement of her curls did nothing to detract from their ebony gleam. She must have been desperate indeed to do such a thing—although Honora's distress wasn't the only thing that sent a skewer between his ribs.

Charlotte. What if she meets Charlotte?

That would be the absolute finishing touch to Honora's living nightmare, he thought rapidly as he watched her scrub at her eyes with the heel of her hand. After everything else that had befallen her, to learn of Frank's final betrayal might be the thing that sent her over the edge into misery so fathomless she might never recover. There would be two lives ruined then. That of Charlotte, whom he loved as a daughter, and Honora, who somehow, by some witchcraft all her own, threatened to make him question things he'd thought settled. It was dangerous to have the two women under the same roof even if they were unaware of the common thread between them—yet Isaac knew he couldn't send Honora away.

Damn it all. Is this what happens when you let yourself be swayed by sentiment?

As if reading his mind Honora raised her head, looking at him so wearily any thoughts of her leaving stuttered and died.

'I know I shouldn't have come and I'm sorry to bring this to your door. I just…didn't know what else to do. There's nowhere else I could think of to go, with no money and the weather worsening by the minute…'

'Of course. Of course you should have come here.' Isaac found his lips moving of their own accord, spurred into action by her uncharacteristic vulnerability. He *shouldn't be doing this,* sailing so close to the wind and risking both Charlotte and Honora's increased unhappiness, but what else could he do? Turn her out into the snowy night? He would have to think up some way of managing the situation and he would have to do it fast.

He stood up. A bell hung beside the fireplace and before Isaac could think the better of it he pulled the rope, gesturing to Clara when her face appeared obligingly round the half-open door.

'We have an…unexpected guest. Would you ready a room for Mrs Blake—?'

The vehement shake of Honora's head cut off the rest of his sentence.

'Not Mrs Blake, if you don't mind. I am Honora *Jackson*.' At Isaac's quizzical look she firmly set her jaw. 'That man took everything and left me with nothing but his name. I don't want it. I'd sever every tie if I could—starting with going back to who I was before I ever had the misfortune of meeting him. I don't want to talk about him, don't want to think about him, don't want to do anything that might recall a single moment of our marriage. He doesn't deserve it.'

Isaac nodded slowly as Clara whisked efficiently from the room. Perhaps Honora took his quiet for something else, for she looked down at her hands with her voice lowered likewise.

'I know Frank was your friend and I'm sorry if my words offend you. Perhaps you were right after all. It was easier for Frank to be a good friend than a husband.'

It was all Isaac could do to prevent his lip from curling.

A good friend was the very last thing Frank was to me. I'm ashamed now we ever had anything in common, a link I'd do anything to sever.

But another thought occurred to him. If Honora wanted to be referred to as Miss Jackson and have no mention made of Frank…mightn't it be possible to conceal her true identity? Frank's name was forbidden beneath this roof anyway, those two syllables never now leaving the lips of Charlotte or himself. He hadn't told his ward why he'd needed to visit Somerset, only mentioning it was on business, so she could have no suspicions that Honora was connected in any way to their nameless enemy. Honora would only be at Marlow Manor for a day or so while they found a way for her to proceed. If Charlotte's previous behaviour was any guide, she might spend that whole time hidden away. It could be they would avoid each other entirely, surely the least complicated solution for the risky situation Isaac found he had strayed into...

But then the door to the study opened once again and, with the sound of light footsteps, all Isaac's hopes of an easy way out were destroyed.

'Oh!'

The dark-haired young girl in the doorway stared at Honora as though she'd seen a ghost. Her eyes flew wide and she took a step back as if wanting to turn and retreat the way she'd come, only hesitating when she caught sight of Isaac half-hidden beside Honora's chair.

'I didn't know you had company... I was asleep when you arrived home and I only learned a moment ago of your return. I won't—I'll go back to my rooms.'

'Please don't leave on my account.' Honora stood up, finding a smile from somewhere to paste on to her lips. In truth the girl's interruption was a welcome one, a blessed distraction from the distress reigning over her innards that had taken hold at the reading of Frank's will. She hardly knew when she had been more ashamed, having to sit before kindly Mr Drew and bear his discomfort at breaking the news of *exactly* how little Frank had cared…although turning up uninvited at Marlow Manor was a close second. Isaac had looked so surprised to see her, vivid alarm crossing his handsome face when she couldn't control her cursed emotion. She *hated* that he had seen her so weak, witnessed her vulnerability with his own eyes, but there was nothing but kindness in his response, and the stirring in her stomach at seeing him again grew stronger with his genuine concern.

'You must be Charlotte. It's a pleasure to meet you.'

Still with the smile stapled in place Honora made to offer a polite curtsy—until a glance down explained at once why the girl had wanted to run away.

The front of her pretty gown billowed to cover an unmistakable bump, the bulge a jarring contrast to her painfully thin arms and hollow cheeks. Her face was almost as pale as the snow outside and her eyes dulled with such misery and fear that a shard of ice lanced into Honora's chest.

Lord Lovell's sorrowful gazing into the fire that night at the inn, his forthright protection of her dignity against the blond stranger's advances and determination to preserve her reputation... All the pieces of the puzzle fell into place as for one heartbeat Honora froze, caught up in the realisation of why Lord Lovell had behaved so strangely. His Charlotte was pregnant, her good name hanging in the balance and teetering on the brink of ruin. No wonder Lord Lovell had been so careful, no doubt agonisingly aware of the perils a woman could face at the hands of an uncaring man. Of course he had seemed so troubled and eager to get back to Marlow Manor and the ward he had come to love as a daughter, the poor child obviously wretched and fading to a skeletal wraith.

She felt Lord Lovell's eyes on her, but didn't turn around. Without even looking in his direction she sensed precisely what she'd find—apprehension and the wary distrust of a parent ready to leap to the defence of their child—and she knew at once she would give him no cause for alarm.

'My name is Honora Jackson. As I said, please don't leave because of me. I'm sure I'd be delighted if you didn't.'

Charlotte cast her a sideways look, uncertain and skittish as a wild fawn. The temptation to flee must have been strong, but reluctantly she stepped inside, hunching slightly as if trying to hide her tell-tale silhouette.

'Hello, my little wren.'

Lord Lovell stood and gathered the girl into his arms, her head barely reaching his shoulder. Honora watched as he held Charlotte close, so gently reassuring it raised a lump in her already tight throat.

I was right. There really is more goodness in him than I first thought.

Something stirred in the pit of her stomach and she found she couldn't tear herself away from the sight of Lord Lovell cradling his adoptive daughter as though she was made of fine china. Her own problems would be resolved in time, somehow. Wasn't she the Honora Jackson who had climbed mountains, scaled trees and learned to hunt at her father's side, even if Frank had eventually come between them? She wasn't some genteel, retiring lady—she was a strong woman and she would find a way out of the hole Frank had flung her into, come hell or high water.

Charlotte, on the other hand... Usually an expectant mother raised a tide of longing in Honora that faded into bitterness and regret, a stark reminder of something she would never possess for herself. In the case of Lord Lovell's ward, however, there was nothing to envy and instead pity so strong it almost choked her rose in Honora like bile. What kind of monster had got such a young girl with child with clearly no intention of marrying her? It was every woman's worst nightmare, and every parent's, too, and as Lord Lovell finally released Charlotte from his hold Honora determined to temporarily set her own predicament aside.

The last thing he needs are my problems heaped on top of his own. I shall stay here tonight and after a goodnight's sleep I shall no doubt think more clearly in the morning.

Lord Lovell helped Charlotte down into his chair. With only two in the room and the other claimed by Honora he leaned against the nearby wall, steadfastly avoiding her eye and keeping his attention trained on his ward's wan face. There was a moment of tense silence as nobody spoke, until Honora leaned forward, Charlotte drawing back with a slight flinch.

'So, Miss Charlotte. Lord Lovell tells me Christmas is your favourite time of the year.

Can you credit it's only just less than two weeks away? I don't know where the time has gone.'

The girl blinked, casting a fleeting glance at Lord Lovell as the faintest hint of pink stole into her pale cheek.

'It's rather crept up on me this year,' she murmured, her voice barely a whisper. Honora wondered if she had always been timid or if it was self-consciousness of her condition that made her so shy, the elephant in the room nobody had yet acknowledged.

'It has a habit of doing that, I find.' Honora nodded encouragingly, determined to put poor Charlotte at ease. 'The wreaths I saw out in the hall were beautiful. Were they your doing?'

'Yes. The holly is from our own grounds.'

'They look wonderful. You clearly have a talent.'

'Oh.' The colour in Charlotte's cheeks deepened. 'Thank you.'

'Not at all. I'm quite jealous. My own attempts at that sort of thing tend to look like I made them in the dark while wearing a blindfold.'

Charlotte hesitated—and then to Honora's delight her bloodless lips hitched a fraction, curving as though she hardly dared let them.

'I'm sure that's not true.'

'It most certainly is. I tried to make a kissing ball once—I still have nightmares about it.'

Out of the corner of her eye Honora saw Lord Lovell's head turn in her direction. The sensation of his gaze resting on her scattered sparks through her veins and her heart began to skip, warmth pooling in her core. It felt so good to see him again, so strangely *right* to be in his presence, and she couldn't help a blush rising to mirror Charlotte's.

'They *can* be difficult. Getting the right shape without pricking your fingers isn't easy.'

'I agree. I end up feeling like a pincushion every time.'

The tentative smile strengthened a little more. Charlotte still sat curved over as if to conceal her shape, but some of the tension had left her shoulders and behind her Honora caught the movement of Lord Lovell's relaxing likewise.

Poor child—and poor Lord Lovell, too, I suppose. Both seeming to dread my judgement, as if after Frank I had any room to condemn others for making bad choices.

She leaned forward again and this time Charlotte didn't recoil. Her periwinkle eyes were still unsure, but some of the fright there had ebbed away. Apparently simple kindness was the way to win her confidence and that shy smile was painfully touching to Honora's maternal heart.

'And Lord Lovell? Was he of much help with the decorations or did he do nothing but get under your feet?'

'He did his best…but Isaac's true talents lie in other areas, I think.'

This time it was Honora's lips that twitched upwards, even as she savoured the novelty of Lord Lovell's newly-discovered Christian name. Beneath Charlotte's reserve she was sure she sensed an innocent sweetness, crushed by humiliation and tangible regret, yet still so wanting to shine through. The atmosphere of the room certainly seemed to have changed since that first unexpected smile. Nothing Honora could put her finger on, yet surely *something* had shifted none the less.

Am I imagining things now? Did that trek through the snow damage my wits as well as my dress?

She'd been too distracted to notice how her skirts were soaked through to the skin, but now the unpleasant sensation of wet linen against her legs returned with a vengeance. The snow had been ankle deep by the time she arrived at Marlow Manor and doubtless there was more to come judging by the brooding clouds and taste of ice in the air. A clean, dry gown was just what she wanted from the bag she'd abandoned in the doorway, as well as to tidy her hair, uncomfortably aware Lord Lovell—no, *Isaac*—had seen her in such an unflattering state of disarray.

She turned to him to ask if she might be shown her room, but the words died on her tongue and the ability to speak fled her grasp as she saw the look on his face.

Their eyes met and it was as though the air had disappeared from the room, Honora's lungs suddenly burning. Isaac watched her so intently, his mouth set and yet no censure in his warm brown gaze as he searched for something in her face—something that with a burst of heat beneath her gown Honora hoped he wouldn't find wanting. Was it her compassion to Charlotte that prompted him to stare so, some appreciation for her helping the girl to conjure a smile? Whatever Isaac was thinking was hidden behind those dark eyes, now softer than she had ever seen them before and their scrutiny stirring flames in her stomach to leap to new heights.

She looked back, the comfortable room around her blurring at the edges until everything except Isaac's magnetic presence faded away. It was the same feeling that had gripped her that night at the inn, when all good sense had fled and to taste Isaac's lips was all she could think about. That desire flared again now and she couldn't help her eyes dropping to survey his mouth, still firmly closed, but its contours no less enticing than they had been in that flame-lit bedroom. The moment between them stretched out as fragile and beautiful as a spiderweb— until Charlotte gave a hesitant murmur, unwittingly breaking the spell Honora couldn't quite understand.

'Miss Jackson, forgive me… I couldn't help but notice your skirts are wet through. I think you must be staying for the night? If so, would you like to see your room and perhaps change before supper? I wouldn't want you to catch cold…'

With a momentous effort Honora turned to her, fighting the sensation of surfacing from some uncanny dream.

'Thank you. In truth I'd be very glad of the chance to swap my gown for a dry one.'

Charlotte nodded and made as if to stand, reaching in the direction of the bell pull beside the fireplace, but stopped when Honora waved her back.

'Please don't exert yourself. I'm sure I can find my own way upstairs.'

'Are you sure? It would be no trouble…'

Honora shook her head, all too aware of Isaac's indistinct figure standing off to one side. Her heart had picked up into a rhythm more suited to a racehorse than a woman and the urge to escape before he became aware of her secret desires was strong. Whatever had just passed between them had felt like lightning, some phantom of it still lingering in the room, and she had no hope of understanding what it meant while he stood close enough for her to reach out and touch.

Chapter Seven

At first when Isaac heard the sounds coming from his library he thought he must still be dreaming.

He'd barely slept—*yet again*—his mind too full of Honora to find any relief in sleep. Her distress when she'd appeared before him in his study, as though summoned by his relentless thoughts of her. How her vulnerability had commanded his protective instinct like a call to arms. And then, the most agonising part, her kindness to Charlotte, dragging a smile to reluctant lips he'd hardly seen move ever since she had discovered Frank's child grew inside her. If Honora only knew the truth… Surely then that complex, heart-pounding look that had passed between them before she fled to change her gown would never have happened, an instant of unfeigned connection he scarcely dared believe. The memory of it had left him staring up at the darkened ceiling until the first fingers of dawn light crept beneath his shutters, trying his hardest to understand what—if anything—the new emotion in Honora's eyes had *meant*...

Isaac pushed open the library door and stood for a moment, taking in the scene in front of him with brows raised in wordless surprise.

Charlotte and Honora sat side by side at the long table that usually held his many maps, now neatly rolled up and set to one side to make way for the great swathe of greenery scattered in their place. Boughs of bright holly, ivy and sprigs of mistletoe gleamed in the light of a cheerful fire crackling in the grate, the dancing flames chasing away the morning chill that had followed Isaac from his rooms. In all it was a picturesque sight—but the thing that most caught his attention were the faces of the two who hadn't yet noticed his presence.

Charlotte was laughing. Actually *laughing*, her cheeks pink and looking more alive than she had in weeks. It was quite possibly the most beautiful sound Isaac had ever heard and his heart leapt in amazement. He'd *thought* he had caught that wonderful chime as he had descended the stairs, but dismissed it at once. Charlotte hadn't laughed for so long it seemed a forlorn hope to think it was her, although nothing could mistake what now came from her pale lips.

What miracle is this? He could do nothing but stare at the transformation that had overtaken his ward. Her skin still had its unhealthy pallor aside from the high colour in her cheeks and her frame was as fragile as it had been the night before, but a hint of the old Charlotte, the girl who had been so happy before Frank blighted her life, peeped through now and Isaac could hardly credit the change. Was this what she'd needed all along? A companion who hadn't yet shown any sign of judgement, only compassion for a damaged soul and determination to make her smile?

'Like this? *Now* do I have it right?'

Still unaware he watched them, Honora held up whatever she was cradling in careful hands, a woefully misshapen lump of holly studded with mistletoe and slices of orange, the rich scent of it unfortunately its only redeeming feature.

'Oh, Miss Honora…no!'

Charlotte's giggle redoubled and Honora joined in, the sound sending a flood beneath Isaac's breastbone.

I've never seen Honora laugh. Just when I thought she couldn't get any more beautiful.

It was a thought he knew he shouldn't allow and yet there it was, the absolute truth. With her eyes creased and her full lips drawn up at the corners her face took on new animation he hadn't seen there before, the strain usually present in every contour falling away to give a glimpse of how she must have looked before she came to England and embarked on the path that would ruin her life. She was a mature woman, surely closer to forty than thirty now, and confident in her skin in a way younger women had to learn, but in this unguarded moment she looked half a girl again and Isaac couldn't drag his eyes away from her radiant face.

How could Frank have spent all those years with Honora and never come to love her? He must have been mad as well as stupid. A wife like that might tempt any man to marry—even the most reluctant...

Isaac froze on the threshold, one hand still flat against the door.

No. Oh, no. I see where this is going and let me state now: absolutely not. He gritted his teeth as a wave of horror washed over him like a cascade of cold water. *One strange look, one laugh and you're having thoughts like this? Don't be ridiculous. You're just grateful she's been so good to Charlotte. That's all. Nothing else comes into it.*

He would not be throwing away thirty-seven years of bachelorhood for Honora Blake—or

Jackson, whatever she wanted to be called now. Hadn't Father taught him everything he needed to know about matrimony by his own disastrous example? More specifically the importance of avoiding it? He'd learned from his father's mistakes, and anyway, the idea Honora might entertain the idea of marrying again was absurd. She'd as good as told him she never wanted to be bound to a man again, so fiercely independent she inspired both admiration and wariness. If she seemed to be starting to dislike him less that meant nothing, perhaps his own weakness making him see things that weren't really there.

Shouldering that particular alarming thought aside, Isaac cleared his throat and finally stepped into the room.

'What have I stumbled upon? Is there any holly left in the rest of Northamptonshire, Charlotte, or is it all here on my map table?'

Two heads turned in his direction, one piled high with ebony curls and the other topped with brunette ringlets. Unalike in every other respect the only tie between them were the smiles— Charlotte's stronger than he would have dared dream and Honora's suddenly a little shy, something Isaac's disloyal heart noticed with keen interest.

'I'm teaching Miss Honora to make a kissing ball.' Charlotte gestured to the lumpen thing sitting on the table beside her own pristine creation, her lips twitching a little. 'She's...ah. It's been...'

'...a complete and utter failure?' Honora supplied helpfully, now carefully avoiding Isaac's eye. 'A colossal waste of your time?'

'Not at all! I think you've made some excellent progress, considering your first attempt...'

Isaac followed Charlotte's glance to a sorry-looking heap of greenery sagging forlornly on the floor near his boots, for all the world as though it had been thrown there. 'At the very least this one is a *kind* of sphere.'

'I think you might be being a little too generous.' Honora prodded her unfortunate handiwork with a doubtful finger. 'This has no place hanging anywhere other than perhaps a pig sty.'

'Oh, no! It will take pride of place somewhere in the house, won't it?' Charlotte peered up at Isaac, some tiny spark of life returned to her blue gaze. There were still shadows beneath her eyes, the work of nights spent crying rather than sleeping, but there was such enthusiasm in her look Isaac knew he couldn't refuse her anything.

'Of course. I'll hang it up in here myself. It'll brighten up that far window.'

Isaac approached the table and held out his

hand for the offending article. Honora passed it to him reluctantly, the kissing ball hanging from her fingers by a red ribbon—and a flit of sensation glittered down his spine as her fingertip brushed his, the most minute of accidental touches and yet as welcome as a monsoon in a desert.

He flinched instinctively at the static jolt and saw Honora jump likewise, a lightning-fast reaction neither could fake nor control. His own start he could understand, but what did Honora's mean, that unthinking shiver the skim of his hand on hers conjured from nowhere?

He turned away swiftly and crossed to the window, uncomfortably aware of his movements as he went. Knowing Honora watched him, he felt ungainly and the feeling didn't abate when he stretched up to slip the ribbon loop over one end of the curtain pole. It hung there, pretty despite its clumsiness with its green leaves shining and red berries peeping out between the thorns.

'Perfect!' Charlotte nodded with satisfaction and even Honora looked grudgingly pleased. 'Now it's just as festive in here as the rest of the Manor.'

'Ah.' Isaac tapped his forehead as a thought resurfaced. 'Festive. That reminds me. Mrs Strimpel was looking for you.'

'Was she? Why?'

'She wanted to consult you before she started on the Christmas pudding. She knows you like to choose the spices.' Isaac allowed himself a quick glimpse in Honora's direction. She was watching him and flushed slightly as his eye caught hers. 'Mrs Strimpel is our cook. As Charlotte is the chief organiser of Christmas at Marlow Manor she's usually the one the servants report to. It's been this way since she was a child.'

He expected Charlotte to smile, but instead she stared down at her lap, the light vanishing abruptly from her face. Isaac saw it go with a start of dismay, about to go to her until Honora gently touched her arm.

'What's the matter? Are choosing cake flavours so difficult?'

Charlotte sighed. Her brow creased and she looked up at Honora with the unhappy, trusting eyes of a child needing direction. In that moment she could have been a girl of nine again, the years reeling backwards in Isaac's memory to when she'd first arrived at the Manor, a sad, motherless scrap who had clung to him and wetted the shoulder of his shirt with a river of tears. He'd vowed to take care of her from that day onwards, determined to protect her from life's dark underbelly even as he himself had once enjoyed its delights—how horribly ironic, then, that the one other person she seemed to find comfort in was the widow of the man who had inflicted the worst upon her, Honora apparently already filling some gap in Charlotte's affections even after so brief an acquaintance. Not for the first time he wondered if Honora's feminine kindness struck the same chord for Charlotte as a mother's would. No wonder his ward looked to her for answers, such unjudgemental warmth doubtless a soothing balm for Charlotte's shattered soul.

'The kitchen servants will see me if I go down to the kitchen. What if they stare?'

Charlotte twisted her slender fingers together like willow boughs bending in a storm. It seemed to border on painful, how tightly she twined and tangled them, and Isaac watched Honora take both hands firmly in her own.

'Is that what bothers you?'

A small nod was the only reply.

'I understand. I know what it is to be stared at and remarked upon, truly I do.' Honora ducked her head a little to look into Charlotte's downcast eyes and Isaac felt his throat tighten at her tender concern. 'Ever since I can remember people have watched me and wondered about my life. My parents were an unusual match and there have always been people who thought those like me, a bridge between two worlds, should not exist. It used to upset me until one day I realised I could stare right back. So can you. Marlow Manor is your home. You shouldn't creep around it as though you had no right to be here.'

She was still holding Charlotte's hands and the girl managed a tiny smile like the fragile light of a match.

'I'm not as brave as you, though, Miss Honora. I don't think I could do that.'

'How do you know? You haven't yet tried. I think you might surprise yourself.'

Charlotte hesitated. She shot Isaac a swift glance and at his decided nod she gave a slow one of her own.

'Very well. I'll go down now. I hope... I very much hope you're right.'

'She probably is,' Isaac murmured wryly. He caught the answering flicker of Honora's eyebrow, but moved to help Charlotte from her chair, lightly squeezing her fingers reassuringly as she took his hand. She seemed to take some strength from him as she straightened up a little more, straightened her shoulders and left the library with quiet steps—leaving Isaac alone with Honora and unsure whether to enjoy the experience or flee.

* * *

Honora toyed with a stray holly leaf, acutely aware of Isaac's tall shape at the edge of her line of sight. Even without looking directly at him she could make out the distinctive pattern of his waistcoat over a broad chest and shoulders that filled his coat very nicely indeed, crowned with his thatch of chestnut hair, always so pleasingly haphazard. The silver threads shot through it made him look distinguished, a scattering of salt and pepper Honora had to admit she'd admired more than once since he'd come barrelling into her life…

'Thank you.'

She started guiltily. For a split-second she feared she'd spoken aloud, somehow revealing her most secret thoughts and mortified Isaac had heard—until he continued obliviously.

'That was very well done. You've been so kind to Charlotte. After only a few hours in your company she seems so much happier. How is it you knew just what to say? I've tried to reach her since this mess began, but nothing I did made much difference.'

Honora bit her tongue on a bitter reply. *Because I know how it feels to know all eyes are on you as though you've committed a crime, when all you're guilty of is stepping outside their narrow expectations.*

What she'd told Charlotte was true, she *had* learned to stare back, but not without enduring such unhappiness she'd run crying to Ma more times than she could count, and still might now, had the gulf between them not been more than mere distance. Charlotte had no mother to dry her tears and something in the orphaned girl called to Honora, all her wasted maternal instincts rushing forth in a desire to protect and comfort little more than a child.

'Just as I said. In a different kind of way I'm used to the judgement of others—I can speak to her from my heart. I suppose Charlotte knows you love her so much you'd say anything to make her feel better, whether it was true or not. That isn't always helpful.'

'You're right. Again.' Isaac huffed a dry laugh, the sound stoking the embers in Honora's innards. He still stood near the window, lit from behind by the cold light filtering through white clouds that caught on his hair and made it gleam like burnished bronze. He was too handsome by half and it made it difficult for Honora to think, distracted at every turn by his dangerous allure.

She looked away. Isaac's love for his ward grew more touching with every moment and she marvelled now how she ever could have thought Isaac and Frank to be alike in any way aside from their disconcerting good looks. Her late husband had never cared for anyone but himself. It wouldn't surprise her if he'd sold his own grandmother for more money to gamble with. How had the two become friends with apparently so little in common? Perhaps Frank had fooled Isaac as he had her, pretending to be a better man to further his own ends. No doubt claiming friendship with a lord would have boosted Frank's ego up to the sky, allowing him to move in the circles he had once hoped Honora's blood-soaked inheritance would buy his entrance to.

With a grimace she dragged her thoughts from the one who'd ruined her life and returned them to poor Charlotte. Who was the man who had taken an axe to *her* dreams for the future? The question had niggled at Honora ever since she'd first seen the bump half-hidden by a modest gown and she wondered now if she had the courage to ask Isaac for an answer.

'Isaac…'

He raised his eyes from the window where he peered down at the unseen lawn below. 'Yes?'

'Would it be too much for me to ask…what *happened*? How did Charlotte come to be in this sorry predicament?'

She watched his face set, the muscles there tightening into some expression she couldn't quite read and obliterating the openness of only moments before. Something flitted across his countenance like a hare fleeing from hunters, disappearing as soon as it snapped into life, but was it a hot flare of *guilt*? Or more specifically guilt he tried at once to conceal? Surely she was mistaken, yet all of a sudden Honora felt her intuition stir.

Is he hiding something?

Isaac didn't speak, instead only gazing back at her for a long moment as the air of the library cooled suddenly beneath the weight of his complex stare.

Perhaps I shouldn't have asked. Honora felt the short hairs on her arms raise in discomfort as Isaac's lips pressed into a tight line. *Doubtless that's the very last thing he wants to talk about, the humiliation of his beloved ward and the damage done to her reputation as a result... and yet, why would that make him seem so suddenly on his guard?*

'It happened as you might expect.' Isaac finally spoke, his voice low and disquietingly measured as if to keep himself in check. 'Nothing out of the ordinary, I'm afraid. A most undeserving man seduced her—she didn't know what he wanted until it was too late, so innocent she didn't see the direction he was leading her in under my very nose. He ran when I confronted him and we won't have his name spoken in this house ever again. That's…that's really all I want to say on the matter.'

Honora nodded slowly. *As I suspected. A tale as old as time.* A man taking advantage of a naive young girl was so depressingly common there was little to surprise her in Isaac's answer, although one thing was out of the usual order.

'You didn't insist he marry her?'

'No,' Isaac stated flatly, eyes sliding away from hers—with another touch of that evasiveness that blew kindling air on the embers of her nameless suspicion. 'I would not have her tied for life to a man who used her for what he wanted and then gave her up without a thought. She's sixteen years old—and only just. Her birthday was October. I'm sure you can work out the sums involved from that.' A flicker of disgust crossed his face and he turned to the window, resting his knuckles on the sill. With his back to her Honora couldn't see his expression, but his hands had balled into fists and she cast about at once for some way to change the subject, his tangible revulsion enough to make her set aside her natural curiosity, or at least for now, that strange look that flickered in his eye something she knew she couldn't so easily dismiss.

'Have *you* never married?'

As soon as the question slipped past her lips Honora wished she hadn't uttered it. Of all the things to ask… Her cheeks grew hot, but Isaac's backward glance was only surprise, perhaps relieved she'd left the topic of Charlotte behind.

'Me? No. Absolutely not. In truth, my father's example wasn't one I wanted to copy.'

At Honora's quizzical look he gave a bleak smile, her eyes instantly drawn to that slightly quirked mouth.

'Tragic, really. After my mother died in childbed he married again, for reasons I never could fathom. They fought endlessly. Nothing she did was ever good enough and nothing he did could ever please her. It didn't leave me with a very high opinion of marriage and I determined from a young age not to try it myself—why would I, if the only outcomes I've seen are grief or bitter loathing? Neither is a future I'd willingly risk, when the alternative is far more appealing.'

Honora inclined her head. 'I can't argue with that wisdom. Matrimony didn't work well for me, either, as I think you're well aware.'

Isaac's smile took on a wry edge as if he thought that something of an understatement.

'I confess I had noticed. But would *you* marry again? It might be second time lucky.'

She couldn't help an undignified snort. *Marry again? He must know that's impossible.* 'Even if I *were* so inclined—which I assure you I am not—I doubt I'd have the chance. After Frank left there were some…impudent remarks. I'm sure you can imagine. That, combined with my lack of wealth and family background, make finding another husband unlikely.'

Isaac turned away from the window and regarded her with interest that caused little flutters in her stomach. 'Your family background?'

'Yes.' Honora picked up her stray sprig of holly again and frowned down at the spiky leaf, the thought of her distant parents as always making her unsure whether to smile or cry. 'My father was born a slave in Virginia. He was freed after serving in the Revolutionary War and soon after that he met my mother at a Pennsylvania church—the daughter of a wealthy tobacco plantation owner. The Baptist churches back home were more welcoming than some others and their congregations often had many different kinds of people mixing together. Not everybody is so accepting of these differences, however, or would be willing to overlook my heritage and the origins of my father. I'm a walking embodiment of something some people are opposed to and that hasn't always been easy to bear.'

Isaac nodded thoughtfully, clearly considering her words. 'That would be their loss, then...' he glanced out of the window, suddenly avoiding her eye '...if they allowed their prejudices to deprive them of your acquaintance. The only people who would be disadvantaged are themselves.'

A curious warmth flooded Honora's innards as she stared at the back of Isaac's firmly turned head. He thought the forfeit of her friendship would be a loss to those who spurned her? Implying he himself thought it a benefit? Her heart skipped over an incredulous beat, her already flushed cheeks growing rosier still.

'That's kind. I'm sure I'll remember you said that even after I leave here today.'

'You intend to go back to Somerset so soon? Have you thought up a plan, then, for how you'll manage now?'

'Not yet.' She began to shred the leaf between her fingers, glad of an excuse not to look up. In truth, she was no closer to knowing how to proceed than she'd been the previous night, but she couldn't impose on Isaac's hospitality for long without feeling as though she'd worn out her welcome. He must want to return to normality as soon as possible and he couldn't do that with Honora under his roof, a grim figure in a black gown who bad luck stalked like a malevolent ghost.

'Well, I think you've a while yet to think about it. Have you seen outside this morning?'

She glanced up to see Isaac nodding towards the window. 'Not properly. It was still dark when I woke up and then we were so busy with our making I didn't think to look.'

'Aha. Come now, then, and see for yourself if you fancy leaving here today.'

Frowning, Honora got up from the table and crossed to the window, Isaac moving aside to let her see out. The moment she came close to him her every nerve stood to attention and her body longed to curve towards him, but she roughly reined in her unconscious desires and forced herself to peer through the cold glass.

Now that the sun was fully up and the Marlow estate was bathed in chilly daylight Honora could see what Isaac meant. Snow covered every inch of the lawns leading down to hedges set about an impressive fountain, the surface of the water spread with unblemished ice and the stonework barely visible above its white blanket. The drifts were so deep it was impossible to see the paths and the world below looked bleached, sparkling and perfect while yet more flakes drifted down to add to the wonderland already stretching out beneath heavy clouds.

'The roads won't be passable under all that. I'm afraid you have no choice but to put up with Charlotte and me a while longer.'

'Oh.' Honora's breath misted the glass as she leaned forward to look down. Her heart, already leaping from her closeness to Isaac, picked up a little more, flinging itself against her bodice as though trying to escape.

I don't have to leave immediately. I can stay with Isaac a few more days.

The realisation flickered inside her like a flame dancing in a breeze and she had to steel herself not to smile. It was a ridiculous, inappropriate reaction, but one she found she couldn't help.

'I'm sorry to have to trespass further on your hospitality. Perhaps I could pay you in more badly made Christmas decorations? I'm afraid I've little else to offer.'

Isaac's lips twitched and he cast a look up at the lopsided kissing ball hanging above their heads. 'Would you? I think I'd like one in every room. They give the Manor a distinctive air, I feel.'

'Very well. I'll get started at once.'

Isaac's smile broadened—and then faded, another expression taking its place that wiped any amusement from Honora's mind.

'You know what traditionally happens under one of these.' He gestured upwards to the cluster of greenery and Honora felt her mouth dry at once. Surely he wasn't suggesting what she thought he might be…? The tick of her pulse became more of a roar in her ears as she tilted her head to look into his face.

'I do.'

'But not in this case, of course. I know last time, at the inn, you didn't appreciate the idea… and there's still the small issue of my being— what was it?—one of the most unpleasant men you've had the misfortune to meet. Probably in my case you'd rather dispense with tradition.'

If she hadn't been able to see his face, she might have thought he was joking. Instead she saw the real question in his eyes, an honest enquiry that demanded an answer, and her voice was uncharacteristically low and quiet when she replied.

'I think you must know my opinion of you has changed given recent events. How I felt when I first met you is not how I feel now.'

'I see.' Isaac nodded and Honora saw the movement of his throat as he swallowed, a reflexive action she couldn't help but copy. All of a sudden it was difficult to breathe, the atmosphere in the library now heavy with something unspoken that surely Isaac must feel, too. 'So we needn't abandon the usual Christmas customs entirely? You wouldn't find this one entirely revolting?'

'No. I think perhaps I could bear it. It would be a shame to have made such a flawless decoration and not allow it to fulfil its destiny, after all.'

Honora's face felt as though it had burst into flame as Isaac's mouth quirked again.

'I agree. In the spirit of Christmas, then, and to celebrate your craftsmanship...'

Time seemed to slow as Isaac bent his head, two wordless gazes locked on to each other in a blaze of cautious desire. Honora could hardly bear the achingly unhurried closing of the gap between them, Isaac aiming for her cheek and brushing it softly—until at the last possible moment all good sense abandoned her and she turned her head, her lips finding his and rejoicing at feeling their touch once more.

If Isaac was shocked at her bold action, he showed no sign. He didn't recoil, or flinch, or behave in any way like a man unwilling to press his lips against Honora's and steal every breath from her melting body with earth-shattering skill. His hand came up at once to steady her

curving waist and she gasped to feel the heat
of his palm through the sombre material of her
gown, scalding as though each of his fingers
contained real fire to burn her yearning skin.

She was a tall woman, but still she had to
reach up to meet his questing mouth with hers,
her own hands now rising to anchor him in
place. With one at his shoulder and the other
tracing the short hair at the base of his neck
she felt Isaac shudder, but surely only with the
hopeless wonder that coursed likewise beneath
Honora's skin at such unexpected, heated contact she'd never thought to experience again.
Locked together in an embrace so tight nothing
could have slipped between them, she nearly
sagged in his hold, her legs weak with longing
and distant amazement at her own nerve. What
was she thinking, turning her head so brazenly
to accept Isaac's kiss? And why on earth hadn't
she sought it sooner, this slice of heaven she
never wanted to end?

He flattened his hand against her spine and
dragged it upwards, leaving a trail of pure sensation in its wake that made her gasp again. She
could have sworn she felt him smile against her
lips, grazing them gently with his teeth before
ducking lower to find where her pulse raced
below her jaw, pressing his mouth to the sen-

sitive spot and with one light nip reducing her bones to water.

Isaac must have been able to feel the rhythm of her heart beneath the thin skin and doubtless relished his effect on her, finally indefensible proof his handsome face had succeeded at last in breaking down her studied indifference. Perhaps the knowledge would inflate his ego, but Honora couldn't manage to care—all she could think was how good it felt to be within the circle of two strong arms, her breath coming fast and shallow and the feeling of Isaac surrounding her completely, in the air she breathed and the scent of his skin and the sound of her own heartbeat thrumming loud enough for the whole world to hear.

With her eyes closed and head tipped back, it took her a moment to realise the library door was creaking open. Only when the rustle of Charlotte's dress met her ears did Honora jolt out of Isaac's grip, cheeks glowing and lips flushed and guilt written all over the two faces that turned in the girl's direction.

She stood on the threshold, looking from one frozen countenance to the other with the distinct impression she knew she'd stumbled across something she shouldn't. Charlotte might have been innocent, but she wasn't stupid. Honora cringed—there was no way she wouldn't realise what she had just interrupted…

Although it's just as well she did. You evidently can't be trusted to behave yourself when left alone with Isaac, a strict little voice at the back of her mind spoke up disapprovingly. *Brazen, that's what you are. And foolish beyond imagining.*

'We were just looking out at the snow.' Isaac waved a hand towards the window, his usual confidence apparently quickly restored. 'It's too deep for Miss Honora to leave us today as she'd planned so she will be staying a few days longer. I thought you'd be pleased.'

'Oh!' Charlotte's face lit up as if someone had lit a candle behind it, prompting a flutter of fondness behind Honora's breastbone even as she struggled to catch her breath. 'I'm more than pleased! In truth… I was hoping to ask you—' She broke off for a moment to cast a pleading look at Isaac, who gazed questioningly back. 'I wanted to ask if you would stay for Christmas? Unless you have other plans, of course?'

Honora's lips parted in surprise and she couldn't help a cut of her eyes in Isaac's direction. To stay until the roads were clear was one thing—might lingering be more than Isaac would want, especially now that second kiss had stirred up more confusion between them?

'Stay for Christmas? I'm not sure...'

'Won't you help to persuade her?' Charlotte turned the full force of her periwinkle charms on Isaac, who stood so tall and straight beside Honora she felt her fingers twitching to reach and entwine with his own.

Stay here for Christmas? Is that wise? And would Isaac even want me to?

The desire to accept Charlotte's invitation was immediate, flaring inside her like a struck match. There was nothing awaiting her return to Somerset, after all. Nothing called her back, her home no longer her own, and the only friend she had doubtless busy with her own family for the festivities. Honora was all alone and the sudden ache *not* to be was more powerful than her usual caution. It was dangerous to grow closer to Isaac, she knew, well aware now of his determination to avoid tender feeling—wasn't it a risk to allow her growing regard for him to continue, doubtless strengthening as each day passed?

In all probability, the little voice agreed dourly, *and yet what other choice do you have?*

She felt Isaac's gaze upon her and met his eye, her skin tingling as his lips curved upwards.

'Well, Miss Jackson. It seems my ward has

spoken and I'm loath to disappoint her. Will you oblige her and stay for Christmas? If you can tolerate another fortnight in our presence?'

Charlotte took a step forward, hands clasped before her so beseechingly Honora knew there could be only one answer.

This could be a mistake. I could well be letting myself in for more heartache I thought I'd never feel again after I lost Frank.

She sensed Isaac at her shoulder, waiting wordlessly for her reply. That kiss had changed things between them, surely—although whether for better or worse only time would tell.

'Thank you, Charlotte. That would be wonderful. I'm delighted to accept.'

Chapter Eight

Snow continued to fall in fits and starts as the days leading up to Christmas passed in a flurry of activity. There were yet more garlands of holly and evergreens to hang on every available surface, filling the Manor with scattered pine needles and bathing it in the light of countless candles burning in every nook and cranny. Oranges and cloves scented the air from pomanders placed at each hearth and delicious smells of spices drifted up from the kitchens as Charlotte's carefully directed cakes and puddings were baked below stairs, making Honora's mouth water each time she passed through. St Thomas's Day was spent making up parcels of food and fairings for the poor widows who came to call, deprived of their husbands by illness or war and glad of the Christmas cheer contained in baskets Honora and Charlotte filled together at the great oak kitchen table. She might be forced to rely on something similar herself in the future, Honora had thought bleakly, but the next moment she'd pushed the idea aside. For now she was in a warm house, by some miracle, her friendship with poor Charlotte strengthening by the day—she should count her blessings and appreciate the here and now rather than fret about what might be to come when the snow finally stopped and she would be forced back into reality. For two precious weeks she could pretend all was well and that was not to be sniffed at.

Standing now at the dining room window, she looked out at the vast gardens stretching behind the Manor, attempting to turn her thoughts away from their habitual bent towards Isaac and the worries that had plagued her since their unexpected kiss. The snowy landscape was almost untouched, only one set of deeply pitted footprints leading away from the house toward a tangled copse of trees to one side of the submerged lawn. Their branches waved wildly beneath iron-grey clouds, the peaceful drifting of white flakes replaced now by the threat of a blizzard that grew with every passing hour. Before long the wind would be whipped into a frenzy and those dark clouds would release their menace on the world below, flinging ice down on the heads of anyone fool enough to venture outside.

Honora shivered. When was the last time there had been a storm so close to Christmas? Not since she could remember, the twenty-fifth usually dawning cold, but not stopping her from making the short walk into the next village for the Christmas Day service. Only on a handful of occasions throughout the year would she brave the stares of the congregation to settle into a pew, both her skin and uncertain reputation drawing attention she didn't enjoy. If the weather stayed as fierce as she suspected it might now, then perhaps she might be spared the same ordeal this year—a different church, but surely the same reaction, mutters following her as she sailed down the aisle with as much dignity as she could muster.

I wonder what Isaac would think of the stares. Might he even spring to my defence as he did in the coach?

Not that she should wish for such a thing, Honora reminded herself sternly even as her heart gave a sharp lurch at the thought. Ever since their lips had met beneath the cluster of mistletoe hung at the library window, a reminder of her moment of poor judgement every time she stepped inside, it had become all the harder to ignore the weakness for her host that muttered to her night and day. *She* had long determined not to fall on the mercy of a man again and *he* had expressed his opinion of romantic relationships as a dangerous waste of time, so why could she not seem to remember those facts now it was more important than ever? There was nothing to be gained by entertaining her foolish weakness for that handsome face, yet it would seem her powers of self-control were still trying to elude her.

Glancing away from the window, Honora felt her ears redden as she recalled the traitorous urge that had whispered for her to turn her head, at the last minute changing *everything*. What had started out as an innocent tradition had morphed into something else and now every time she closed her eyes the same moment came back to visit her, the image of Isaac bending towards her with such gentleness in his expression it made her throat dry with sudden thirst. Her glimpse at his hidden kindness had made her want to know more, a perilous desire that could so quickly spin and consume her just as Frank's cruelty had swallowed her whole.

A movement on the other side of the glass caught her attention, a flicker of blue among white and standing out against the darkening sky. She frowned for a moment, squinting into the gathering dusk, until a rush in her chest recognised what she was looking at before rationale caught up with her instinct.

Isaac was struggling through the snow, retracing the single line of footsteps towards the Manor and dragging something along behind him. He was bent over, gripping his burden with both hands and his face screwed up against the chill wind throwing snow into his eyes. It pulled at his hair, rippling across the warm chestnut and tugging at the blue coat flapping on his back, but he didn't stop, continuing onwards until he disappeared from view behind a box hedge covered in sparkling frost. He was making for the kitchen door, if she wasn't mistaken, and after a moment of hesitation Honora left the dining room. Isaac looked as though he might appreciate some help and the notion of providing it was more pleasing than she knew she should allow.

Be careful, Honora. You're in ever greater danger of letting yourself get carried away— and what's worse, you know it.

Isaac sat down heavily on the soaking log and waited for his breath to stop sounding like a winded horse. All around him the kitchen hummed with activity like bees in a hive. Mrs

Strimpel was the queen at the very centre and cast him sidelong looks that left no room for interpretation.

'I'll be taking the Yule log out in a moment. Just catching my breath first. No need for alarm.'

The cook bestowed a gracious smile on Isaac as if he was a little boy who had given the right answer to a question. She'd been a fixture at Marlow Manor since Isaac was in short trousers and he could well remember sneaking down to beg a piece of gingerbread or fresh-baked roll as a child, all while his father turned a blind eye. What would the previous Lord Lovell think of the current state of affairs at his ancestral home? Isaac wondered now for the first time. His son's ward carrying the illegitimate baby of a perturbing guest's errant husband, neither knowing the real truth of the other, but becoming closer friends every minute that ticked past. Father's eyes would have lit up on seeing Honora, Isaac knew as he waited for his pulse to slow. An intriguing woman who any fool could see had piqued his son's interest and might even question his ridiculous determination not to marry. Isaac's reluctance to take a wife and expect her to weather the storm of labour had been a source of unspoken tension between the two generations of Lovell men and now Isaac tightened his grip on the sodden wood beneath his palms.

What Father would have seen is the very reason I should spend as little time in Honora's presence as possible. If only I could make myself listen to my own good sense. He would have been right to pin his hopes on her creeping beneath my defences and I won't be so arrogant as to ignore that danger.

He no longer worried Honora would spread news of Charlotte's pregnancy. That wasn't the danger he recognised. The poor, motherless girl had clearly drawn Honora in with her unfeigned sweetness and obvious yearning for acceptance, doubtless touching the void in Honora's maternal heart and filling some gap there like sand flowing into an hourglass. The threat he saw now was of a different kind and one he knew loomed larger every day.

The more time Honora spent at Marlow Manor the more his esteem for her blossomed like a stubborn bloom, unfurling its petals as though she was the sun that sustained it. Her kindness to Charlotte showed what lay beneath that caustic exterior and it called to him, her lack of judgement and compassion as attractive as the fine lines of her countenance. When she'd turned her cheek and let his lips touch hers under the kissing ball it had been all the delightful, unexpected, terrifying encouragement he needed to think his feelings might be returned—which was exactly what he feared.

If she came to care for me as I do her and then discovered I had concealed Frank's involvement, along with the distasteful similarities that once existed between us...wouldn't she hate me and resent Charlotte, and above all be devastated the child she longed for was given to another by the very man she had pinned her hopes upon?

The memory of her face when she'd told him of her sadness came back to taunt him and he couldn't help an unconscious grimace. Any possibility of tenderness would be stripped away the moment she learned of his deception, warmth he had no business hoping for anyway. He didn't want to form an attachment and neither did Honora—both of them with unarguable reason to avoid such complications—so why were they dancing around the very thing they professed not to desire, an entanglement that would only lead to pain? It was confusing and enticing and risky beyond measure, the chance of Honora discovering the truth about Frank making Isaac feel as though he walked on eggshells in his own home.

Unless... He recalled the flicker of suspicion in Honora's eye that day in the library, before her lips on his had made all else fall away. If he hadn't known better, he might have thought she could tell he was hiding something, that sharp mind leaping to conclusions he might never guess. *Unless, of course, I looked that fear in the eye and told her anyway. Perhaps the certainty of her reaction might be better than my prediction. She might surprise me—heaven knows Honora has never been predictable so far and, if she suspects a secret already...*

'What do you have there?'

A voice rose above the noise of the kitchen and Isaac's heart shuddered over a skipped beat as Honora emerged through a cloud of heavily scented steam, followed close behind—as always, these days—by Charlotte.

Isaac stood up, uncomfortably aware of his limbs at her unexpected appearance. He was a lord, for heaven's sake, a full-grown man who had reduced countless women to blushing wrecks and enjoyed every moment of it at the time, yet the sight of Honora before him, inspecting his trophy with a raised brow, somehow managed to make him feel almost a lad again.

'The Yule log, of course. Why else would I have dragged half a tree into my house?'

The dark brow flickered. 'Yule log? What's that?'

'You must know!' Charlotte peeped round her shoulder, looking younger than ever beside Honora's tall frame. If it wasn't for the half-hidden bump beneath Charlotte's gown it might have made a touching tableau so reminiscent of a rosy-cheeked child looking up at her mother it made Isaac blink. 'It's brought in on Christmas Eve usually, although given the weather Isaac dragged it home early, and then burned until Epiphany. Surely you must know that?'

Honora shook her head. 'We didn't do that in Virginia and my English Christmases have always been…' She paused, cutting a glance at Isaac who waited for her to finish with suddenly bated breath. Would she mention Frank, with one word plunging all three of them into misery only he had foreseen?

'…underwhelming. Lacking in tradition, I realise now.'

Isaac felt himself relax a fraction.

A temporary reprieve. But for how long? When will the time come that a slip of the tongue, an unthinking hint, will reveal everything? Unless I reveal all first?

He bent to take hold of the log once again, glad of the excuse to hide his face. He shouldn't think like that. If they could make it through the festive days until January without incident all might be well, when Honora would leave for Somerset and the danger would be past. How he felt about her leaving Marlow Manor to disappear he couldn't quite tell, although a sharp pang at the thought of her departure *should* have been all the warning he needed their parting couldn't come soon enough.

'I can't leave this lying in here, getting under Mrs Strimpel's feet. I'll take it out into the corridor and have the steward see it's taken care of.'

Honora watched doubtfully as he heaved the log away, a frown clouding her face.

'You'll never manage by yourself. Let me help you.'

She moved to his side and pushed her sleeves up from her wrists—something that somehow didn't surprise Isaac one bit, although he caught Charlotte's eyes widen. The same forthright action from any other lady would be unthinkable, but Honora merely seized a curve in the bark and began pulling alongside him, putting her back into it with unselfconscious effort he had to admire.

'Honora! You really needn't…we have servants that can do this…' Charlotte ventured anxiously, darting uncomfortable looks at the maids who had paused to watch.

'It's no trouble. I've chopped my own wood for years—I don't mind getting my hands dirty.'

The maids didn't seem convinced of what they were seeing, the sight of an otherwise dignified lady with mud gathering under her fingernails and cheeks growing ruddy as she helped the master drag a great log through the kitchen door not something anyone would have expected. *Except me, perhaps,* Isaac acknowledged, all too aware how Honora's shoulder bumped against his as they pulled in tandem. The huge chunk of wood made a horrible grinding sound as it scraped across the flagstones, but bit by bit it moved along.

I know Honora wouldn't let something as silly as decorum stand in the way of getting a job done.

'She's right,' he managed to say, breath coming harder with exertion. 'You needn't bother yourself. I'm perfectly able...'

'...to break your back, insisting on doing this alone?' Honora's voice was strained as they stepped backwards into the corridor, leaving the maids to stare after them. 'Dragging it through snow is one thing, but along a stone floor is another entirely. Unless you intend to spend tomorrow with your doctor?'

Isaac couldn't help a gruff laugh. 'Have you

looked outside recently? There's a blizzard closing in as well as the darkness. Half an hour and it'll be pitch black with so much snow you wouldn't know which way you were walking. No doctor would be able to get through that, even if I broke my back clean in two.'

'All the more reason for me to...*help*...then.'

With a final grunt Honora rolled the log round to rest against one wall of the corridor between the kitchens and the rest of the house. Straightening up, she pushed both hands into the small of her back, arching to release the tight muscles. The movement showcased the hidden lines of her figure so clearly Isaac couldn't help but stare, his eyes fixing on her slim waist barely concealed beneath black bombazine and blind to all else but that secret curve. Would it be as warm today as it had been in the library, when he had snaked a palm up to rest there and felt his skin burn against her gown? She'd been like a willow bough, so fragile looking, but strong and only ever bending, never breaking under strain. And she'd been under strain, hadn't she? First a miserable marriage to a man who never loved her, then abandoned, and then left penniless and alone, but she didn't complain, didn't shatter, didn't give in. She was determined and capable and worthy of anybody's admiration, and certainly not just because of that tantalising sweep of waist to hip he ached to reach out and trace with wondering fingertips.

Honora gave him the same small smile that always succeeded in scattering stars through his nerves and then turned to Charlotte with a sigh.

'There. At least now I can say I've been of some use during my stay here.'

Charlotte smiled back, her small hand slipping into the crook of Honora's arm. 'You can't think that's the only thing you've done to help, surely. For my part I've much to thank you for.'

'Have you?'

'Of course.' The wan little face was suddenly earnest and Isaac felt a wave of love for the girl he'd come to see as his own wash over him like a tide. 'Before you came I felt so unhappy, sure nobody would want to know me again. But you've been so kind—a friend who appeared just when I needed one most. It might almost be fate.'

Isaac said nothing as Honora reached to pat Charlotte's fingers with real fondness. A complex combination of pleasure and pain swirled inside him to make speech quite impossible. On the one hand it delighted him Charlotte had found some comfort in her hour of darkest need, but wariness tempered any relief. There was so much at stake that neither his ward nor Honora so much as suspected, so much that could go wrong—and with his weakness for his guest showing no sign of abating surely it was only a matter of time before somebody was cut to the bone.

If it were only me who stood to be hurt I could bear the tension. It's not knowing when the axe will fall—and on whom first—that I can't stand. Surely I have no choice. I'll tell Honora as soon as the moment's right.

The panes in Honora's bedroom window shook with the ferocity of the gale outside, great flakes of snow hurling themselves against the glass as if they'd shatter it if they could. Moaning gusts of wind echoed eerily in the darkness, but Honora merely stretched beneath her warm blankets, snuggling deeper like a forest creature in its nest. Timbers creaked and somewhere a loose shutter banged closed over and over again, although floating deliciously between waking and sleep Honora barely heard it.

What had roused her from the deeper slumber she'd been enjoying a few moments before? She didn't know and hardly cared, sleep creeping over her again to return her to oblivion. Some noise, probably, some howl of the wind down a chimney had disturbed her, but no matter. Soon she would be gone again, curled up in the most comfortable bed she'd ever slept in, and the next time she opened her eyes it would be another day closer to Christmas.

From somewhere in the murky depths of her unconscious Honora became aware of something else, some other intruder from the waking world that stopped her from sinking back under. Her brows twitched together and she frowned without opening her eyes, trying to ignore the nagging sensation that *something* stirred out there in the night that she should be aware of.

It's nothing. One of the maids moving about, perhaps. Go back to sleep.

She rolled over, burying her head until only a cluster of dishevelled curls showed atop the covers. So warm, so contented, Honora couldn't help a little sigh as she surrendered to the velvet voice of sleep.

Her eyes snapped open like a china doll's and she lay still, staring into the darkness as the noise that had woken her came again to fling her pulse up to the ceiling. It was a faint cry, long and drawn-out like an animal in pain, and the moment she heard it Honora knew exactly what it meant.

She was out of bed and flying across the carpet before she realised she'd moved, not even stopping to catch up a shawl to cover her thin nightgown as she flung open her door. The sounds of the blizzard outside accompanied her down the landing to Charlotte's rooms, the soft cry ended again, but replaced by uncanny shrieking of the wind that did nothing to calm Honora's thumping heart. All around her Marlow Manor was cloaked in night, not a flicker of light to be found as she raced to Charlotte's door and burst through without pausing to knock.

'Charlotte?'

Searching through the gloom, Honora *just* made out the shape of Charlotte sitting up in her bed, her face the vaguest pale smudge in the darkened room. Although she couldn't make out her expression Honora heard the gasping breaths as the girl fought back panic, her voice high and terrified when she spoke.

'Oh, Honora—help! Please help me! I think… I think I'm dying!'

Honora was at Charlotte's side in a moment, feeling for her hand and taking the icy fingers in a firm grasp. Charlotte was shaking, both with fear and the storm of weeping that squeezed her in its fist, and Honora felt her own nerves tighten with concern.

'Shh. Shh, now. You're not dying.' She slid an arm around Charlotte's back, intense pity rising inside her as she felt every rib of the poor girl's tiny frame. There was no substance to her at all and she was like a bird in Honora's hold, skinny shoulders shuddering with each sob.

'I think I must be. I was woken by a great rush of something coming out and now I keep having these pains I've never felt the like of before… oh, and another…'

Charlotte gave a whimper and curled into Honora's side, clutching her hand so tightly Honora felt her knuckles grind together. She didn't pull away, however, only waited for the crisis to pass and until Charlotte sat upright again with a deep breath.

'You're not dying, dearest. Your labour has started. The baby is coming now.'

'The baby? Now?'

Another flood of compassion flowed through Honora at the wild dismay in Charlotte's thin voice.

'But… I don't know what to do! How am I to manage? I have no mother to tell me what to do, what to expect…' The pale face turned in Honora's direction, shadowy eyes glazed with desperation. 'Will *you* stay with me? Will you help with what's to come?'

Honora swallowed. Her heart still leapt like an untamed horse and the darkness felt suffocating, worry circling despite her soothing words. It wouldn't be the first time she'd attended a labouring woman. Back in Virginia she and Ma had helped many neighbours through their births, bringing the child forth and sharing in the family's joy. This time, however, there was no joy to be found, only the terror of a young girl thrust into a situation she should never have known. 'Of course. Of course I will.'

She felt Charlotte sag against her and tightened her grip on the frail body, pressing a kiss on the tumbled curls.

Poor girl. Poor, motherless scrap. Whoever the man was that did this to her deserves a punishment I can't even dream of.

'I'm so afraid.'

'I know. But you can do it. You're stronger than you think.'

Chapter Nine

Isaac paced back and forth in front of Charlotte's door like an angry cat, hating himself for his helplessness. Every cry was like a dagger to his heart, every groan twisting the knife, yet he could do nothing but wait as more than one life hung in the balance.

When Honora had appeared at his bedroom door for a moment he'd wondered if he was dreaming—until one look at her face made his heart stand still.

It's time.

He cast a desperate glance now out of the landing window, ice flooding his veins as yet another awful sound came from Charlotte's rooms. Snow still flung itself against the glass, the noise of the wind cutting through the darkness, and Isaac passed a hand across his eyes. There was no possibility of going for the doctor while a blizzard ruled the night. With the gale whipping up the white drifts he would be snow-blind in moments, turned about and confused and hardly able to tell which way was which in the midnight gloom. He would go at first light, but until then there was nothing to be done but pray Honora knew what she was doing, the fate of his beloved girl in her capable hands.

And if Honora hadn't been here? What would have happened then?

The thought made him shudder. What *would* they have done without her stepping into the fray, taking control with such calm authority his admiration for her had swelled inside him?

I should have planned better. I should have engaged a nurse to stay here in case of a situation exactly like this one—anything rather than force Honora to deliver her own husband's baby, even if she doesn't know it...

Guilt circled in Isaac's stomach to mix with the worry already there, an uncomfortable brew that made him wince. It was cruel of him to maintain his deception and he knew it, his growing regard for Honora chafing against his dishonesty. She deserved better than to be taken for a fool, first by Frank and then by himself, and his resolve to come clean swelled ever larger—but then that truth was driven from Isaac's mind by a cry louder and more agonised than any before.

'Charlotte!' Her name was torn from his lips and he stood, staring at the heavy wooden door that lay between them as if he would see straight through it. A birthing room was usually no place for a man, but what was that to him, when the one he loved as a daughter lay frightened and desperate and beside herself with pain?

'"Usually" be damned,' he growled, striding for the door. Nobody could tell Lord Lovell what to do and he hardly hesitated as he seized the handle and pushed inside. Charlotte needed him, her terror tangible in that wild scream, and nothing and no one would keep him from being at her side.

His first thought was how warm the room was. A fire blazed fiercely in the hearth, throwing strange shadows up against the blue-papered walls, and too many candles to count stood on every surface, bathing Charlotte's chamber in a comforting orange light. They were clustered most densely around the bed, the hangings pulled back and the fine embroidered coverlet kicked to the floor. Clara hovered to one side, but it was the two figures on the bed that caught Isaac's attention like an arrow: Honora sitting at Charlotte's head with the sleeves of her hastily donned gown pushed up and her hair hanging loose about her shoulders, one hand gripping Charlotte's, whose face was so white she might have been carved from marble. Three sets of eyes turned to fix on him—one pain-filled periwinkle, another determined hazel, the last frightened brown—and with a nod of his head toward the door Isaac dismissed Clara from the room. She slipped out with a weak, grateful smile, only pausing to direct one final look of heartfelt sympathy for her young mistress lying limply on the bed before vanishing, pulling the door shut behind her and making the candle flames dance in the closing draught.

'My little wren.' Isaac stepped towards the bed, noting with a leap of dismay how feebly Charlotte reached for his hand. Despite the warmth of her chamber her hand was like ice, her face pale although sweat slicked a curl to her forehead. He cut a concerned glance at Honora, who returned his gaze with steady seriousness that did little to dim his fears, but assured him she felt them just as acutely.

'I'm so glad you're here.' Charlotte gripped his fingers and moved to brush them with her cheek like a kitten seeking comfort. Her voice was faint, far weaker than he would have liked, and he tensed his jaw on a sudden thrill of fear.

Was it normal for a labouring woman to sound so frail? Surely she would need more fight than this, to keep about her task until it was mercifully at an end?

'Of course I'm here. Nothing in the world could keep me from you now.'

He tried to twist his lips upwards, but they hardly moved, the muscles of his face frozen by worry so acute he could barely breathe. Out of the corner of his eye he saw Honora get up from the mattress and lay Charlotte's hand down with care that raised a lump in his throat.

'You're staying for the duration, then, I take it?'

'Yes. I'm going nowhere.'

He caught Honora's grimly approving nod. 'Good. We could do with the help. I never understood why men should be excluded in the first place. They're responsible for bringing a woman to childbed after all—it only seems right to me they should play their part in the final outcome.'

Charlotte's grip on his fingers tightened suddenly and a high moan came from somewhere deep in her throat. Her face closed in on itself, agony written in every line, and she curled forward, shoulders hunching and knees lifting towards her chest.

'You're doing so well. So, so well, dearest.'

Honora's voice sounded as though it were coming from underwater, so deeply was Isaac submerged in his concerns, and he spared one quick look in her direction. She'd moved round to the end of the bed and was gently lifting the blankets that covered Charlotte's legs, careful yet completely in control in a way that sparked such intense gratitude in Isaac he couldn't find words to speak.

I've never known a woman like her in all my life.

He watched with silent wonder as Honora dipped out of sight, reappearing again a moment and wiping her hands on a strip of stained linen.

She knows exactly what she's doing and isn't a bit afraid. Her bravery and competence is something anyone could learn from—as well as her kindness. If I ever needed proof my first impression of her was wrong, I need look no further than her actions since arriving at Marlow Manor.

It was hardly the time or place to examine his feelings for his unexpected guest and yet Isaac was powerless to ignore how they coiled inside him. Far from the aggravating woman he'd encountered in Wycliff Lodge's parlour, he couldn't now deny Honora's place in his mind and—worryingly enough to make him pause—

heart, pushing her way past the walls he had erected to break through his defences as if they were no stronger than paper. She was still just as stubborn, sharp and independent as she'd always been, but now as she knelt at Charlotte's side the goodness within shone out of her face and Isaac knew he had never seen a more beautiful sight than her quiet, determined strength. If anyone could help Charlotte through this ordeal it was Honora. For the first time Isaac saw past her mask to the true softness within, a core of steel wrapped in velvet, and his respect for her climbed higher than it had ever climbed before.

'Charlotte? I need you to listen carefully for a moment.' With gentleness that clawed at Isaac's throat Honora stroked a damp curl back from the girl's face, crouching at the side of the bed and reaching for Charlotte's freezing hand. 'You've done wonderfully so far. With the next pain I want you to push—you're ready for the baby to come now.'

'Hasn't it been coming already?' Charlotte's thread of a voice wavered, half-buried beneath barely restrained tears. 'All those pains and nothing happened? Was I doing something wrong?'

Her face crumpled and Isaac caught Honora's eye, a look passing between them too complex to fully explain but understood by both. Charlotte had no more idea of how a baby was born than a baby itself, orphaned before she was ten years old with no mother to explain the facts of life. No wonder she was terrified and confused, although the next moment some of the horror left her expression as Honora squeezed her fingers.

'You did everything perfectly. All we need from you now is to pass the final hurdle. I have every faith you'll do it—don't you, Isaac?'

'I've no doubt whatsoever.' Isaac managed a smile, stiff and unnatural, but a smile all the same. Nauseating anxiety gnawed at him but he would rather die than let Charlotte see—or Honora, for that matter, her courage an example he would have to follow and one he admired now more than any other. In that warm, flame-lit room with the wind howling outside they might have been the only three people left in the world and he *would not* let Charlotte see any fear on the faces of the two she looked up at for assurance.

I must thank Honora for this somehow. She came here thinking she was the one whose debt must be repaid—and yet it is I who owes her more than she could ever imagine.

He sensed her on the other side of the bed without even raising his head to look, his awareness of her so intent it was more instinct than design. He was helpless in the face of it, an almost animal reaction to her he couldn't control, and despite the heat of the room his skin prickled to know she was close.

I should begin that repayment with the truth. It's the least Honora deserves once this terrible night is over and what I ought to have done from the start.

Honora held the baby as carefully as if he was made of glass as she washed the worst of the blood away and wrapped him in clean white linen. His scattering of dark hair was soft beneath her fingers and his mouth formed the most delicate little O as he yawned, clearly exhausted already from the messy business of being born. Honora looked down at the bundle in her arms and felt her heart swell with happiness for Charlotte—and then with unexpected grief so sharp it took her by surprise, almost making her stumble as she approached the bed.

It was years since she'd attended a birth and the sight of a newborn baby, so small and breathtakingly vulnerable, seized her throat and gripped without mercy. She was delighted for Charlotte's sake, but that unhappiness for herself welled up so violently it might have drowned her, rising up to drag her beneath the surface.

Gritting her teeth on her emotion, Honora found a smile, hard won but passably genuine. 'You have a son—a beautiful, healthy son.'

She heard Isaac's breath of relief, but didn't look at him as she gently laid the baby in the crook of Charlotte's thin arm. Isaac's eyes were too sharp by half—she knew he would see the turmoil in her face at once, no doubt remembering the secret sadness she'd let slip weeks before, and instead she kept her attention firmly on the new mother lying spent in the bed.

'Charlotte? Did you hear me? I said you have a son.'

The girl's eyes were closed and her chest rose and fell with rapid breaths. At the placing of the bundle in her arm her lids fluttered open and she gazed down at the tiny face, silently drinking in every detail of his plump cheeks and little creased forehead.

'It's all over? I have a son?'

'That's right. What will you call him?'

On the other side of the bed Isaac leaned over and softly moved the linen to see the baby's face. In the low dawn light he looked tired and drawn, but a spark glowed in Honora at his expression, giving way to a rush of fondness she was too exhausted to deny. He looked every inch the proud grandfather—at the ripe old age of thirty-seven—and a flutter of wonder swept through her as he stroked the miniscule nose. How many men would be so tender to their ward's illegitimate child, its existence sure to bring shame on his name and household? There was no shadow of reproach in Isaac's look, however, and once again the goodness Honora had once been so sure didn't exist showed itself so obviously she had to shake her head.

I can hardly believe I ever thought him to be like Frank. To have sat all night with Charlotte, holding her hand through her pains and now looking at the baby as if pleased to meet him...

The dangerous regard for Isaac that had grown within her like a great tree spread its branches ever wider, challenging her to fell it with an axe of good sense, but she found she couldn't even lift the blade, let alone swing it. The kind soul concealed behind confidence that could be confused for arrogance had won over her hesitation and now Honora felt exposed, unable to look away from his face or make herself listen to the nagging voice inside her that still muttered for caution.

'I think I'll name him Christopher. Christopher Isaac.' Charlotte's voice was little more than a whisper, almost lost amid the crackling of the fire in the grate. She traced the line of little Christopher's chin with wavering fingers and Honora felt her brow contract into a frown. The hand Charlotte lifted shook violently. When Honora placed her own against Charlotte's forehead, she found it burning hot where previously it had been cold and clammy.

That isn't right.

Slowly Honora moved to the foot of the bed, conscious not to let her thoughts show on her face. A gleam of alarm had begun to shine at the back of her mind, but she forced herself to lift the blankets drawn over Charlotte's legs quite calmly, praying she wouldn't find what she suspected, with growing fear, might meet her worried eyes.

To her horror, she saw she was right.

The sheets beneath Charlotte were sodden with blood, far more than could usually be expected for a straightforward delivery and enough to make Honora catch a strangled breath. It was the nightmare every doctor and wise woman dreaded and, replacing the blanket, she moved discreetly to Isaac's side.

'Isaac.' She bent to speak directly into his ear, hardly noticing how he stirred at the sensation of her closeness. 'You need to send a servant for the doctor. It's light enough now for him to find his way here. You must do it this moment.'

'What? Why?' He turned his head to murmur back, Charlotte too weak and intent on Christopher's face to pay them any mind. 'Surely the danger is passed now the child has been born?'

'Charlotte is bleeding—a great deal too much to be safe. If the doctor doesn't come quickly...'

She tailed off, but there was no doubting what she meant. Isaac's face turned the colour of sour milk and he lurched to his feet at once, only stopping when Honora seized his arm. Their eyes met, hazel looking up into brown, and a spark leapt into the gap between them to dance over so much left unsaid. Despite their shared fear there was something else, something that bound them together in one snatched moment, a connection neither one of them could fully understand or deny.

'Don't go for him yourself. Send a footman. Charlotte needs you here with her to reassure her all will turn out well.'

'Of course. Of course I'll stay with her. Let me go to find Taylor. He's our fastest rider—if the situation is as bad as you say there isn't a moment to lose.'

Cutting the uncanny thread of their locked gaze, Isaac turned to Charlotte and stared down at her, a skeletal figure in a bed far too large for her tiny frame. He looked on the verge of saying something, his mouth working silently, but instead he stooped to press a kiss to the damp forehead and left the room at once, his joy of moments before doubtless turned to ash and his fear for his ward overcoming all other thought. In a matter of seconds the atmosphere had changed and the rapid alteration made Honora's head spin, horror rushing in to push aside everything else—apart, perhaps, for the echo of that long look, that silent exchange of *something* for which Honora had no name.

She watched him go with pity so stark it pained her to feel it. The life of the one person he loved in all the world was threatened at the very moment he'd finally thought it safe… there was no justice in the world and as she took up Isaac's vacated position beside the bed she could have cried at the cruelty of a girl so young forced to endure such suffering, and for the man who would be devastated beyond words at her loss.

'Where has Isaac gone?' The thin reed of Charlotte's voice quavered up from her rumpled pillows.

'To fetch a doctor. I'm afraid… I'm afraid there's been a complication.'

'Ah.' Charlotte sighed dreamily but didn't relax her hold on her sleeping son. 'I thought perhaps there was. Somehow I knew something wasn't quite right.' She closed her eyes briefly. 'I feel strange. Almost as though floating away on a warm tide.'

Honora looked at her in alarm. She sounded so unlike her usual self, so weak and talking such nonsense that real fear flared in Honora's stomach. She'd seen this once before, in a carpenter's wife she and Ma had attended some twenty years ago. Sapped by a bad bleed after a long and difficult delivery, the poor woman had babbled incoherently until she simply gave up. There was nothing they could do to save her and Honora knew how Ma had been haunted ever since, wishing she'd somehow been able to conjure a miracle. The similarity between the young woman and Charlotte was almost too much to bear—the same pallor yet feverish heat, the same insensible speech and the same crimson stain on sheets growing ever deeper. Charlotte hadn't been strong even before the birth, thin and pale as a graveyard wraith. If the doctor didn't come soon there would be only one outcome, one Honora couldn't bear to look in the eye…

'I'm going to die, aren't I?'

It was a statement so close to the train of Honora's terrible thoughts for a moment she was unable to reply.

'Of course not,' she lied through gritted teeth. 'Neither Isaac nor I will let that happen.'

'But it's out of your hands. You can't stop it if that's my fate.'

Honora steeled herself against a shiver. Charlotte's voice had taken on a vague quality so like the unfortunate carpenter's wife that it was frightening.

'Don't talk like that. The doctor will be here before you know it.'

'You're a good friend. You've been so kind to me even though I didn't deserve it.' With obvious effort Charlotte swapped the swaddled baby into her other arm, her shockingly cold fingers finding Honora's in jarring contrast to her heated face. 'That's why I'm going to leave him with you.'

'Who?'

'Christopher. When I've floated away he'll stay here with you and Isaac.'

Charlotte's chest still shuddered with those quick, shallow breaths and she seemed to be fading before Honora's horrified eyes. 'You *will* marry Isaac, won't you? As a parting gift to me—so my poor boy has two parents to love him?' She looked up at Honora with such sudden, clear hope it was all Honora could do not to flinch back, away from those shining, feverish eyes. '*I* could never give him that. I'm not even allowed to mention his father's name. Can you believe such a silly thing?'

Honora hesitated, confusion and uncertainty crowding her already clamouring mind. She could hardly believe she'd heard correctly, Charlotte's unexpected request surely too silly to so much as consider—but what was that about Christopher's father? It took her straight back to that day in the library, when Isaac had seemed so evasive and his reluctance to speak had roused her suspicions at once. Those same suspicions whispered again now, hinting at some secret loitering *just* out of view…

Why is Charlotte forbidden from uttering the man's name? And what was it Isaac seemed so keen to conceal?

But then Charlotte's head turned painfully to look down at the baby cradled in the crook of her arm and all thoughts of mystery and intrigue fled. Honora heard her begin to hum brokenly under her breath, tender and nightmarish at the same time, and felt her innards roil with dismay.

This can't be happening. She's descending into delirium so quickly…where's Isaac?

Still holding Charlotte's hand, she swallowed down the metallic tang of fear. Marrying Isaac? Bringing up Christopher as her own? It was the rambling of a sick woman, but that didn't stop

Honora's heart from beginning to rail inside her chest. 'Charlotte, this is madness. You don't know what you're saying.'

'Oh, I do.' Charlotte almost sang her reply, gazing down at Christopher with unfocused eyes. 'I've thought about this since that day in the library when I saw you with Isaac. If you two married, Christopher would be raised in a stable home with parents who love him. Would you deny him that? An innocent child—' She broke off and one solitary, heartbreaking tear slipped down her cheek to wrench Honora's chest. 'I let him down before he was even born. With you and Isaac he would have a chance at a good, respectable life with good, respectable people. It's what I want. Won't you promise to do it before the tide carries me away?'

Honora sat frozen to the spot, lips parted, but no words starting from them to explain the depth of her horror. The grey dawn light had grown stronger, trickling beneath the heavy velvet curtains, but still she felt as though she were trapped in some terrible dream.

She truly wants me to marry Isaac. And raise her baby as my own.

It was impossible. Charlotte was merely babbling, her rationality stolen by exhaustion and pain, and making her say things she couldn't possibly mean. Once the doctor had stopped her bleeding she would recover and all would be well, and the memory of her absurd request would be no more than that, a bizarre moment of madness she probably wouldn't even remember once her strength had returned.

Before Honora could answer the door opened and Isaac entered, ashen with worry, but the sight of him enough to gladden her heart and somehow calm the worst of her fear. He came to the bed and sat beside Charlotte, his hand moving at once to smooth back her wild hair.

'Doctor Harcourt will be here very soon. Taylor has taken my own horse to fetch him—between them they'll be there and back in no time, snow or no snow.'

Charlotte's eyelids had closed again, dark lashes sweeping pallid cheeks, and Isaac threw Honora a questioning look. Sitting on either side of the bed, they were like a pair of matching statues, bound together by their desperation, but each taking comfort from the other, a curiously heartening feeling Honora could hardly explain. Now Isaac was before her the world seemed the smallest fraction less bleak, although worry still gnawed at her like a hungry beast she knew stalked them both.

'Any change?'

She shook her head. 'I'm afraid not. She doesn't seem to be in any pain, although she's clearly delirious...'

'I'm not,' Charlotte spoke up, unsteadily and still with her eyes firmly closed. 'I meant every word and what's more I'll say them again, to Isaac this time.' Still she didn't look at them, remaining oblivious to Honora's start of dismay.

'What words? What do you have to say to me?'

'Christopher. I want him to stay here with you and Honora when I go to be with the angels. When you marry her and raise him in a family. You'll do that for me, won't you?'

She asked him as simply and trustingly as one might request some ribbon to be brought home from market and Honora saw Isaac's face tighten with shock. He didn't frown or exclaim or do anything else but sit quite still and look down at his ward's peaceful face, doubtless every reaction made impossible by disbelief. Whatever he'd been expecting her to say it certainly wasn't *that* and when his gaze sought Honora's she saw her own feelings reflected back at her in his granite face.

The colour rose in her cheeks and she looked swiftly away from him, feeling Isaac's incredulous stare like a physical touch to her skin. Was he horrified by the notion Charlotte might pass away or the suggestion he marry her? Likely both, neither something he'd ever wish to dwell on.

'I know there's something between you. I saw it in the library when you were so insistent all you were doing was looking out at the snow. I'm a foolish girl, but I'm not entirely blind… together you could make Christopher's life very happy and his family complete.'

The baby stirred and Charlotte rocked him gently, her face creasing for a moment with a flicker of pain. Honora longed to reach out, but her limbs were too heavy, shock and bone-deep tiredness stealing any hope of movement as Isaac dropped his head into his hands.

She thinks there's something between us.

Of all the confusion and dread that spun through Honora's mind that one phrase leapt forward before she could wrestle it back. Of all the things to ask for—how could Charlotte think Isaac would agree? Even if his feelings for her *had* grown a little warmer that didn't mean he would want to commit himself to her, tying himself to a wife he'd already stated he had no intention of taking.

And the baby? Honora couldn't allow herself to think of it. Her yearning for motherhood had never been at the expense of another. For her to take the baby Charlotte would have to die and the very idea of it rose bile in her throat.

'My little wren...' Isaac's words were between a murmur and a sigh, holding such anguish Honora wanted to take him in her arms and help soothe his raw agony. 'Don't say these things. You don't—'

'Please,' Charlotte interrupted weakly. 'There's nobody I love more than you, but my boy will need a mother. Let it be Honora. There's no other I would trust.'

Honora found she was shaking her head. It was madness, pure and simple. Charlotte couldn't die. She just *couldn't*. She couldn't be snuffed out like a candle, leaving Isaac to his fathomless grief and no doubt blaming himself. The thought of two lives wasted washed over her like a grim tide and she felt her throat tighten with emotion as Charlotte settled more comfortably against her pillows.

'I think I'll rest a while, now I've told you my plans. I'll sleep easily in the company of my three favourite people in all the world.'

She smiled then, such a sweet, contented smile Honora could hardly bear to see it. Isaac must have felt the same, for without a word or even so much as a glance in Honora's direction—whose desire to hold him close bloomed inside her like a dark flower—he returned his head to the cradle of his hands and didn't raise it again until a knock at the door announced the arrival of the doctor.

Chapter Ten

Absently Honora stared up at the bunch of mistletoe that gleamed below the parlour's crystal chandelier, its white berries catching the feeble light. The whole room was festooned with holly and ivy, mistletoe and boughs of evergreen, but that seemed such a pointless thing to notice when she could *just* overhear the doctor speaking quietly to Isaac beyond the half-open parlour door. She sat alone, cold and aching and trying to catch every word she could.

'The bleeding has stopped, thank heaven, and the sleeping draught I administered should bring her much-needed rest. I must warn you, however, that your ward is extremely weak. I'm afraid you should prepare yourself for the worst—I'll do all I can for her, but her chances of survival...'

'I see.' Isaac's voice was desperately hollow and Honora closed her eyes in yet another silent prayer. 'Her condition is as serious as that? You're certain?'

'I fear so. Had she been of a stronger constitution, less frail before the birth, her prognosis might not be so bleak, but that's hardly relevant now. You must focus on keeping her calm and comfortable. She mustn't be allowed to become aggravated again. Any whims, any strange fancies should be humoured to make her mind easier.'

'Humoured?'

'Yes. It's vital her nerves are soothed if there's to be the slightest hope of recovery. Hysteria in women is a very real problem. They lack the rationale of men and their nerves can be their greatest enemy. If you can work to put her mind at rest, you'd be helping more than any medicine I can give.'

At any other time Honora would have rolled her eyes at the doctor's misinformed views on female capability, but as she sat in the chilly parlour any indignation deserted her. There was only one thing Charlotte had requested that might be termed a 'fancy' and the idea of Isaac entertaining *that* was too unlikely to believe.

'And the child?' Beyond the door she heard Isaac continue, his voice still taut with rigidly repressed emotion. 'Is he well?'

'A strong baby. I'll send for Mrs Glenn—a very good woman and extremely discreet. She's just weaned her sixth and will be glad to nurse your...your...'

'Heir,' Isaac supplied firmly. 'Thank you, Dr Harcourt. I'd be grateful if you could make those arrangements as soon as possible, if as you say this Mrs Glenn isn't given to gossip.' There was a shuffling that might have been the noise of two men bowing or shaking hands—and then the subtle clink of coins. 'For your services this morning and a little more to thank you for *your* continued discretion.'

'Of course, Lord Lovell. You can always rely on me to respect the privacy and dignity of my patients. I'll call again this evening. Good day to you.'

Honora listened to the retreating sound of boots with her head bowed, trying to ignore the burning behind her eyes. Charlotte lay upstairs, teetering between this world and the next, her future hanging by the finest of threads, and there was nothing Honora could do to help. She was powerless—just the same as Isaac, who stood now on the parlour threshold and regarded her narrowly.

'I suppose you heard all of that.'

The only response she could manage was a silent nod.

'So you understand Dr Harcourt's recommendation. What is your opinion?'

Confused, Honora frowned up at the man closely watching her every move. He seemed to be waiting for something, or perhaps searching was more the right word, but there was nothing to tell her quite what it could be. 'His stance on women's abilities isn't something I agree with, but I suppose for the remainder he must know best. He's a well-established doctor, after all, from what you told me when he arrived. I imagine his advice will be sound.'

She saw Isaac's throat move as he swallowed with difficulty, her confusion only growing with his curt nod. 'My thoughts exactly. If there's anything to be done to ease Charlotte's distress, I would like to attempt it.'

He sat down opposite her on a luxurious striped sofa, directly below where the mistletoe spun gently on its ribbon. The thin light of the winter morning lit one side of his face, illuminating his firm jaw and his brow creased with suffering.

'I know it's an enormous step to take. I don't think either of us could have foreseen this, but I don't see any other way to proceed. It's what she wanted... I never could refuse her anything and now her very life might depend on it I find myself weaker than ever.' He ran a large hand over his face and then looked Honora unflinchingly in the eye. 'So you're truly in agreement? You would really do this for my poor girl? I'm not ignorant of the fact you wouldn't have chosen this path, but I hope the idea isn't as abhorrent as it might have been once. You would be doing me a great honour.'

Slowly the wheels of Honora's mind began to turn and as the truth unfolded her eyes grew wide.

He's talking of Charlotte's wish for us to marry.

There was no other explanation that made sense.

He's talking of Charlotte's wish for us to marry! And he wants me to accept!

Her dawning understanding must have swum through her expression, as Isaac rubbed his forehead with heavy unease and shifted position on the sofa.

'I see you understand me now. Well?'

'I hardly know what to say.' Honora was having trouble making her lips move, so tightly had her face frozen. Not in a hundred years would she have thought Isaac would take Charlotte's absurd request seriously, yet there he was, watching her unblinkingly and waiting for her reply. 'This isn't something I ever expected.'

'Nor I. But you heard the doctor as well as I did. *Anything* to soothe Charlotte's mind might help her—knowing she needn't worry about Christopher's future could help her rest more easily. In truth, I can see her reasoning.'

'Can you?' She heard the disbelief in her voice and was surprised to see Isaac's mouth twist in a bleak, humourless smile.

'Can't *you*? Think of it. Charlotte knows I'd do my best for Christopher, but I couldn't guess where to begin raising a baby on my own. With you here he would be loved almost as if he were your own—and we would have to marry to make the arrangement above all suspicion. No doubt for Charlotte there's the added appeal of knowing I wouldn't be left to rattle round this big old house alone without her if I had a wife. Did you know she's always wanted me to marry?'

'No…'

'She has. Interfering little miss.' He looked down at his hands. They were clasped together in front of him in the same praying motion he'd adopted that fateful night at the inn when his lips had first met Honora's and set her running down a course she'd never dreamed of. That had been the first time she'd seen a glimpse of the real man behind the confident façade, a man with real feelings and the ability to love, and now as she gazed at his downcast face she felt something tug at her heart.

This is folly. We shouldn't waste a moment talking of it. And yet...

The tugging at Honora's heart grew stronger as she watched him sit so quietly, so obviously in the greatest of pain. Isaac loved Charlotte as a daughter and the idea of her slipping away must be agony. No wonder he grasped at the slightest of hopes for her salvation, even if it meant going against his own firmly entrenched beliefs.

'But you don't want a wife. You told me that yourself only weeks ago.'

'That was before I faced a situation where, unless I marry, I cannot win. There are two outcomes I can see. The first: my marriage soothes Charlotte's worries for the future of her son and her contentment allows her to recover. The second: she is lost to me, but her final hours were peaceful and I have a wife to act as a mother of sorts to my heir, a child I would otherwise be hopeless to know how to raise.' He looked up at her, so wounded and despairing it made Honora flinch. 'I know it's no romantic proposition. I know you deserve more than this. But I ask you, in all humility, to consider. You would have a home here and a family of your own, and that's more than awaits you if you were to return to Somerset. Perhaps there's something in that you might accept. You would be valued and cared for and my gratitude would be deep as an ocean.'

Honora felt her chest tighten as Isaac's words hit her like a shower of broken glass, each one stinging in its undeniable truth. Because he was right: nothing waited for her in Somerset but a tumbledown house no longer her own and the ghosts of past regrets that wouldn't leave her be. Mary was there, that was true, a staunch friend and until recently the only one Honora had, but she was busy with her husband and sons and the new baby just arrived, and she had enough to attend to without anyone else added to her burden. Honora recalled her ache not to be alone any longer when Charlotte had invited her for Christmas and how pleased she had been to accept. At Marlow Manor she could do some real good, a comfort to Charlotte and maternal figure for Christopher—and as for Isaac...

It was pointless to deny her feelings for him any longer. Ever since she'd seen the kindness inside him, his ability to care for those other than himself, the danger of her falling under his spell had grown in strength and now there was no question that she had succumbed. His face was handsome and his title might impress some, but it was the light in his soul that called to Honora and made hers cry out in return.

I was so determined never to rely on a man again. I was so sure I'd never return to the position Frank reduced me to—but in my heart I know this is different.

Becoming Isaac's wife would be nothing like shackling herself to Frank and Honora's lip could have twisted at the thought. There was a world of difference between the two men, but more than that Frank had married her for what he could gain, while Isaac's offer would benefit her as much as himself. She would be acting out of mercy for Charlotte, compassion for little Christopher and sympathy for Isaac, and she knew no better motive than to help others in their darkest hour. In turn she would be saved from a life of poverty and disgrace and above all given her greatest wish: a family around her with no secrets or deceit.

The idea of losing Charlotte filled Honora's veins with ice and she still couldn't look the possibility full in the face. If there was *anything* she could do, surely she ought to attempt it? With a strange quiver in her stomach she looked again at the swaying greenery above where she sat, aware of Isaac's eyes upon her, but suddenly unable to meet them.

'I'm not a fool, Honora.' He spoke quietly. 'I know in my heart Charlotte won't survive this suffering. I failed her and now I must watch her die…but can you see why I'd try *anything* to save her? No matter how absurd it might sound?'

'Yes. I can understand.'

Gathering all her courage, Honora lifted her chin and looked in Isaac's face. It was pale, exhausted—and the most dear to her, a fact that had crept up so gradually she hardly knew when it had begun. From a condescending, intolerable lord to a thoughtful, vulnerable man, Isaac's transformation was uncanny, or perhaps it was she who had changed, the walls she'd built around her heart since Frank's betrayal blinding her to what had been before her very nose.

She set her shoulders and straightened her back. Ma would have been proud to see her posture and Pa her steady hands, she thought with a stab of wistful yearning, as Honora took a breath and leapt with senseless daring into the unknown.

'Very well. I accept. Will you shake to make it binding?'

Honora saw Isaac's quick look: relief, gratitude and a hint of wariness she well understood. The same feeling stirred inside her, until the faintest gleam of amusement in those brown eyes made her pause.

'Another bargain to be sealed with a handshake? We're to be married, Honora. I think we ought to be less businesslike in our dealings with each other than two farmers agreeing the sale of a horse.'

'Well? What do you suggest instead?'

His gaze flickered upwards and she followed it, coming to rest on the bunch of mistletoe hanging from the light above their heads. At once her stomach flipped, an uncomfortably gymnastic movement she couldn't control.

'A more suitable symbol of agreement than a handshake, considering we're to be husband and wife. Wouldn't you agree? After all…' He stopped, as if speaking was a sudden effort that caused him great pain. 'Considering how much time Charlotte spent on these decorations I wouldn't want them to go to waste. I don't know that she will ever see another Christmas.'

Honora swallowed—but then she found she had nodded and her legs had unfolded to bear her up, and she was standing before Isaac beneath the mistletoe before she truly understood what she was doing. All she could think was the strangeness of it. On one hand a tragedy, while on the other sparks lit her from within as Isaac gently cupped her cheek and tilted her face up to meet his, more tender than she'd ever known him before and the emotion in his eye something that couldn't be faked. Perhaps it was the magic of the Christmas mistletoe or the severity of the situation, but as Honora and Isaac clung together, giving and taking with questing lips, neither seemed to want to let go. They were tied now, for good or ill—both twined together in Honora's mind so tightly it was impossible to separate the two.

Isaac hated himself as he took Honora's hand and helped her from his carriage on their return from church, the hastily procured wedding band shining on her finger. For the princely sum of a few shillings he had secured a common licence allowing them to marry only two days after Charlotte had given birth, now the day before Christmas Eve, and with Honora as his wife his gratitude to her was eclipsed only by his guilt.

You deceitful, conniving wretch.

He'd made up his mind to tell her before everything had gone so spectacularly wrong, unable to bear the weight of concealment any longer. Watching Honora tend Charlotte with such care and kindness had driven a spike of pain into his gut. How could he keep secrets from her now, when her goodness was so deserving of the truth? His respect for her, already snaking upwards like a vine, had long since twined itself around his heart—alongside feelings for his new wife that were something altogether different.

But I didn't tell her, so wildly did events go awry, and after Charlotte's request all good sense seemed to desert me.

He chanced a glance at Honora, walking beside him up the snow-laden steps of Marlow Manor. Her head was high and she moved with the same purpose as always, but there was a subtle tinge to her cheeks and when she returned his look he saw something linger in the depths of her fine hazel eyes.

'You look troubled. Don't tell me you're regretting this already.'

Isaac shook his head, realising with a jolt it was apprehension he saw in her expression. How could she think any man would regret taking her as his wife? Any with a particle of sense would know how lucky he was to have found such a woman and therein lay the trouble.

He'd lured her into marriage without knowledge of the full facts and that hardly made him any better than Frank, another selfish man acting in his own interests rather than hers. Honora might gain a home and family from their bargain, but how much would that matter to her when she discovered Christopher's parentage?

Damn it. Damn it all to hell and myself along with it.

'No. There can't be a man alive who wouldn't consider himself fortunate to have you at his side.'

She almost smiled, a tiny curve of full lips Isaac could have stared at all day. He had no right to think it, but he couldn't help wondering if she'd allow him to kiss them whenever he pleased now she wore his ring, the once clear boundaries cursedly blurred. Were they a truly married couple now, or merely friends? And what would they be when Honora learned her new husband had concealed the sins of her first and that the baby she'd already come to care for was that first husband's son?

It was a fine mess and no mistake, and as Isaac stood back to let Honora enter the house ahead of him he felt bile rise in his throat. Charlotte still lingered somewhere between living and death, every day repeating her wish for Christopher to pass to him and Honora to raise together. She'd become agitated more than once and only the news of their engagement had soothed her, the fight bleeding out of her feeble body and her pale cheek relaxing against her pillows once more. The chance of Charlotte recovering should have made his deception worthwhile, but he couldn't shake his foreboding as he followed Honora inside and heard the door close firmly behind them.

It's done now. You never wanted a wife, never intended to marry, but now you must work at being the best possible husband you can be. Honora deserves that much and more.

'Ought we go up at once to see Charlotte? She'd want to know all about the ceremony. There's nothing that cheers a young girl like a wedding.'

Honora unbuttoned her coat and Isaac watched her out of the corner of his eye. She wore the only light-coloured gown she'd brought with her from Somerset, a sprigged muslin that had clearly seen better days, but a vast improvement on the sombre mourning she'd worn previously. As the wife of a lord she could have her pick of expensive gowns—not that he thought she'd considered *that* for a moment.

How many society ladies could one say that about? That their reason for marriage had nothing to do with the contents of their purse?

He became aware his new wife's attention had strayed from him and followed the direction of her gaze, turning to look behind him at the grand holly-swathed staircase sweeping into the hall. Mrs Glenn was descending slowly, holding a tightly wrapped bundle carefully to her. Isaac could just see a little nose poking out among the swaddling as the wet nurse reached the ground floor and dropped a curtsy, a sweet-natured woman close to Honora's age whose face invited confidence.

'Good afternoon, Lord Lovell. I brought the young master down to give you and Lady Lovell his warmest congratulations.'

In spite of the unpleasant feelings currently swirling through his innards Isaac couldn't help a dry laugh. 'His warmest congratulations? Such manners for a child of only three days old.' He nodded at Mrs Glenn, who stepped forward and held Christopher out for Honora to take. 'There now. He can offer his good wishes in person.'

Honora took the baby from the wet nurse's sturdy arms and cradled him gently against the bodice of her gown, moving the wrappings slightly aside to reveal his rosy cheeks. Little Christopher stared up at her, his eyes the brilliant unseeing blue of a newborn, but seeming to roam her features as if solemnly drinking her in. Honora gazed back, her face softening beneath that innocent scrutiny and glowing with such genuine tenderness Isaac felt his heart skip a beat. There was a suggestion of the Madonna and Child about the scene before him, two faces suffused with perfect contentment in each other's company, and another flare of gratitude leapt within him. If the worst were to happen and Charlotte slipped away, there was no doubt Honora would raise the baby with love, her affection for Christopher's mother and naturally maternal heart making any other outcome impossible—until she learned the truth.

What if she sees some trace of Frank in the child's countenance? What if, as he grows older, some hint reaches her ear...?

Isaac felt a cold finger of guilt run the length of his spine. If Charlotte died, the truth would die with her, no one else able to reveal the name of her seducer, but that outcome far too high a price to pay for secrecy. He was caught now in a web of his own lies with no way out but to confess all and the net was closing around his neck to strangle him where he stood.

'Is Miss Charlotte awake?' Unaware of her husband's tortured thoughts Honora spoke to the wet nurse, still holding Christopher in a warm embrace. She rocked him in a gentle rhythm that made it difficult for Isaac to look away, so oblivious to whose child she was holding a savage wave of shame rose up to soak him to the skin.

'No, ma'am. Doctor Harcourt came to call and administered a particularly strong sleeping draught when he learned you'd gone to church to be married. He thought her excitement might be too much for her to bear—like as not she won't wake fully until tomorrow morning, he said.'

'Oh. That's a pity.' Honora's voice was heavy with disappointment. 'I'd hoped the news might cheer her. Still, I'm sure I can wait another day to see her smile. An early gift for her on Christmas Eve.'

Isaac nodded stiffly, hoping Honora wouldn't notice the rigid set of his expression. Almost an entire day until he would have to stand before Charlotte and pretend he felt no regret for what he'd done, luring a good woman into a marriage based on the shifting sand of deceit. He could try to soothe his conscience as much as he wished, but that was the raw truth, and he had less than twenty-four hours to learn how to stop his face from betraying the turmoil in his heart.

Mrs Glenn was correct. Charlotte slept soundly for the rest of the day, not even stirring when Honora opened the bedroom door a crack and peered inside, hoping her friend might have awakened at last. For Isaac her continued unconsciousness was a relief, but one that lasted only until night fell, when he entered his own chamber to find his wife sitting alone in the vast expanse of his four-poster bed.

His mouth dried at once. It was a scene so startlingly similar to his most secret dreams that he stood for a moment in the doorway, fleetingly unable to force his limbs to move. Honora was clad in nothing but her demure nightgown, the most tantalising hint of her shape hidden under a scant coverlet. He'd seen her in such a state of undress on more than one occasion, it was true, but never before had she been *waiting* for him, *in his bed* and looking back at him by the light of a single candle with its shadow moving across her watchful face.

'Sorry. I didn't mean to startle you. I assumed, as we're married now...'

She tailed off, shrugging one shoulder beneath the thin linen. In the dim light her eyes were darker than usual, guarded and more like those of the defensive woman he'd met that fateful night at Wycliff Lodge. They'd come so far together since then, some strange regard growing between them Isaac knew Honora felt, too, but as she waited for his reply she seemed almost unsure.

'Yes. Naturally you should sleep in here with me. It wouldn't be the first time we'd shared a room, would it?'

He meant to put her at ease, but all he succeeded in doing was to bring the memory of that night to the forefront of his mind, when he and Honora had drunk each other in with such unexpected passion that took them both by surprise. By the look that flickered over her face she must have recalled the same thing and she tactfully busied herself with arranging the covers as he undressed and slipped in beside her, only the subtle colouring of her cheeks suggesting she wasn't quite as calm as she appeared. Isaac leaned over to extinguish the candle and then there they were, man and wife together in a great oak bed, cloaked in darkness that did nothing to dim the desire to reach out and touch that was so tangible between them it made the atmosphere of the room feel stretched dangerously taut.

Every nerve in Isaac's body blazed as he lay unmoving, listening to Honora's steady breaths at her side. She was so close he could feel the warmth of her creeping over the sheets and his fingers itched to cross the slim gap between them and make contact with her skin, doubtless smooth and heated and soft beyond imagining— not that he hadn't tried. From the first moment

Honora had melted into his arms he'd barely spent a night without attempting to guess how she would feel beneath his palms, willowy yet strong and a delight he longed to discover. The fervour with which she'd returned his kisses and even seemed to seek them had to mean *something,* give him some clue to the secret desires hidden behind her cool façade, but with a sudden, unwelcome icy shock of reality he knew he shouldn't seek it.

He didn't deserve her intimacy or trust and he had no right to enjoy the attentions of a beautiful wife when he held some part of himself back from her. Wouldn't giving in to his yearning for Honora make him no better than Frank, taking from her so shamelessly while giving so little in return?

If you do this, you'll be every bit as selfish as he was. She deserves to be loved completely—not with secrets and half-truths from a guilty heart.

The heart in question sank at the thought, but it couldn't be denied. He'd be taking something he had no right to and would have to find a way to stem the craving that had begun to tighten its grip, the woman next to him so entirely oblivious to the power she wielded to make him forget his restraint...

'This isn't my first wedding night, you know. I can explain how to proceed if you're not sure how to go about it.'

Honora's quiet voice caressed his ear, a hint of amusement hidden somewhere in its depths, and despite his resolve Isaac felt himself stir. Surely only a granite statue could remain unmoved with that low murmur coming from so nearby, its owner's intoxicating smile unseen yet clear in every word.

He took a breath and steeled himself against the disloyal workings of his body. The temptation to give in to his desires and pull Honora closer was like a siren's call and he closed his eyes in an attempt to block it out. 'I think I've a fair idea, thank you. I'm hardly a maiden either.'

'No? Not a shy young damsel?'

Isaac felt the covers shift as Honora moved on to her side. Although the room was dark he could make out the shape of her face now mere inches from his own and his heart leapt helplessly from its former place in the pit of his stomach to rail against his waistcoat.

So close. She's so close I could kiss her if I chose.

'I can't say I've ever been called one of those.'

'I see. So it must be me that makes you pause.'

His nerves sang at the sensation of her breath

on his skin, lighting the side of his neck as surely as if she'd run a fingertip across it. The tide of desire inside him rose up again to crash against the rocks of his determination to resist—Honora thought he didn't *want* to draw her into an embrace and count every arching rib, smiling against her throat when he heard her sigh? She thought for a single, solitary second *she* was the reason he kept his distance?

He lay for a moment, feeling the tide of yearning return over and over again to beat at his defences. He ought to stand firm. He ought to keep his resolve, his respect for Honora the most important thing in the world and to be protected at any cost—but then she reached out a hand to trace his jaw and every sensible thought fell from his mind like rain from the sky, leaving behind nothing but hopeless want.

'Have you decided you regret our marriage after all? You've realised you should never have taken me as your wife?'

There was no reply Isaac could make but to seize the hand that touched him and pull it upwards, drawing Honora towards him as though she weighed nothing at all. He settled her along the long, lean length of him and his own hand came up to tangle in the hair at the nape of her neck, warm curls that smelled of soap and honey and the unique, secret scent of the woman he adored. His other hand pressed her to him as his mouth found hers and it was as if a match was struck inside him, the flame blazing into life and scorching him from within.

'Does this answer your question?' Isaac heard the feral longing in his voice and a snatched breath was Honora's only response, a short, shuddering thing gasped against his lips and making him tighten his hold. Perhaps he'd taken her by surprise with his bold advance, perhaps making her blush, or perhaps not, as the next moment she'd slid a palm over his chest and gripped his shoulder with a force he had to admire. Any notion he might have had of her prim modesty was flung away as her mouth moved over his and opened to accept his kiss, his blood heated past boiling point and scalding in his veins.

The hand that pinned her to him moved to explore the hidden landscape he'd dreamed of for so many nights, still covered by thin linen, but the promise of what lay beneath rendering him almost insensible. It was the most uncanny thing, some vague part of him had to acknowledge: he'd been with women before, many times, but never had he been driven so close to the brink by one still wearing her nightgown. Something in the shape of Honora and the heat that came from her skin tempted him, called his name and made him drunk with delirious desire for her touch, and touch him she did, her fingertips at his neck and his collarbone and then moving to linger at the top button of his nightshirt with delicious intent.

Slowly, so teasingly she must have known how it made him shiver, Honora twisted the first one loose and slipped her finger between the collar and his neck, stroking softly at skin that cried out for her caress. She pushed herself gently out of Isaac's grip and ducked below his jaw, following the progress of her fingers with tiny kisses to his neck and throat that made his every muscle strain and coil, the desire to catch her up again so strong it was frightening. How was she *doing* this? he wondered with the only shard of consciousness not yet completely consumed by passion for the woman in his bed. It shouldn't be possible for him to be unmanned so effortlessly—but Honora must have known some magic his other encounters had not, skilfully unfastening one button after the next with no shame or hesitation, moment by moment revealing more of his firm chest and growing closer to the point of no return...

Before Isaac knew what he was doing he had

flattened Honora's hand against his chest and held it there, preventing her from moving any further. His breath was racing and his heart pounding as if he'd run a mile, but the fog was lifting from his mind and a half-second later he was dismayed by how near he had come to making a terrible mistake.

Stop. Stop now. You know this isn't right.

Honora stilled, the sound of her breathing as fast as his own, but uncertainty entering her voice that Isaac wished he could chase away. 'Is something the matter? Is something wrong?'

He hardly knew how to answer her. Regret so sharp it cut him beneath his ribs rose up within him, the knowledge he'd almost strayed too far painfully real. Another few moments and he would have taken all Honora had to give, just as he would in the days before Charlotte's fall had shown him the need to be a better man.

You almost lost control. You were almost as free with Honora's feelings as Frank was—and that can never be allowed.

There came a soft sigh from his side, a low breath as if Honora had realised something a heartbeat too late. 'Of course. I should have known.'

Confused, he felt Honora retract her fingers

from his. It wasn't the swift whip of rejection, however. Instead the movement was smooth and kind, and when she placed her hand back on top of his with such gentle care his confusion only grew.

'It's Charlotte, isn't it? You've no desire to cement our marriage while she's so unwell.' She shook her head in the darkness, the sound of her hair moving on her pillow a tell-tale sign. 'I'm sorry, Isaac. I should have realised your mind is too full to consider anything else.'

Unseen in the dim room Isaac's face hardened. First Honora thought she was the reason for his distance and then she apologised when he took his chance? The injustice of the situation made him clench his jaw, the same jaw which only minutes earlier had been lucky enough to feel Honora's lips, and lying there Isaac hated himself more than ever. Dishonest and untrustworthy, that was him, and entirely undeserving of the woman who pressed a chaste kiss to his cheek with quiet sympathy he hadn't earned.

'Try to sleep now. It's been a long, strange day and I wager we'll have much to tell Charlotte in the morning.'

He felt her settle beside him, the warmth of her flooding out to touch him. She was curled

close enough that he could fit himself against her
as he dreamed, although it was to be hours until
Isaac's whirling mind allowed him the mercy
of sleep.

Chapter Eleven

'What a lot of fuss. I'm sure nothing can be that bad.'

Honora settled Christopher carefully in the crook of her arm as she paced the holly-strewn parlour, rocking him in time with her unhurried steps. His face was crumpled with temper and his thin little voice was like that of a lamb, indignant and insistent on his demands being satisfied at once. Honora couldn't help a smile at such rage contained in so small a body and she felt a rush of affection steal over her for the wailing creature in her arms.

If the worst happens and Charlotte slips away, I might have to be as a mother to this child. Loving him would come so naturally.

The smile slid from her face at once as cold fear rose in her stomach. Wouldn't that be the most painfully bittersweet answer to the prayer she'd whispered more times than she could re-member? The chance of a child to love—but at the cost of Charlotte's life?

Nothing I desire could ever be worth that price. I would never trade that poor girl for any selfish wish of my own.

Christopher's grizzling showed no sign of stopping and Honora tried to ignore the chill spreading through her innards. There was no point in thinking like that and as she patted the baby's back she searched for a suitable distrac-tion—both for him and herself.

'Did you know it's Christmas Eve, Christo-pher? Perhaps a carol might cheer you.'

She cleared her throat, slightly self-conscious. Normally Honora would rather eat coal than sing in front of an audience, but she supposed she was safe enough with Christopher. If he didn't appreciate her talents, he had no way of saying so, after all.

'"While shepherds watched their flocks by night, All seated on the ground, The angel of the Lord came down, And glory shone around. 'Fear not,' said he, for mighty dread had seized their troubled mind. 'Glad tidings of great joy I bring, To you and all mankind."'

Honora felt the baby still a little in her arms, his cries growing slightly less passionate. She swayed to the parlour's window and stood with her back to the room, holding him to the light as she continued.

"'To you, in David's town this day, Is born of David's line, The saviour who is Christ the Lord, And this shall be the sign: The heavenly babe you there shall find, To human view displayed…'"

Christopher gave a great yawn and fell silent, his eyes closing in sleep now instead of fury. Honora rocked him soothingly, pleased with her success as she gazed out at the Manor's grounds. Snow still covered the grass, rising in strange heaps where it skimmed a hedge or low wall, and for the first time she wondered what Mary would say if she were to see her old friend's new home. She'd be happy Honora had found a place in the world, no doubt, and delighted it included a handsome husband who treated her with such care. For her part Honora could scarcely believe the wild turn her life had taken, throwing her into Isaac's path and making her reconsider every fiercely sworn oath she'd ever made not to fall for a man again—

'All meanly wrapped in swathing bands, and in a manger laid.'

The sound of Isaac's voice behind her made her jump and she turned to see him just inside the doorway, finishing the verse in an unselfconscious baritone that vibrated through her chest. As always when catching an unexpected glimpse of him, Honora felt her heart leap up into her mouth and her pulse began to hum beneath the thin skin of her throat, an insistent flit she was surprised he couldn't hear.

'How long were you standing there!'

'Long enough.' He came fully into the parlour and stood before the fire to warm his hands. By the ruddy cast of his cheeks he'd just been out in the snow and Honora admired the way the high colour contrasted with the soft brown of his ruffled hair. 'Teaching the boy his Christmas carols already?'

'I certainly wouldn't have if I'd known you were loitering about, listening at keyholes.'

He huffed a laugh, eyes crinkled appealingly at the corners, and not for the first time since their confusing wedding night Honora longed to trace the contours of that face. She fully understood why Isaac hadn't the resolve to finish what they'd started—but that didn't make it any easier to bear. Honora had barely slept, all too aware of the warm body next to hers and every sinew screaming to touch him. Her self-control was stretched to its limit. A more prudish woman might be ashamed of such desires, but Honora remembered what it was to lie with a man and her longing for Isaac far outstripped any such feelings she'd ever had for Frank. Now they were married there was no shame in indulging those desires she knew Isaac shared, but Charlotte still lying so pale and weak was enough to give them pause.

You're bound together now for the rest of your lives. There's plenty of time to explore whatever might be growing between you—both in body and soul.

'I was hardly loitering at keyholes. I beg your pardon if I embarrassed you, though.'

Honora shifted Christopher carefully into her other arm, transferring his solid weight from one aching shoulder. He was making good progress even if his mother wasn't and she caught Isaac's satisfied glance at the baby's sleeping face.

'There's one way I'll forgive you. I'd like to ask a favour.'

'What's that?'

'May I borrow the carriage this afternoon? There's somewhere I feel I must go.'

Isaac snorted. 'You needn't ask for things like that, Honora. It's your carriage now as much as mine and entirely at your disposal. Where is it you're thinking of going? A last-minute Christmas errand?'

She hesitated, taking a moment to rearrange the linen that swaddled Christopher's tiny frame. In truth, her mission was one she'd wanted to complete for some weeks, but something inside her had held back.

'I want to visit Frank's grave.'

Isaac's face tightened and for a split-second Honora saw an expression flee across it she didn't understand. Was it displeasure? Jealousy? Or something different she couldn't quite name? It brought to mind the same look she could have sworn she'd seen when she had asked the identity of Christopher's father, that same flit of sudden secrecy that put her immediately on guard.

But that would suggest some link between Frank and Charlotte—surely that can never have been the case.

She tried to dismiss the notion at once, but to her discomfort it refused to be brushed aside so easily. Unless she was very much mistaken there was *something* Isaac conspired to keep from her and the idea was more unsettling than she wanted to allow. It caught at her with its claws, irritating but insistent and determined not to be ignored.

'It isn't from sentiment. Not really,' she continued firmly, trying to blot out the creep of uncertainty. 'I've been considering it for some while and I don't think I can truly rest until I feel I've closed that door for ever. After everything he subjected me to, all that passed between us… Do you understand? Can you see why I want to meet him one last time?'

She watched him carefully, although whatever she'd seen in his face had gone. Perhaps it had passed through or perhaps he was hiding it, but he seemed composed as he nodded.

'I understand. You'll want me to accompany you, to show you where he lies.'

'If you would.'

'Of course. That's the least I can do.'

Honora tried to smile. 'Thank you. I thought you wouldn't mind visiting him. You were such friends, after all.'

The tiniest flicker of movement twisted Isaac's lips—miniscule but still stoking the fire of Honora's kindling suspicion. He made a low sound that might have been of agreement and looked away to the window that bathed Honora in wintry light, the snow gleaming in the weak sun that illuminated holly boughs about the room to gleam like emeralds. His back seemed to have stiffened and a beat of unexplained tension threatened to stretch out between them, until Honora shifted the baby forward.

'Will you take Christopher for a moment? I'd like to speak to Clara about my warm cloak. It tore last time I wore it and I need to mend the hem—she must have some thread I can use before we go out.'

'You don't need to do your own mending any longer, you know. You're Lady Lovell now—I'll buy you ten new cloaks if the fancy takes you.' Isaac turned to take the swaddled bundle from her, brushing her fingers accidentally, but all the same sending soft fire to lick where he touched. Christopher looked smaller than ever cradled in Isaac's strong arms and she couldn't help but stare, captivated by the gentleness on his carved features and the tender ease with which he held such a fragile burden.

He looks at Christopher as if he loves him. An illegitimate child, fathered by some nameless villain Isaac must despise and the cause of his ward's deepest shame, yet he cares for him all the same and holds him as though he has the world in his arms. A man like that is hard to find...surely it's no wonder I grew to love him. He gave me no other choice.

Honora took a breath and allowed the truth to roll over her as strong and unstoppable as the crashing of a waterfall. It was the first time she'd allowed herself to admit it, but there was a kind of strange peace to be found in accepting what she couldn't fight.

I never wanted to let a man into my heart again after how Frank tried to grind it into dust and caused such a gulf between me and my parents, those who actually loved me. I never intended to make an exception for Isaac—but how could I do otherwise? A kind man with compassion for an orphaned girl, a child born from shame and a widow without a penny to her name?

She felt the quickening of the blood rushing through her veins, but didn't try to push the thought away. By some miracle she'd found a man *worth* finding, one who treated her with the respect and care Frank had never bothered to attempt. In time perhaps Isaac might come to see her in the same light, his regard for her deepening to join the desire she knew he already felt.

Stranger things have happened, she thought as she watched Isaac begin to pace the flame-lit room with kissing balls hung at every corner, rocking the child as he walked with such beautiful patience she felt her yearning for him soar up to the sky.

There's no knowing how my luck might change and if this husband might come to love me better than the first... But first I must determine what secret he keeps. I won't be made a fool of again.

'Down here. Towards the fence.'

A cold breeze nipped at Isaac's nose as he led Honora through the graveyard, careful to keep his face as impassive as it had been in the carriage. It wasn't the pretty church they'd married in that they skirted around now, instead a smaller chapel just outside Carey's boundary, and he thought again how glad he was that Frank had been nowhere near the place where Isaac had taken Honora for his own.

I didn't need his spectre following me down the aisle. After all the pain he caused I'd rather forget he existed. However...

He knew there was no chance of hoping for that until Honora had made her peace with the past and he had little choice but to lead her among the frosted graves to where Frank lay. Apprehension writhed inside him, dogging each step across the snowy ground, and he could hardly bear to glance at his wife as they finally stood side by side before the place her first husband would wait for ever in endless silence, Honora growing still as she recognised the name carved into a simple stone.

She leaned forward to brush a light dusting

of snow off the ingrained letters and with a sharp twist of his innards Isaac saw her hand shook. It was the smallest of tremors but he wanted to catch her up none the less, to hold her against him and comfort her in what must feel so uncanny a moment. He couldn't see her face, only the back of her bonnet as she bent her head, but her vulnerable neck rose out of her collar to catch his eye, so smooth and warm he longed to lay a hand on it. What would he see in her expression if it wasn't hidden from him? Would there be grief there—grief Frank didn't deserve?

Unseen by his distracted wife Isaac took a step back, partly to give her the illusion of privacy, but also to hide his grimace as he lifted his hat and raked a hand through his hair. Memories of the man lying beneath the soil turned Isaac about until he hardly knew which way was up, Frank's final moments coming back to torture him at the worst possible time.

Isaac had thought the villain was acting at first when he'd watched Frank fall to his knees, a few scant paces ahead with the distance between them closing by the second. Blood and fury had bellowed in Isaac's ears and he had kept running, tearing through the darkness of the night until he'd reached where his prey lay gasping for breath on Marlow Manor's frost-scattered lawn, clutching his chest and moaning like a felled beast.

It had only been when Isaac had tried to haul Frank to his feet that he'd known it was too late and now, standing in a windswept graveyard at Honora's back, he could recall every detail of the moment he had realised Frank was as good as dead.

'Have mercy, Lovell, please—I have a wife. Honora...at my old Wycliff Lodge...'

'The fact you have a wife hidden away down in Somerset doesn't move me, Blake. Where was your concern for her when you dishonoured my ward?'

'But she needs me. You wouldn't make an innocent woman a widow before her time?'

Isaac clenched his teeth, a dark shadow of the rage he'd felt that night sweeping over him. As far as Isaac was concerned the world had lost nothing with the passing of Frank Blake, but the quiet figure of Honora still sent a dagger through his heart and he stepped back to her side.

'Is there anything I can do?' His voice was almost lost to the wind that picked up the stray curls escaping from Honora's bonnet, making them dance as if they were alive.

'No. I don't believe so.' She looked up at him,

head lifting to see into his face. Her eyes met his and all at once Isaac felt as though he was falling, that hazel gaze so direct it knocked him off balance and made him lose one jagged breath. 'There's nothing else. You've done so much already.'

Isaac's heart stumbled over a beat as he felt her take his hand, Honora seeming suddenly shy as she laced her fingers with his. Her lashes swept down as she watched her grey glove entwine with his black, his hand so much bigger, but gentle all the same.

'I wanted to come here today to finally lay the past to rest. Until I did that I couldn't fully embrace my future…or you, in truth.' A glimmer of fresh colour suffused her cheeks and Isaac steeled himself against the urge to cup them between his palms and bring her face up to meet his. Instead he remained still, listening with his pulse leaping as she pressed on.

'I know we met under strange circumstances. I know you never wanted a wife, and I certainly didn't make it easy for you to warm to me at first. But I wanted *you* to know…how much it means to me that you saw past all the things that made others sneer and took me as I am. After Frank I thought there could be no good men left in the world—apart from my father, who deserved better than my stubbornness—and that they all lied and deceived for their own ends. Thanks to you I see now that isn't so.'

She snatched a glance up at him. With her tawny cheeks grown rosy and a gleam of uncertainty in her eye she looked so much younger, so different from the self-assured woman he had come to love.

'Because that's the truth, isn't it? There's nothing you'd hide from me? No secret you would keep?'

Isaac felt his mouth dry abruptly.

Of all the questions she could ask...

There would never be a better time to come clean, he knew with crystal clarity as all other sensation but that of slender fingers gripping his fell away. The perfect moment didn't exist, but wasn't this as close as he would ever get, Honora standing before him with such openness in her face it inspired him to do the same? She half suspected already, he could tell, although *exactly* what stirred the rushes of her curiosity neither he nor even she truly knew for sure. It was instinctive, he supposed, the sharp consciousness of an intelligent woman—like a bloodhound she'd picked up a scent and she followed it now to wherever its origin lay.

You always meant to tell her and now she's

*given you the chance. Do the right thing, Lovell.
Be the better man you vowed you would be.*

'You think I'm hiding something?'

'I think it's possible.'

Isaac gave a dry laugh. Trust Honora not to
give too much away. She was too shrewd for that,
even now—another reason he loved her, as if he
needed any more.

He sighed. By the keen look in his wife's
eye he couldn't speak soon enough, although
the words clung to his lips as though trying to
save themselves from being set loose upon the
world. Once he'd uttered them there was no turning back. He would have to face whatever form
Honora's shock, surprise, horror took, with no
excuse and nowhere to hide from her emotion.
What would it be? he wondered, trying to ignore
the thrill of dread that flared inside him like a
cold flame. Disappointment? Anger? Unhappiness she'd been tricked into marriage without all
of the facts? There were so many avenues she
might charge down and none of them good, but
her honesty deserved honesty in return. After
everything Honora had done for him, the very
least she was owed was the chance to make up
her own mind.

'You'd be correct. I'm afraid it concerns the
man we had in common.' Isaac took a breath,

collecting himself under a cloak of unease. Honora watched him closely, never faltering, and in the face of her patience Isaac took the final leap.

'He didn't die in my arms because we were friends. I don't think we ever were.'

Isaac swallowed and felt his dry throat contract. Beneath his coat he sensed a chill that had nothing to do with the winter wind snapping at his face. It went deeper than that, wending its way into his bones. It might be the last time Honora looked at him with anything other than disgust and he wanted to remember her as she was that moment: windswept and beautiful, a woman of courage and substance he knew he didn't deserve.

'Honora, Frank was—'

'I knew it.'

Isaac blinked, caught out by her unexpected response. 'What? What did you know?'

'That you and Frank could never truly have been friends. You need never have pretended, in some misguided attempt to spare my feelings.' She held up her free hand, the other still twined with Isaac's that he never wanted to let go. 'I know what Frank was: a wastrel and a rake. How could you ever have liked him? You had nothing in common. His gambling, his poor treatment of women, careless attitude to life—all his flaws are alien to you. You would never behave like that and I'm more glad of it than I can say. Those kinds of men deserve nothing but contempt.'

Her grip on Isaac's fingers tightened and she looked up at him so frankly, with such truthfulness in her lovely eyes, that he had to bite back a grunt of pain.

Gambling. Poor treatment of women. Careless attitude... All the things on which Frank and I based our cursed friendship.

Honora had just described him to the letter, or as he had once been, before Charlotte's fall from grace had made him re-examine his place in the world. Her disdain for feckless men was plain in every syllable and Isaac felt himself flood with a chill that seized his very heart.

But Honora wasn't yet finished, oblivious to the sudden ice in her husband's gut. 'I never felt I truly belonged before I came to Marlow Manor, to live among those who have treated me with such real kindness and care. We may not know for certain yet if Charlotte will recover, but I pray for her every day and God willing she'll rally. So thank you, Isaac. Thank you for giving me this fresh chance at happiness and the hope of a family I thought lost to me for ever. Thank you for being, in the end, nothing like the man I wed before.'

She rose up on to her tiptoes and pressed a kiss to his cold cheek that spread like flames beneath Isaac's skin. He wanted to hold her to him, capture that strong, willowy frame and keep it for ever, but he was frozen with a mixture of wonder and despair that robbed any words from his disloyal tongue.

Oh, my love. How can I tell you now?

By some hideous twist the situation had *worsened,* actually found a way to become even *more* complex, and Isaac's confession died in his mouth. Only a second before he'd seen the way so clearly, but he had to turn back, the prospect of revealing all to his trusting wife now surely impossible.

If I tell her about Frank's role now it will destroy everything she's come to hold dear and she will never look at me the same way again. Her home, the family she hopes to build around her—it will all be ruined if she knew how Frank tainted it and how similar I was to that wretch. I'd be pulling the rug out from beneath her feet just as she was starting to feel safe...how could I ever be so cruel as to hurt her like that, when she's suffered so much already?

The answer was that he couldn't. He couldn't

shatter the haven she thought she'd found and there was nothing in the world that would convince him otherwise—and neither could he bring himself to face her contempt, knowing without question it was more than he deserved.

His conscience struggled against yet more deception, but Isaac bullied his lips into a brittle curve. Under any other circumstances he would be overjoyed to hear Honora's affection for him spelled out so clearly, something once upon a time he never would have believed. It was the granting of his dearest wish and yet he couldn't rejoice in knowing she returned his regard, his dishonesty sucking the joy out of what should have been a moment he never forgot.

'I'm glad you feel Marlow Manor is your home after such a short time. I'll admit I wasn't always sure you'd like it...or me.'

'Oh, now you're a different thing entirely. You deserve a category completely your own.' Honora returned his smile with one of her own, one so sweet and hopelessly shy Isaac knew what she was about to say before she even said it and felt his every nerve cry out to repeat her declaration back at her and mean every word. The churchyard around them seemed to retreat somehow, growing distant and faint and the graves disappearing as he looked down into Honora's face and watched her pretty lips.

'I think that's why... I think that's why I've come to feel...'

Her sentence was cut abruptly short by the sound of boots crunching over snowy ground and Isaac felt a hand on his shoulder before he heard the voice.

'Sir! Lord Lovell!'

He turned, still holding Honora's gloved hand, but alarmed now to see Taylor, the manservant, standing behind him.

'Taylor? What are you doing here?'

The red-faced manservant straightened up. Some distance behind him, at the edge of the churchyard, Isaac saw one of the horses tethered to a rail, blowing hard. How he'd failed to hear the approaching hooves was hardly a mystery— he'd been so intent on hearing Honora and what he suspected she was about to say he'd been deaf and blind to everything else, even now cursing the servant for interrupting.

Was she about to say she loved me? And was I about to say it back? In spite of the secrets I must now keep the rest of my life?

'Well? What is it?'

'It's Miss Charlotte, sir.'

Belatedly Isaac realised Taylor's expression

was one of grave worry and he felt his insides turn to ice.

No. No. It can't be that.

'Miss Charlotte? What about her? She hasn't…? She *can't* have…'

'No, sir. It isn't that.' The man shook his head, glancing at Honora as if she could spare him the ordeal of breaking whatever news he had to Isaac.

'Then what? What is it?' Sharp relief turned in Isaac's stomach, but couldn't eclipse his increasing dread. Charlotte hadn't slipped away, then, his worst fear by miles—but why then had Taylor come to find him, looking for all the world as though he'd rather be *anywhere* else?

'She hasn't passed on, sir, but—' Taylor broke off unhappily, only forced to continue by the fierce gleam in Isaac's eye. 'It's difficult to explain.'

'Damnation, Taylor—will you not put me out of my misery and just *speak*?'

'I'm sorry, sir. It seems Mrs Glenn went in to speak to Miss Charlotte and found the bed empty. We searched all over, but I'm afraid I have to tell you…we couldn't find her anywhere. Miss Charlotte has disappeared.'

Chapter Twelve

Isaac stared down at the rumpled sheets of Charlotte's bed, its embroidered coverlet still hanging from his hand where he had torn it from the mattress. The pillows bore soft indents where a head had recently rested and a half-empty glass of water sat close by on the bedside table, but there was no sign of the occupant herself and Isaac passed a hand across his furrowed brow.

'Could you tell me again, Mrs Glenn—when did you realise Charlotte had gone?'

Behind him the wet nurse held Christopher close to her as if fearing he, too, might be spirited mysteriously away. 'About a half-hour after you'd left, sir. I came upstairs to lay the baby down and then thought of something I wanted to say to Miss Charlotte. I peeped through a gap in her bed-hangings to see if she was awake and that's when I saw she wasn't there.'

'Did you talk with her before that?' Honora spoke from Charlotte's wardrobe, opening the door to check briefly inside. 'She was sleeping when we left this morning, but perhaps you caught her in a lucid moment?'

Isaac glanced at Honora, but she was too intent on Mrs Glenn's reply to notice. All trace of the rosy, girlish creature he'd been captivated by in the graveyard was gone now, replaced by the same capable, clear-minded woman who had taken control on the night Christopher was born. If she'd been about to confess her feelings for him, as he had hoped so hard it took his breath away, there was no chance of that now Charlotte had vanished—worry and dread coiled inside him like snakes, but shot through with a thread of regret he couldn't ignore.

Would she have uttered the words I've wanted to hear for longer than I even knew myself? And would I have returned them, knowing how little I deserve even a moment of her time after my deceit?

'I only spoke with her briefly this morning, ma'am. She complained of being particularly hot. I opened her window and asked Clara to bring a fresh glass of water. In truth her face *was* flushed despite the chill outside and it seemed to me as though her fever might be peaking. I thought I'd recommend Dr Harcourt to be sent for on your return, but now...' Mrs Glenn patted Christopher's back unhappily. 'I should have acted sooner. She was speaking quite wildly, more animated than I've seen her in days, and her cheeks were brilliant pink. I should have known something wasn't right, but when she said she was going to sleep a while I thought perhaps that was best. I never dreamed she would be gone next time I checked.'

'You have nothing to rebuke yourself for.' Isaac touched her vaguely on the shoulder, his mind too full to take in all of what she said. 'None of this was your doing.'

'Wait.' Honora moved away from the wardrobe, her face clouded with some thought. 'You said she complained of being hot? Did she *ask* for her window to be opened?'

'Yes...' the wet nurse nodded '...she even left her bed for a moment to put her face into the fresh air, although she got back under the covers again when I warned she might catch cold.'

Isaac watched as Honora crossed to the window in question and looked out at the white-swathed grounds below. Charlotte's rooms were toward the back of Marlow Manor and boasted one of the best views of the estate, showing the copse of trees standing to one side of the lawns and running parallel until it reached the park beyond. From there the treeline curved round to hide a gentle slope leading to a small lake, unseen from the house and a breathtaking surprise Honora had found one day on a snowy walk. Now as she surveyed the grounds Isaac could have sworn he heard cogs moving beneath her pile of black curls, her busy mind working on something he would probably never have considered.

'Has the whole estate been searched? Or just the Manor?'

'Just the Manor. Surely Charlotte is too weak to have wandered any further afield.'

'I wonder…' Honora's eyes narrowed with the thought Isaac knew had been coming. 'She was hot and delirious by Mrs Glenn's account. The desire to cool herself must have been torturous and her confusion could help spur her on… Isaac, we need to search the grounds at once.'

'You truly think there's a chance she could have ventured outside?' Isaac eyed her doubtfully. 'She could barely walk, let alone struggle through all this snow.'

'A determined woman can do anything, as I think you already know,' Honora countered firmly. 'Charlotte is not in her right mind. There's no knowing for sure exactly what she's capable of.'

Isaac ran his hand yet again through his thatch of chestnut hair and looked down at Honora's set face. She was right. There was no limit to the things a woman could do if she set her mind to it and if that mind was disturbed... There wasn't a moment to lose.

He nodded, suddenly more grim than ever before. Charlotte could be out there somewhere, confused and alone and turned about by her weakness and fever. If they didn't find her soon, it might be too late and he would never forgive himself for not acting more quickly to save her.

'You're right. As always.' He shot Honora a dark, humourless smile and caught her answering gleam. 'I'll take Taylor and the footmen and start combing the park. If she's out there, we'll find her.'

'And me. I'm coming out to look as well.'

Isaac had turned for the door, but at Honora's voice he looked back over his shoulder. 'I don't think that's a good idea. The woods are dangerous after the blizzard. You might slip and fall, or a damaged tree might come down on top of you...'

Even as he was speaking Isaac realised his words were in vain. Honora's jaw had set and although she waited for him to finish he knew he might as well have said nothing at all.

'You're warning me about the dangers of trees and snow? Knowing I grew up in the forests of Virginia, where there was far more to worry about than losing one's footing?' She raised a dark eyebrow. 'There were bears, Isaac, and wolves, too. I spent more time climbing trees than I did getting squashed by them. I'm not afraid and I want to do my part in finding Charlotte.'

'Honora...'

'This conversation is wasting time that we can't spare. Tell me, do you truly think you can stop me? Knowing me as you do?'

Isaac gazed at his wife, looking straight back at him with unflinching determination, and his admiration for her swooped inside him like swallows in spring. Her steely spine was something most men could learn from. Her courage and strength of conviction was unmatched by anyone he'd ever met, and in that moment he knew there would never be another woman in all the world who could eclipse her in his heart.

'No. I don't think that. You'll do as you will, Lady Lovell—I wouldn't expect anything else. Come, then, if you're coming. We leave at once.'

The wind whistled around Honora as she stepped among the snow-laden trees, her skirts flattening against her legs and the ribbons of her bonnet flying back over her shoulder. She scanned the swaying branches that danced on all sides, hoping to catch a glimpse of her quarry, but there was nothing but frozen trunks and snatches of white lawns peering through them, and the far-off sound of footmen calling Charlotte's name. They had been searching for an hour already with no luck and even splitting into different directions hadn't brought as much as a clue, the girl apparently disappearing from the face of the earth.

I'll find her. I'll find her if it's the last thing I do.

The memory of Isaac's pale face as the carriage had borne them back from the churchyard was burned into the forefront of Honora's mind. To take his hand in hers and hold it with fierce sympathy had been so natural she hadn't known she'd done it until he had squeezed back, that tiny movement just as thrilling as a hundred kisses from Frank. Ironically enough it was her first husband who had convinced her to be honest with her second—but that was before Taylor had come running in to shatter the moment, snatching Honora's declaration of love from her mouth and replacing it with fathomless worry. Now the best thing she could do for Isaac was help find his ward, hopefully wiping the fear from his blanched face. There would be plenty of time for talking after Charlotte was safe and sound again in her warm bed, when Honora could seize her courage with both hands and tell Isaac the secret workings of her heart.

I can't say for sure how he'll react. I know he never wanted a wife, but his behaviour has never been that of an uninterested man—and I can't stay silent any longer.

Moving among the trees on the hunt for elusive prey brought memories of Virginia flooding back and at another time they might have made her smile. Walking beneath the Blue Ridge Mountains was the last time Honora could remember feeling free of worry, the trees not caring about the shade of her skin or where her father was born. The only shadow of that freedom she'd experienced since had been here at Marlow Manor, living with Isaac and Honora as Christmas Day drew closer by the hour and feeling part of something *real*, so far removed from Frank's false regard it was laughable. She'd been right about Isaac's secrecy. He'd never liked Frank, the differences between them so stark she could hardly believe she'd thought they could ever be alike. There was nothing between Isaac and Frank to bind them, she knew now, and Honora quickened her step as she came to the edge of the trees and the glass-topped lake hove into view before her.

She stopped, chafing her gloved hands together as she surveyed the icy majesty of the still water. It stretched out silently at her feet, dully reflecting the grey sky above and the only movement that of the clouds mirrored on its surface. Now she was out from the protection of the trees Honora felt the wind cut across her face with added spite, snapping at her nose and trying to pull her cloak away from her body. It was bitter. Even wrapped in layers of wool she felt the chill creeping over her skin, sliding a finger down the back of her neck to cool the column of her spine. Looking out across the frozen lake, she was gripped by a shiver that had nothing to do with the cold.

If Charlotte wasn't found soon there would be no hope for her, none at all, and the realisation turned Honora's stomach. The light would begin to fade and then all would be lost, the only possible outcome that of finding her poor, lifeless body somewhere, huddled alone in the snow and breaking the hearts of both Honora and Isaac, never to be repaired. Christopher would indeed be left motherless and all he would have to remember her was a portrait and a lock of hair, a sad collection of relics that could never capture the likeness of the girl they honoured…

And then Honora saw her.

Charlotte was standing quite still, cutting a bleak little figure on the lake's iced surface. She was draped in one of the blankets from her bed, but even from a distance Honora could see it was soaked and filthy, dragging along the ground, and a wet stain spreading up to cover Charlotte's body. It must have chilled her to the bone, but she didn't seem to have noticed, only hovering with her back to Honora and looking across the frozen water as though entirely alone in the world.

'Charlotte!' Relief so intense it could have brought Honora to her knees surged inside her and she hurried closer to the lake's edge. 'Charlotte, thank heaven! We've been looking all over for you! Come back from there, it isn't safe!'

The girl didn't turn.

'Charlotte?' Honora called again, but again there was no response. The sad, blanket-draped figure didn't move and Honora frowned, thinking quickly.

I'll have to fetch her. I don't think she'll come on her own.

She snatched a glance at the back of Charlotte's tousled head, its brunette ringlets swaying in the wind. A bird was singing in one of the trees behind her, the sweet notes in perfect contrast to the unease unfolding in Honora's innards as she tested the ice with the toe of one boot, concentrating hard.

It's thick enough to bear Charlotte's weight, but mine, too?

She hesitated. The ice certainly seemed stable, but one false move would send her crashing through into the water below, possibly taking the girl along with her to sink without trace. If there was any alternative Honora would have snatched it, but there wasn't, and with her heart beginning to hammer she carefully set one foot on to the ice, as slowly and as gingerly as if her life depended on it.

Which, you know, it does.

Pushing the unpleasant thought aside, Honora gritted her teeth and took a step, ears trained all the time for the tell-tale crack that would spell disaster. It didn't come, however, and she stepped again, slipping away from the bank towards the centre of the lake and the young woman standing on it oblivious to the danger all around.

Little by little Honora inched closer, placing her feet with the greatest care. A swift look down showed reeds and driftwood trapped beneath the glassy surface and she swallowed an instinctive thrill of fear—she could so easily plunge through to join them, the dark waters closing over her head and pulling her under…

She shuddered, but kept moving forward, every step taking her further and further from the safety of the snowy bank. A few paces more and she'd be close enough to take Charlotte's arm and guide her back, and she clung to that promise as the ice slid under her boots and tempted her to fall.

'Charlotte?'

With her heart still beating like a drum Honora watched the girl turn, slowly as though in a dream and a hazy smile spreading across her face.

'Honora, what are you doing here? Were you too hot as well?'

She stepped closer and Honora immediately slid an arm around Charlotte's back, not wasting a single moment in guiding her towards solid ground. They could talk properly once off the ice, although the relief that wended its way through Honora as Charlotte allowed herself to be shepherded away was so strong she could have sighed out loud. Her heart still leapt, but she had firm hold of Charlotte, her arm tightly clamped against the sodden blanket, and as the bank grew nearer she felt some of the tension leave her frame. Isaac would be beside himself that his ward had been found unharmed and as she herded Charlotte gently up on to the snow-covered grass Honora was barely any less delighted herself. The girl was safe. Sweet, kind-hearted Charlotte was alive and, if she was strong enough to walk so far, she must be recovering at last from the ordeal of her labour, although the vague look in her eye and strange tone of her voice still suggested delirium that made Honora pause as Charlotte murmured something in her ear.

'What was that? I couldn't quite catch…'

'Slipper. My slipper. It came off.'

Honora followed the shaking finger pointing back at the lake and her stomach fell into her boots as she saw Charlotte was right. Sitting proudly out on the ice was one bedraggled slipper, and a glance down showed only a stocking covering Charlotte's left foot.

Honora closed her eyes for a moment, summoning all her exhausted strength not to groan.

She can hardly struggle back to the Manor with one shoe. I'll have to go and fetch it—back on to the death trap that could crack at any moment.

'So it did. How rude of it.' Honora found a smile from somewhere and carefully helped Charlotte down on to a felled tree near the water's edge. She arranged the filthy blanket around her more warmly and nodded with a confidence she didn't feel. 'Stay just here and wait for me. I won't be a moment.'

Leaving Charlotte sitting obediently on her perch, Honora took a steadying breath and ventured once more on to the still waters. The wind attacked her as soon as she inched away from the bank, but she lowered her head and continued her slow, precise progress towards the slipper lying some distance away. If it had possessed a face she might have suspected it was taunting her, Honora thought sourly, still listening hard for any alarming sounds. The wind tugging at her bonnet made it difficult to hear clearly and she could only hope her luck—and the ice— would hold.

She closed in on her prey and bent to retrieve it, victory bringing a curve to cold lips. At last. At last she could take Charlotte and get out of this damned freezing weather, to sit beside a roaring fire and defrost her poor aching bones. Mrs Strimpel would make sure tea was sent up, probably with a pile of hot toast to accompany it to celebrate their triumphant return. Honora could almost taste the butter and her mouth began to water as her fingers closed around tattered satin and she straightened up again, turn-

ing to retreat back to the safety of the bank with
her quarry held firmly in one hand…

But then from beneath her boots came the
most almighty *snap* and Honora was in the water
before she even had time to scream.

It hit her with agonising force, shock pushing the air from her lungs. The water was just
so cold. It surrounded her, above and below and
on every side, in her eyes and her ears and her
mouth that opened to cry out but the words mercilessly drowning beneath the ice. She kicked
and fought, struggling towards the daylight that
filtered in fragments through the gloom, scrab-
bling at the glassy roof above her with numb
hands that caught and tore—but her cloak tangled around her legs with every abortive stroke
and instead of swimming she was sinking, still
fighting, but trapped by her skirts and weighed
down by the saturated material that conspired
to drag her under. Blind panic gripped her and
she shook from side to side like a terrier would
a dying rat. Was that what she was now? A terrified creature facing its end, thrashing and helpless and clawing with every ounce of its strength
to escape? Her bonnet had come loose and her
hair swirled into her face, clamping against her
nose and mouth as if trying to end her suffering,
but when she tried to fling it away her scratched

and bleeding hands were just too weak to do anything but drift through the water like weeds.

The faces of her mother and father flitted through Honora's mind as she flailed helplessly, her chest bursting and lungs screaming for breath. They would never be reconciled now. Isaac wouldn't even know where to address a letter to let them know she'd died, she thought, somewhere vague and seemingly distant from the crisis racking her poor body. She'd never see Isaac again, either, never run her hands over that lovely jaw and tell him how her heart leapt when he was near, that he was a hundred times the man Frank had ever been and that living with him at Marlow Manor had felt like coming home at last. She would die there beneath the ice, cold and frozen and alone—but at least she'd saved Charlotte. When they dragged her body from the water she might have a smile on her face because of that and, with her mind circling on that final thought, Honora felt her eyes flutter closed and darkness overcome everything else.

At first when Isaac hauled Honora on to the lake's bank she lay quite still, eyes closed and wet hair fanned out around her like an ebony halo. The snowy ground was cold beneath him as he knelt at her side, a different kind of cold than the biting water he had plunged both arms into and locked around her waist, and for one brutal moment he wondered if he'd been too late. She didn't stir as much as a fingertip—until without warning Honora lurched upright, expelling a great gout of water and coughing and coughing as though she might bring up a lung.

Isaac felt his heart turn over, a giddy somersault that snatched away his own breath. He wanted to shout or laugh out loud, but instead he could do nothing but crouch there in his sopping shirt, staring down at Honora with the same two words resounding in his mind.

She's alive. She's alive!

Fierce relief roared up within him like a burning flood as he reached for his hastily discarded coat lying on the snow. With numb fingers he draped it over Honora's spasming shoulders, her eyes still closed, but his never leaving her face for even a half-second. If he looked away she might disappear back beneath the ice or somewhere else he couldn't follow, the jaws of death doubtless enraged to have been cheated of such a prize. If he lost sight of her, he could wake from this dream and find he hadn't been fast enough, and that in some other nightmarish reality he would never see Honora again.

So close. I came so close to losing her for ever. When I saw her fall through into the water...

A ghostly hand wrapped freezing fingers around Isaac's throat and tightened its fist. He could hardly bear to think of it. If he hadn't emerged from the trees at that precise moment, seen her wild look of alarm as the ice gave way...

He pulled the coat around her and gathered her into his arms, lifting her from the snowy ground. The soft weight of Honora against his chest made it swell with emotion so strong it almost choked him, fear and stark gratitude assailing his flagging composure. With his wife cradled in his arms, shivering but reassuringly *real*, he still hardly dared believe the danger was over. Might she still be stolen away by cold or shock, the light of his life extinguished by her selfless sacrifice?

Isaac turned for the house, Honora settled against the front of his shirt and grasped so tightly not even a whisper could have slipped between them. Nothing would be allowed to take her. He would fight anyone or anything that tried to snatch her from him. The prospect of a life without her in it was no life at all. As he strode back towards the Manor, with Taylor carrying Charlotte close behind, he knew the time had come for her to know it.

He glanced down at her, all coughing subsided now and her face serene and quiet. With her eyes closed she might have been sleeping, so it was with only a murmur Isaac spoke into her ear.

'Stay with me, Honora. I couldn't bear to live without you now.'

'Thank you, Clara.'

Honora wrapped herself in the linen drying sheet the maid held out to her and stood before the fire, luxuriating in the feeling of heat on her skin. It tingled from the scalding bath she'd stepped from, but still she couldn't completely escape the chill in her bones, coldness that sat inside her like a block of solid ice.

Perhaps I never will. Perhaps coming so close to death will stay with me for ever.

She shuddered. If Isaac hadn't dragged her out, wouldn't she be lying on the murky lakebed now instead of drying after a hot bath, the water freezing her blood rather than warming it again? The sensation of drowning, of suffocating and her lungs filling with burning cold returned to remind her how near she'd come to the ultimate disaster and she felt herself sway sickeningly despite the safe comfort of her familiar bedchamber. Isaac had saved her life. A few moments more and she would have been lost, drifting away to join Frank in whatever afterlife awaited those who passed before their time.

A quiet tap at the door interrupted her horror, giving way to a different emotion entirely when it opened and Isaac slipped inside. His face was drawn and pale, wearing a look of concern that carved new lines into his already weathered brow—until he realised she wore nothing but the drying sheet, and his gaze dropped with impeccable good manners to the carpet. Clara cast one swift, knowing glance at him and with a hastily dipped curtsy left the room, closing the door behind her and leaving Honora alone with the man who had snatched her from a watery grave.

'I'm sorry. I didn't mean to interrupt your bath.'

Honora shook her head, holding the sheet in place and supremely aware its scant cover was all that stood between Isaac and her bare skin. Her damp shoulders gleamed in the firelight and she saw him snatch a glimpse of them before averting his eyes once again, his fingers fidgeting at one cuff.

'I was already finished. Somehow I feel I've spent quite long enough submerged in water for one day.'

'Yes. I imagine you would.'

He frowned down at his hands and Honora

couldn't help a reflexive swallow. They were the very hands that had pulled her from certain death and she owed them her endless gratitude— as well as the man they belonged to, whose rigid face made her want to smooth away his troubles with gentle fingertips. Not for the first time that strange day her heart began to skip, but this time not with fear. Love and wonder caused it to jump now, along with the vaguest recollection of his murmur as he'd carried her back to the house.

What was it he said? He never wanted to be without me?

'You might have died today.'

His voice was low and Honora blinked at the tortured edge she heard below its surface. It was the voice of a man pushed to the brink by pain and worry and she could only find a nod in reply.

'You almost sacrificed yourself to make sure Charlotte did not. That ice could have broken at any time and yet you ventured out anyway—' He bit off the end of his sentence as if he could hardly bear to speak it, one hand tunnelling through his hair. Isaac turned, pacing away from her in a manner frankly alarming until he stopped again just as abruptly and shook his head.

'By heaven, woman—do you know if I wasn't

already under your spell I could have fallen in love with you all over again for that bravery alone?'

Honora's lips parted and she stared, her concern of moments before evaporating like frost in sunshine. Isaac gazed back, with such absolute conviction in his face she could have watched him for ever to see the different tides of his expressions shift across it, each as perfect to her as the last, but none of them helping her to summon the words to respond.

'Even aside from your mind, your beauty, that quick tongue—against what you did today my heart has no defence.' Taking advantage of her uncharacteristic silence, Isaac pressed on, still pinning her to the spot with the fierce adoration in his eyes. 'If you had slipped through my fingers, my soul would have followed you. Tell me now without any pretence. Can I hope my feelings might one day be returned?'

The drying sheet had become unpleasantly damp tucked around Honora's body and her hair steamed as it dried in the fire's heat, but she was unaware of either sensation as she gazed at her husband and drank in his declaration with breathless surprise.

He took the words right out of my mouth. What I'd intended to tell him in the churchyard he's just said himself—he beat me to the finishing post!

Isaac's eyes never left hers as she moved slowly towards him, hardly able to move her feet. Every limb felt weak beneath the rush coursing in each vein and Honora could scarcely believe she wasn't in some wonderful dream, the man she'd admired now the husband she loved and his confession mirroring the one that had clamoured to flee from her own lips.

'You can do more than hope, Isaac, and a good deal sooner than *one day*.'

She rose up on to her toes and, before anything else could happen to stop her, laced her fingers together at the back of his neck, the sheet now precarious without a hand to anchor it in place. That seemed such a silly thing to waste time thinking about, however, when she had so many other things to consider—and so with every sinew cheering her on Honora pulled Isaac's face downwards and covered his mouth with hers.

There wasn't even time for her heart to take one more shuddering beat before Isaac's arms were around her, anchoring her against him with ardent strength. She felt the tendons in his neck strain beneath her fingertips and the silk sweep of hair at his nape, hard and soft combining to thrill her with their contrast. His own hands were busy on a mission of their own, sliding to capture the back of her head and cradle it, leaving her nowhere to hide from his merciless kiss.

But Honora didn't want to hide.

She didn't *want* to escape from the prison of Isaac's muscled arms—*not now, not ever*, she vowed as his fingers tangled in her damp curls and held her still, her breath coming harsh and ragged and Isaac's just as short. Like two fighters in a ring neither one wanted to give way. Honora's sigh was tinged with victory as she triumphed and Isaac's mouth opened wider under hers, with one movement deepening the kiss and breaking down the dam holding back any glimmer of restraint Honora might still have felt. She was falling now, tumbling into an abyss of sensation so instinctive and pure, and when Isaac's hand strayed from the back of her head to trace the path of her spine she shivered with helpless delight.

His fingers skimmed lower across the sheet caught between them, the only thing preserving Honora's last shred of modesty. It was fighting a losing battle and with every movement it slipped a little more, beginning to pool at Honora's feet, and for the first time she felt the smooth slide of Isaac's shirt across her bared skin. The adventurous hand crept lower still, following the curve of her waist and then flattening against the small of her back, to sketch tiny circles on the sensitive flesh still covered by the sheet until she murmured against Isaac's lips.

'What did you say?' he mumbled into the vulnerable crook of her neck, dipping down to explore the soft skin with his mouth and send spikes of longing lancing through her insides. Every breath, every tiny sweep of his lips, made her tremble and when he gently traced the delicate shell of her ear with the very tip of his tongue she thought she might fall apart completely. He was skilled and dangerous and *hers* now, against all the odds, and she couldn't help the need in her voice when she opened her eyes and saw how his contained the same longing, carefully kept in check until she gave the final word.

'I *said*, you need to take this off.'

Isaac gave a shuddering breath and released her, his face flushed and chest heaving just as hard as Honora's. He took the smallest step back, unsteady hands working the buttons of his shirt free to reveal the scattering of hair she already knew lay beneath. She'd long since wanted to touch it, to feel his heart pounding beneath heated skin, and now that there was nothing to stop her she was in his arms again the moment he dropped the shirt on to the floor.

'Lady Lovell. You appear to have lost your sheet.'

His mouth was on her neck again, the feel of his questing lips making every hair at the nape stand on end. Slowly, so slowly Honora thought she might run mad, he nipped lower and lower, bending to chase the shivers that raced across her skin until he reached the secret hills and valleys uncovered by the sheet—and grazed them with his tongue to make Honora gasp.

He pulled back then, sinking to his knees and looking up at her with eyes clouded by desire. Honora could barely stand, let alone manage to mind as Isaac's gaze raked across her, as reverently as if her body was a priceless work of art. She stood before him and was not ashamed. For the first time she had a husband who loved her, truly loved her, without the selfish deceit of Frank's false regard. With her hair curling around her shoulders and the sheet abandoned at her feet Isaac saw her for what she was, *who* she was. Her body wasn't perfect, but it was hers, every single inch *hers*, with no artifice or pretence, and by the wonder she saw in his face she could tell he understood.

'Beautiful.'

Isaac knelt a little closer and Honora felt her breath claw at her throat as he smoothed his palms over the line of her hips, tracing the strong length of her legs and back again as though trying to commit the shape of her to memory. Her knees weakened at his touch and she placed a hand on his shoulder to steady herself, biting down on her lower lip to stop herself from gasping aloud when his fingers drifted higher along her thigh. She wanted to pull him closer and feel the length of his body pressed against hers once more, but she couldn't seem to move and could only snatch one short breath when gently, exquisitely softly, he dipped the tip of his tongue into her navel and laughed darkly at her answering jolt.

'Shall I pass you your sheet while I'm down here?' His voice held a wicked edge beneath the hoarse want and Honora was powerless to stop a small smile as she closed her eyes.

'I don't think I'll need it again tonight. Do you?'

Chapter Thirteen

Kneeling carefully, Honora placed another handful of kindling into the parlour grate, attempting to bank it around the Yule log in an ordered pile, although there was little hope of concentrating while Isaac insisted on trailing soft, delightful kisses down the back of her neck. Each one turned her bones to water just a little more until she turned to him with a stern frown, the impact of which was dented slightly by the twitch of her lips.

'Isaac. *You* were the one who said this thing should have been lit yesterday—Christmas Eve instead of Christmas Day, I believe is the tradition. I was too busy drowning to light it last night, so if you don't let me get on with it now I'll go for my flintlock. You know it's still in my reticule, just *itching* to greet an aggravating husband.'

Isaac's mouth curved in return, but he stepped away from her with a bow, his parting shot one gentle finger caressing her nape to make her shiver. 'My apologies, madam. The very last thing I'd want to be is a distraction.'

Honora watched him out of the corner of her eye as he dropped into an armchair pulled up to the fireplace, sinking back with legs outstretched. For a man who claimed not to be trying to draw her attention he was failing miserably. His crisp white shirt gleamed in the Christmas Day sunlight streaming through the window opposite where he sat. When he brought both arms up to rest behind his head he only succeeded in displaying the outline of muscles concealed tantalisingly beneath. In all Honora would much rather have abandoned the Yule log and gone about the enjoyable business of removing said shirt from its owner, but the lump of wood wouldn't burn itself and she knew how keen Isaac had been to include her in the tradition.

'So? What happens now?'

'You take a splinter from last year's log…' he leaned forward to offer a sliver of wood taken from his waistcoat pocket '…and use it to light this year's. Once it's aflame we'll keep it burning all throughout today and then smouldering until Twelfth Night.'

'For what purpose?'

'Prosperity for the New Year and the warding off of evil. Keeping a shard of the previous log is supposed to protect the household all year until a new one is burned next Christmas.'

She took the splinter and carefully set it alight, a spark from Isaac's tinderbox leaping up to claim it. A vulnerable flame flared into life, dancing at the tip of the shard of wood and illuminating Isaac's face as he smiled down at her. 'Although I'm not sure I need a felled tree to bring me prosperity this year. You've given me more than I deserve already.'

Honora flushed. It made her pulse flutter to hear Isaac speak so tenderly, the memory of the previous night still vivid at the forefront of her mind when he had spoken similarly intimate words to thaw any last vestiges of doubt she could have had. Ever since that moment happiness had chased away the shadows of her lonely past, even Charlotte's condition strengthened by yesterday's foray into the outside world. Doctor Harcourt had decreed she had finally turned the corner, perhaps something in the shock of Honora's accident jolting Charlotte out of her daze—stranger things had happened, he'd said sagely, and Honora hadn't the heart to disagree.

'Is that right?'

Honora stole a peep at Isaac, taking in the streaks of grey scattered through his chestnut hair and the pleasing shape of his profile. If anybody had told her, on the freezing night he appeared in her house, how he would transform her life she wouldn't have believed them and yet he had. The man she'd disliked at once for his arrogance and similarity to Frank had proved her wrong and now when she looked at him it was with love that made her heart feel full to bursting. She'd never expected this paradise, never sought it, but he had given it to her none the less—a home and a family, and the perfect acceptance she'd never dreamed would come to her.

'Of course. Perhaps a little more mightn't hurt, however. If you'll do the honours.'

Isaac gestured to the cold grate crowned with glossy holly. The Yule log sat proudly below its spiky bower and with a flourish Honora touched it with the burning splinter, a slow smile crossing her face as the small flame licked outwards and began to grow.

'Your first proper English Christmas tradition. What do you think?'

'I like it.' Honora knelt before the flames, their warmth caressing her skin and casting orange light across the carpet. At her back she felt

Isaac reach out to play with a stray curl, the soft sensation capturing her attention at once.

'I'm glad. The first of many.' She heard the smile in his voice and tipped her head back to rest against his palm, feeling warm fingers sliding through her hair. 'Why don't you sit up here with me? We can watch the evil flee together, tail between its legs.'

With a raised brow Honora got to her feet, the rich skirts of her new Christmas gown rustling as she went. Wrapped in creamy yellow, her clear skin shone and her curls gleamed in beautiful raven contrast, something Isaac had made sure to tell her as he'd watched her dress that morning from the warmth of their bed.

'I'm a thirty-five-year-old woman, Isaac, and you're not far from forty yourself. I'm not sure this is a dignified way to behave,' Honora reprimanded her husband as he held out a hand to guide her down into his lap, but she took it all the same and the now familiar sense of peace washed over her as she settled against his chest. No doubt it was foolish to act like two young things in the first flush of love, but that was exactly what she felt like, and when Isaac's arm came comfortably round her waist to draw her closer she knew he thought the same.

'I'm glad you are. You're a woman of experience and wisdom, not some green young girl— and none of them can match your loveliness.'

'Such pretty words.'

She dropped a light kiss on his cheek and felt the arm around her waist tighten. His fingers trailed the length of her arm, finding the pulse ticking below the thin skin of her wrist and stroking invitingly. 'And I meant every one.'

He gathered her closer against him, trapping her arms and taking advantage of her imprisonment to nibble one sensitive ear, scattering stars through every nerve. Her breath caught for a moment at the melting sensation and only the prospect of one of the maids coming in to bank up the Christmas Day fire stopped her from sinking completely into Isaac's embrace and allowing him to do as he would.

'That's certainly more than Frank ever did. I wonder now if my parents saw his dishonesty at once, long before I realised it myself. They had the measure of him in no time at all.'

She straightened the skirts of her cowslip dress, for the briefest of flickers allowing the moment she had introduced Frank to her parents to surface in her mind. She'd been so desperate for them to like him, in her weakness for that handsome man entirely blind to his faults. He'd been offhand to Pa and hardly more civil to her mother, Honora recalled now with a twist of shame, but at the time all she could see was Frank's blue eyes and all she could hear was his deep voice, and the look of distaste her parents had shared had only made her angry.

'But I'm not Frank.'

As he so often seemed to manage, it was as though Isaac could sense the direction of her thoughts. He gathered her to him again, but this time with more protective than roguish intent as he captured her hands. 'He was a low creature who only ever thought of people in terms of how useful they were to him. It doesn't surprise me in the least he never valued your parents—you weren't to blame for falling for the charming mask he so often showed to the world, conceal-ing the ugliness behind it.'

With her head resting just below Isaac's chin Honora couldn't see his face, but she blinked now at the sudden and unexpected bitterness she heard rumble through his chest. Surely there was no reason for Isaac to sound so personally slighted, so vehement in his language it made her pause, and yet there it was, real loathing that seemed more than some casual dislike. It was a strange response—unless, perhaps…

Did Frank do something to wound Isaac? Is that why his contempt for him sounds so severe?

'You speak as though you hated him.' She traced a pearl button on his cuff, attempting to keep growing curiosity out of her voice. 'Why would you feel so strongly? I know you had little in common, but why would that make you dislike him so?'

For a heartbeat Isaac didn't reply—and in that half-second span Honora's suspicion flared like a lit match, sparking into life to burn with bright concern.

'His treatment of you is something I find difficult to forgive.'

'But you spoke of a mask?' Honora tweaked the button a little harder, her thoughts beginning to turn. 'And the ugliness behind it—as though you'd seen it for yourself?'

Isaac moved his position in the chair, still holding Honora close, but a fraction less tightly than before. If she hadn't already wondered whether he was being evasive, his hesitation now would have roused her interest at once, the slight reluctance to respond to her questions more revealing than any answer.

'There were occasions…certainly one occasion when I saw how he could be.'

'What happened? What did he do to reveal himself?' Honora ducked out from beneath Isaac's chin and tried to catch his eye, resolutely turned away from her and fixed instead on the fireplace.

She saw a complex expression pass over Isaac's face and for the first time her curiosity segued into a beat of worry, a gripe in her stomach she didn't want to address. Why was he being so coy? What was it he was thinking that he obviously didn't want to share? Unease crept up inside her to threaten the simple happiness of only minutes earlier, when she'd curled into her husband's lap and felt the warmth of knowing she was safe and loved at last.

'Isaac? What *is* it? Is there something you're not telling me?'

He glanced down at her, dark eyes taking in the clear worry creasing her brow, then shook his head. 'There's nothing. I spoke without thinking, that's all.' Isaac smiled, but with another pang of uncertainty Honora saw it was too stiff to be genuine. 'I hope in all ways to be a better husband to you than Frank ever was, Honora. I would never have you feel that unhappiness again.'

'Oh, Charlotte, that one's beautiful!'

Isaac followed the sound of female voices that echoed along the top corridor, coming to a predictable halt outside his ward's rooms. From beyond the half-open door came the rustle of silk and appreciative giggles that would usually have made him smile, if the conversation he'd had with Honora two days previously hadn't still been playing on his mind.

She'd looked for all the world as though she knew he was hiding something from her and the same anger he'd felt at his mistake then returned to goad him now. He should have guarded his tongue and kept his contempt for Frank off his lips, but his real feelings had slipped out before he could stop them and now he feared Honora *knew*, that same suspicion she had harboured before bursting into new life. She was sharp and canny at the best of times. How could he hope she hadn't noticed his evasiveness, when every glance told him she missed nothing with those bright eyes?

All it would take is one more unguarded comment and the family we've built would lie in ruins. Honora's heart would be smashed to pieces and she would never trust me again.

Isaac paused with his hand flat against the door, listening to the merriment that issued from behind it, and felt his stomach tighten with the bitter regret never far from his thoughts. How long could he truly hope his deception would last? He should have told Honora in the graveyard, or even on the night Christopher was born as he'd intended—but he'd missed his moment and still the truth lay inside him like a canker, festering away until the time came for it to wreak havoc. The wife he had come to love would be devastated and there was nothing he could do to prevent it, her suspicions no doubt already raised and on keen alert for even the smallest of dropped hints to explain his clear dislike of Frank. He'd prided himself on how far superior a husband he would be to her first, but wasn't he just as bad as that damned Blake, keeping Honora in the dark even if his reasons for doing so were to spare her from pain?

'Is there somebody outside the door? It's safe to come in!'

Honora's voice drifted from Charlotte's chamber and Isaac's insides knotted further at the note of happiness it contained. Honora must feel she finally had everything she'd ever wanted: a home, a family, a husband who loved her and whom she loved in return… But that joy would turn to ash once the events of the past months became known, causing agony for both Honora and Charlotte that could have been avoided had Isaac kept them apart. Instead he'd brought them together, fool that he was, and as he reluctantly pushed open the bedchamber door he had to fight to bring a curve to his lying lips.

'What's this? A masque ball?'

He watched two faces turn in his direction, both wreathed with smiles that only made his own feel all the more false. Honora kept her place seated at the foot of Charlotte's bed, Christopher lying contentedly in her arms, but Charlotte spun across to meet him, the pretty worked hem of her new dress flaring out as she moved.

'I'm looking at my Christmas gowns for the first time. This one is my favourite so far!' She twirled again to let him see how the pale blue silk danced like a wisp of smoke, although Isaac reached out in alarm when she seemed in danger of overbalancing.

'Be careful. You're still not back to full strength. What would be the point in my ordering new gowns if you fell and broke your head while trying them on?'

Charlotte threw him the indulgent look countless generations of girls gave fussy fathers, but she allowed herself to be guided to sit beside Honora and carefully take Christopher on to her lap. She settled the baby's little cap more comfortably on his head and rocked him so fastidiously Isaac's smile almost relaxed into something genuine, but then from the corner of his eye he saw how Honora watched him, studying him without wanting to be seen, and the ice circling in his stomach redoubled its vigour.

She knows something is amiss. Or at the very least she suspects.

'Are you well today, Isaac? I've barely seen you all morning. You must have slipped out of bed before I awoke.'

Honora spoke mildly enough, but Isaac wasn't fooled for a moment. To anyone else it would seem her attention was more fixed on Charlotte and the warm bundle on her lap, but Isaac knew beneath those clusters of shining curls his wife's ears were pricked for his reply.

'I'm very well, thank you. And yourself?'

'Oh, fine. There's certainly nothing on *my* mind.'

The pointed inflection in that one word almost made Isaac wince, but he affected not to notice the none-too-subtle hint. Apparently one look was all it took for his wife to see some trace of the worries that scurried through his mind like insects, however, his face or actions showing *something* was taking place within. How did she do it? he wondered as he nodded vaguely, not trusting himself to answer further. It must be some female gift he would never understand, but there was no denying Honora's suddenly piercing gaze made him feel exposed.

'Charlotte? Why don't you take another look in the trunk? I think there are a couple of dresses you haven't yet tried.'

Honora spoke pleasantly to Charlotte, but her eyes remained fixed on Isaac's, not wavering even when Christopher was deposited gently into her arms and his mother hastened across the room with girlish glee to see what further riches were waiting to be discovered. Isaac returned her steady stare, feeling his heart begin to skip, but concentrating with manful effort on keeping his face perfectly still.

Careful. This feels as though it might be a trap.

'Isaac?' Still seated on the end of Charlotte's bed, Honora peered up at him, her determined chin lifted, but for the first time a shadow of doubt robbing her of some of the confidence he had always admired. Her eyes sought his and in their depths he saw hesitation, the tiniest gleam of fear that fled straight to his chest and forced itself between his ribs. When she spoke her voice was lowered, shielding Charlotte from the murmured words. 'Isaac, what is it you're not telling me? You all but ran from our bed this morning and you haven't been natural with me for two days. Don't deny something troubles you. I'm not a fool.'

Christopher gave a quiet whimper and Honora held him a little closer, arms coming round him, but with more than a suggestion she was also protecting herself. Whether it was from harmful thoughts that plagued her own conscience or from those she feared Isaac harboured he couldn't tell, but the urge to catch her up and soothe her worries flooded through him like an unstoppable tide and unseen behind his back he clenched his hands into fists of dismay.

'Nobody would ever think you a fool, my love. Who would dare?'

He thought to make her smile, but Honora's lips remained pressed into a straight line. 'Then don't treat me like one. If there's something that disturbs you, I would have you tell me. I don't want another marriage where secrets make it rot from within.'

The eerie accuracy of her words stopped Isaac dead in his tracks. Looking down at his wife on her perch at the end of the bed, he could have swayed, horrified by how closely she had pinned down the truth. A secret that stretched between them, unspoken and yet with the power to destroy everything they had built. It was exactly what he feared and in her wisdom Honora had touched the very nerve Isaac had thought to guard.

'Honora…' He snatched a glance across at Charlotte, feeling the insistent tick of his pulse at his dry throat. If his ward overheard this conversation, decided to get involved… She'd always obeyed his orders not to mention Frank's name within the walls of Marlow Manor, forbidden by disgust and the desire to erase the past. It lingered like a silent ghost, however, never uttered but doubtless thought of every day—and never more than a whisper away from guilty lips. Any talk of secrets was sure to intrigue Charlotte and risk breaking the taboo, the spectre of Frank surely one that haunted her more than anyone could know. Now, though, she seemed happy enough—distracted as any sixteen-year-old girl would be, her attention was entirely absorbed by the trunk of dresses she delved inside, deaf to all else but the occasional grumble of her son that Honora quickly soothed. Currently the only part of her Isaac could see was her back as she drew out another silky creation and he turned to his wife, slightly more assured they weren't to be overheard.

'What is it you think I'm hiding?'

'I don't know. You tell me.' Honora shrugged, but it was an unhappy gesture that tore at Isaac's soul. 'All I know is that two days ago you seemed to stumble into saying more about Frank than you intended and now I can't help but feel you're avoiding me. So what is it? What happened in connection with Frank you think you have to conceal? Your venom was so strong and yet you denied it. I want to know why.'

Isaac opened his mouth, but only air came forth, a soft sigh that must have told Honora more than any words. She watched him so closely, her frame so rigid at the end of that great bed, and the ache inside him to finally abandon the lies that had bound him for so long grew unbearable. It twisted through his insides and wrung out his chest, a weight within him suddenly exhausting. It would be so much easier to confess, to pay Honora the ultimate compliment of the truth—and as he stared down into her waiting eyes he knew he could deny her nothing.

She'll hate me. She'll be distraught, for what I'm about to tell her and by the fact I kept it hidden for so long—and the knowledge I was once almost as undeserving a man as Frank. I ought to have told her long ago, but I can't look her in the eye now and lie. Not when she sits before me as everything I ever wanted, the only woman I know I'll ever love.

He pushed a hand through his hair, searching in vain for the wisdom of how to begin. The tense wariness on Honora's countenance grew by the moment, her attention never straying from him as he took a short step away and back again like an animal in a cage. More than once he saw her lips twitch as though she wanted to ask a question, but each time she stopped short, waiting for him to speak with the same nervous energy he recognised from the first moment he had seen her.

I wonder if she wishes she had her pistol on her now? Fortunate for me she doesn't have it to hand. I wonder how many holes I'd be left with if it was beside her when I finished.

'Isaac? Why are you pacing like that?'

Charlotte's puzzled glance shot through Isaac like a bullet from Honora's flintlock and he stopped at once, head whipping round to see her standing at the other side of the room with a pretty green muslin hanging from her fingers. She raised her eyebrows questioningly, so innocently unaware of his turmoil it made his stomach clench.

Charlotte. I almost forgot she was there.

How would she have felt to overhear the horrible truth issue from his lips, her most shameful secret laid bare before Honora's cautious stare? If he was to finally take that plunge, the most dangerous path from which there was no way back, it must be private, to spare Honora's horror and Charlotte's distress, although no matter how carefully he broke the news he knew there was no way of avoiding pain completely—

But his scheming was in vain.

Honora glanced from Isaac's set face to Charlotte's open one and in that single look seemed to make up her mind. Before she even opened her mouth to speak Isaac knew it was too late, absolute certainty that he had just lost his one chance blinding him like a beacon of forlorn light.

'Isaac was about to tell me of his dealings with Frank Blake, Charlotte. Perhaps you know why such a thing might make him seem so ill at ease?'

Isaac watched helplessly as the colour drained from Charlotte's cheeks. At the very mention of that name all light died in his ward's expression and she froze, the dress still clutched in her fingers, but sagging limply like an empty sack.

'Frank Blake? What…what do you know about him?'

'More than I'd like to, in truth. Did you know him as well as Isaac?'

Charlotte's eyes flickered around the room like a rabbit's might when caught in a trap, trying to find a way out. Isaac took a step towards her, but Honora rose, too, dodging neatly round him to hasten across the room.

'Dearest, you've gone white. Sit down at once. Whatever's the matter? Do you feel ill?'

The girl shook her head, her eyes seeking Isaac's and locking desperately on to him as though he could save her from Honora's unwitting cruelty. 'I'm not... I'm not allowed to talk about Frank.'

'Why ever not?'

As if seeing it in a dream Isaac watched Honora's head turn in his direction, confusion and—worse, so *very* much worse—dawning distrust breaking over her beloved features. He wanted to reach out for her, to gather her against him and *make* her see he would never have chosen to hurt her, but his arms wouldn't move and all he could do was plead.

'Honora. Honora, wait a moment—'

'Why, Charlotte?' Honora backed away from him, wariness radiating from her now that cut Isaac to the bone. 'Why aren't you allowed to talk about him?'

Charlotte had sunk down on to the lid of the trunk of dresses and reached out to take Christopher with shaking hands. She seemed to quail beneath Honora's strange calm, its unnaturalness a sign to anybody that something was dangerously wrong. 'Isaac forbid his name.'

'And why would he do that?' Honora pressed on, quietly but giving no quarter. 'Was something amiss between you?'

'Yes. Yes, it certainly was.'

Like one trapped in a nightmare Isaac could predict exactly what was coming, but was powerless to prevent it. Only minutes before they'd been laughing at Charlotte's delight, but now as he saw his wife's rising fear he thought he might never laugh again. Her breathing seemed to have speeded up and the bodice of her gown rose and fell quickly, reminding him of someone having just finished a race, but there was no running from what he knew was about to fall from Charlotte's lips.

'How so?' Honora prompted the poor girl, fixing her with an unblinking stare that excluded Isaac completely. 'In what way did he offend you so grievously?'

Desperation rose up inside Isaac's very core and with one final push he freed himself from the paralysing spell that bound him. 'Honora, please!' He reached for her, tried to seize her hand and make her look up into his face. If she would only see the true feeling there surely she couldn't hate him—if *only* she would let him explain—but she shook him off, coldness blazing from her now as icy as the driven snow, and when she stooped down to catch Charlotte's shame-filled whisper Isaac felt the ground shift beneath his feet.

'Mr Blake. Frank. He…' Charlotte swallowed, tears rising that clawed at Isaac's tattered soul and surely told Honora all she would ever need to know. 'Heaven forgive me, as well as him. He was Christopher's father and he died running for his life from Isaac's rage.'

Chapter Fourteen

The clasp of Honora's case bit into her finger as she pushed it closed, but she didn't feel its sting. Her senses seemed to have stopped working and she was hardly aware of anything other than the kernel of pain lodged deep inside her, a glowing ember of agony that burned brighter with each breath. Her entire existence had shrunk to fit into the terrible space that throbbed and ached as though part of her soul had been torn out.

It was all a lie. Every last word of it. He never loved me at all.

The truth repeated itself over and over again, twisting through Honora's mind like an echo that wouldn't end. The facts were so clear to her now she could have kicked herself for not seeing them sooner. Frank had fathered Charlotte's child and, in order to stop Honora from spreading the scandalous story, Isaac had made her believe he loved her, silencing her with false regard and the prospect of a family that now lay in tatters. Of course there had never been a true return of the feelings that had melted her cold heart. She'd been tricked again, lured into dancing to a handsome man's tune by sweet words and broken promises, and now she was set adrift once more to be borne away by suffering and the knowledge everything she'd thought she had found was lost.

Leaning over the case, she closed her eyes, for the briefest of moments allowing her body to sag beneath the despair that pulled her down. Her strength was in danger of leaving her just when she needed it the most. It was a long walk to the nearest coaching inn and, although she had left the gowns Isaac had bought her hanging in the armoire, the bag was still a dead weight. Given the choice she wouldn't make the gruelling trek down muddy roads, dragging her luggage with her—but there *was* no choice. She was leaving, putting the hulking shadow of Marlow Manor behind her, and she determined there and then that she wouldn't look back.

But Isaac seemed equally determined he wouldn't let her go.

Dimly Honora heard another round of hammering on the locked door of their bedchamber.

The numbness that had invaded her body the moment Charlotte uttered that tearful confession still covered her like a cloak of disbelief, blunting the full horror she knew would consume her soon enough. For the moment it was as though she was floating through a bad dream, watching the sickening truth unfold through a pane of frosted glass that could splinter into piercing shards at any time.

'Honora, please. Open the door!'

The handle turned fruitlessly and the door shuddered a little on its hinges as Isaac's voice came again to beseech her through solid wood. It was amazing how genuine he sounded, some far-off part of her thought, considering his regard for her was as false as Frank's had ever been. No wonder she'd been fooled, Isaac's gift for play-acting so convincing it had brought her to her knees.

At least I know Charlotte had no part. Her unhappiness couldn't be faked by even the most talented liar—she never knew my connection with Frank and I imagine she feels as much an idiot as I do for trusting Isaac's word.

The handle gave a particularly violent rattle and Honora watched it in impassive silence. Isaac would break the door down at this rate, although what he hoped to achieve by forcing her to speak to him she couldn't possibly guess. The damage had been done, the truth was out, and all that was left was for Honora to wait for the first fog to lift, when the full severity of what was happening would hit her like a punishing blow.

'Please, my love. Open the door and I can explain. If you would only listen…'

Dazed as she was, some of Isaac's pleading managed to penetrate Honora's hazy mind. She still felt numb, detached somehow from the reality that snapped at her, but something else began to creep between the cracks in her shattered heart to fill her with icy shame.

'My love'? I was never his love. I was only ever his pawn.

Humiliation lapped at the edges of her consciousness and she took a deep breath, the stretch of it painful, but helping her stand in the face of her misery. Under the façade of Isaac's 'love' she had thought herself accepted, drawn into the tapestry of life at Marlow Manor, but it had all been a lie she'd been too idiotic to see. There was nothing left for her now Isaac had blown apart her hard-won happiness. For him to persist in trying to fool her was more than she could bear.

With another steadying breath Honora heaved her case off the bed and turned resolutely away before the sight of the great four-poster could wound her further. It was the very bed in which she and Isaac had expressed their love for each other. She had found surety in the embrace of his strong arms and a purpose in the press of his lips on hers—but with a hot rush of shame she clenched her jaw. There had been no love after all, only false coin on Isaac's side and a hopeless yearning on hers, and the ruins of her dreams for the future circled round to taunt her as she squared her shoulders and with the greatest reluctance opened the door.

'Honora. At last.'

Isaac's gaze was anxious as he immediately stepped to her side, his sharp eyes roaming her face and then lower to spy the case gripped in her fist. At once he shook his head, one hand coming up to pass over his forehead and his cheeks pale with what a more naive woman might take for dismay.

'I know what you're planning to do, but please. You can't. You can't leave me.'

Honora's stomach lurched at the entreaty in his voice, but she jerked her bag away from his fingers when he tried to take it. Whatever sense of disbelief had shielded her was swiftly evaporating now Isaac was before her, attempting to block her way, and the shame that curdled her insides ebbed slightly to make way for rising grief.

'Can't I? Why not?' She spat the words as though they tasted foul in her mouth, cursing the tremor of emotion that accompanied them. She *would not* allow Isaac to see the tears she feared would soon begin to fall, the beloved face of the man that stared down at her one she would never show vulnerability to ever again. 'You know I can't stay. You know there's nothing here for me now. Everything I thought I could count on was a lie—and you the creator of it all.'

She turned resolutely away, snatching up the skirts of her dress so not even the hem brushed Isaac's boots as she passed. No part of her would touch him again, she vowed desperately, not now he had betrayed her—he was a Judas and deserved none of the ache that dogged each beat of her broken heart, lying in pieces that scattered to the wind.

'But it was *all* real, aside from my dealings with Frank. I should never have tried to keep that truth from you. I wanted to protect Charlotte and then I was too ashamed to admit our real friendship when I saw how much you'd despise me... I'm sorry. I'm more sorry than I can say.'

Isaac tried once more to get between her and escape, his face white and hands ready to reach for her, but she shouldered past him and, with her teeth set so hard it hurt, made for the staircase at the end of the landing. Each step was an effort, every placing of her foot an ordeal she had no choice but to make even as her spirit wanted to return to sink into Isaac's arms. It would be so easy to believe his sweet persuasion and allow herself to be drawn back under his spell, so wonderful to pretend it could all be made better—but when he strode ahead to bar her way she turned on him like a lion, bitterness and shame forcing her lips into an agonised grimace.

'No!'

She watched with fierce despair as he took half a step backwards, the passion in that one word sure to make a lesser man flinch away completely. His mouth opened to answer her harsh rebuke, but she didn't let him speak, cutting across him and wishing the prickling behind her eyes would stop.

'You let me think I was wanted here, needed even—when really you were just keeping me close to protect Charlotte's secret. Did you really think I'd do anything to expose her? Did you truly think so little of me to fear that?' Honora heard the rising of her voice, but couldn't stop it, sick unhappiness stealing away all restraint. 'You must have had scant regard for me—just like Frank did. You lied to me—just like Frank did. You made...' A sob rose in her throat and she tried to swallow it down, although another came at once to finally free the tears that threatened to roll down her cheeks. 'You made me fall in love with you when you knew you had no use for my heart—just like Frank did. For all your promises you were the same in the end, or worse, even, for he never gave me everything I wanted only to rip it away and my feelings for him were never anywhere close to what I felt for you. You have ruined me, Isaac, and now the best thing you can do is to let me go.'

The tears slid down her face and angrily she cuffed them away, determined Isaac wouldn't see. His eyes burned into hers, taking in the sight of her misery and some reflection of it creasing his own brow—but she wouldn't be fooled again. Isaac might pretend to care for her, but she knew better and there was nothing he could say or do to stop her from leaving now with the fragile scraps of dignity she still possessed.

'Please don't do this.' Once again Isaac tried for her hand, but she moved away, her arm hanging heavy and barely responsive. Only the very tips of his fingers brushed hers, contact she both hated and craved, knowing it would be the final time his skin ever touched hers.

'Honora, don't go. Please. Stay and give me

the chance to prove myself,' he implored her. 'I love you.'

She looked up into his earnest face and felt the pieces of her heart grating inside her like broken glass. He sounded so sincere.

And yet for the entire time we've known each other he has hidden the fact Frank is Christopher's father from me. He would have let me help raise the child without a clue, as if it didn't matter at all.

'I don't believe you,' Honora stated simply. 'If you loved me, you wouldn't have kept me in ignorance. You could have told me at any time, but you didn't. That isn't the action of a man in love.'

With finality that drove a knife into the raw cavity behind her breastbone she slipped past Isaac's outstretched hand and descended the stairs, her case bumping behind her. She heard Isaac's heavy tread at her back, but stumbled on, feeling that at any moment her legs might give way beneath her.

'But where will you go? You said yourself you have nowhere!'

'Back to Somerset. I have a few guineas about me. I'm sure you'll let me keep them for my coach fare and lodgings. Mary will take me in. Even if I have to sleep on the floor of her cottage it will be better than staying here.'

A stifled sound of anguish followed her into the hall, but Honora didn't turn. She kept her eyes on the towering front door of the Manor, closing in on it like a hound on its prey. Her cheeks were wet and her eyes stung, but she couldn't stop, the necessity of escaping the man tempting her to stay something she wouldn't fight.

She paused on the threshold, one hand tight on the brass handle. To heave open the door would be to leave behind everything she'd ever wanted, the place she thought she'd found in the world and the family she had always yearned for—and the man she'd believed worthy of her heart. He'd taken it into his keeping, only to tear it apart; so it was that, without looking back, Honora put her shoulder to the wood and half fell out into the freezing December wind, the cry that rang in her ears one she wondered why Isaac had bothered to make.

By the time Charlotte came to find him Isaac had lost count of how long he'd sat on the bottom step in front of the silent front door. It could have been hours since Honora had disappeared through it or perhaps even more, each minute that passed meaning nothing to him now he had allowed the love of his life to slip through his fingers like water through a net.

You fool. You utter, contemptible fool, the cruel voice in his head sneered once again, but he knew he deserved every word. *See where your lies brought you, in the end? 'You've ruined me', that's what she said—and wasn't it the truth?*

At the sound of rustling silk he raised his head wearily from the cradle of his hands and peered up at Charlotte, standing a few steps above him on the staircase into the hall. Her eyes were red and the pale skin of her cheeks mottled and without a word he held out a hand to guide her to sit beside him. She came at once, settling beneath his arm and leaning into his shoulder as though he was the answer to her troubles rather than their maker.

'I'm so sorry, my little wren. I should have told you from the very beginning who Honora really was.' Isaac's lips barely moved, his face too rigid to allow any expression but empty misery. Even as much as speaking Honora's name sent a spasm flickering through him to join the agony already crowding every fibre of his being, wave upon wave of regret and remorse strangling each breath. 'I thought at first to protect you from feeling shame at meeting Frank's wife, but after that… There's no excuse. I shouldn't have kept secrets from you and I apologise from my heart.'

At his shoulder he felt Charlotte shake her head. 'That's right. You shouldn't have concealed the truth—but I understand why you felt you had to.' She rubbed her eyes, sparkling now with unhappiness. 'It was my fault, though. If I hadn't believed Frank's lies, allowed myself to be taken in by him…wouldn't he still be alive? Poor Honora! I've wounded her so grievously and now I'll never have the chance to tell her I'm sorry.'

At the sight of her tears the lump in Isaac's already tight throat grew even more and he took her little hand in his, gentle but so firmly Charlotte stilled.

'It was *not* your fault. None of this was. The only people who did wrong were two men who should have known better.' His free hand lay on his knee and he closed it into a fist, feeling the nails bite into his palm. The picture of Honora's face the moment she realised his deceit flared before him with a swift kick to his stomach that made him want to groan aloud. 'Honora wouldn't blame you. I can see that now even if I couldn't at first. The only person who owes her an apology is me—and it is I who will never get that chance.'

The river of agony that flowed under his skin was nothing compared to what Honora must be feeling, he thought with desperate shame. His pain at losing her was what he deserved for his actions, but she had done nothing to warrant the sting of seeing all her hopes dashed by the one person she thought would help her realise them. Every particle of suffering Isaac had wanted to spare her had rained down on her anyway. Worse than that, she no longer believed he loved her, thinking his regard had been a calculating sham, and that was torture he could hardly endure. He wanted to chase after her, make her see how she was everything he'd ever wanted and more, but she'd run from him and now he could only sit helpless and wishing he could turn back the clock.

'Do you love her?' Charlotte gazed at him, tear tracks still shining on her cheeks but her curiosity plain to see. 'Even though you only married to please me in my ravings? I should never have asked it of you, although I suspected from the first moment I met Honora that your feelings for her ran deeper than you would admit. Was I right?'

Isaac allowed her a broken smile filled with fathomless pain. Was she right? Was she *right*? Of all the possible questions... Memories of

Honora broke over him like a wave, one after the other in a relentless stream of bittersweet moments he would treasure for ever.

The first time I saw her, all flintlock and fire wrapped in a nightgown. Our first kiss at that shabby inn. Singing to Christopher in front of the window, sunlight shining on her curls. The shape of her in nothing but a sheet, and then not even that...

'Yes.' Isaac rubbed the bridge of his nose. His head ached along with his heart, each throbbing as if in sympathy with the other. 'I love her. How could I not?'

'Then why not go after her?' Charlotte sat up straight, new hope creeping into her formerly dull eyes. 'Why don't you tell her how you feel? You could explain everything! Surely she'd listen? Surely she didn't want to leave us?'

'It's not as simple as that.' If the situation had been different Charlotte's naive surety might have amused him. Instead it stung. 'She knows I love her—I've told her so many times. Unfortunately she no longer believes me and I have nobody to blame for that but myself.'

He looked around the hall, anywhere to avoid meeting Charlotte's reproachful eyes. She seemed displeased by his answer, but what else could he say?

Honora wanted me to let her go—demanded, in fact. If I were to go after her now, wouldn't it be flying in the face of her wishes? I've already hurt her so much. Chasing her when she has no desire to be caught would only make things worse.

Through the tall windows Isaac saw the sky had darkened and dusk had begun to fall. He must have been sitting alone on the stairs for hours, he realised, hunched and cold and haunted by the mistakes that had snatched all happiness from his future. It wouldn't be long until night had crept in completely, and then…? Honora was out there somewhere, friendless and distraught—the thought of her blundering in the darkness chilled him and he longed to know she was safe. How far had she got? Was she comfortable at some inn now, sequestered away in her room? Or was she still struggling along with her case behind her, following an unfamiliar road without a clue to where she might end up?

The possibilities clawed at him and Isaac closed his eyes. Wherever she was, Honora believed she was better off without him—and she was right. As much as it tore at him that was the truth. He had brought nothing but suffering into her life and the least he could do was leave her alone now to try to salvage something from the wreckage. He would pine for her the rest of his days, but she was free from him now and the damage he could wreak, and that was the only trace of comfort he might ever find.

'So that's all? That's the end?' Charlotte's pretty brow was furrowed. 'You won't go out to find her? After everything Honora did for us you're content to let her disappear without a trace?'

'What choice do I have? She didn't want to stay here. I couldn't force her and, if she was so set on leaving, the least I could do was let her go.'

'You could fight for her!'

Isaac felt his own face screw into a frown that only made his headache worse. 'Fight *how*? What do you mean?'

'You could try one more time to apologise. Honora loves you as much as you do her—even I can see that. Surely that's worth one more try at rescuing?'

He tried to smile, but his mouth would not obey. It was so like her to think the best of the world, so innocent she thought happy endings could ever be real. 'I can't fight for somebody who doesn't *want* to be. Honora no longer wants or trusts me. The only thing I can do for her now is let her go in peace.'

He returned his face to rest in his palms, almost but not quite missing the flit of disapproval that crossed Charlotte's countenance. Isaac heard the swish of her skirts as she got to her feet, but he didn't look up, unable to bear the censure he knew he deserved.

'There's nothing else I can say, then. I see your mind is quite made up. All I can think is Honora must have been right. You can never have loved her as you claimed. If you did, you'd try harder to mend what was broken and wouldn't give up so easily.'

Unseen behind his hands Isaac grimaced at the unfamiliar coldness in Charlotte's voice. For years it had held nothing but trust and adoration—and so the disappointment in it as she turned and walked quietly away, leaving him alone in the darkened hall, was more than he could stand.

Chapter Fifteen

The relentless snoring of the man opposite her ought to have been annoying, but Honora barely heard each snuffling breath. All her focus was on preventing herself from crying out with the pain that gripped her in its cruel jaws, her mouth clamped shut and muscles tight with the strain of self-control. Sitting in one corner of the coach's chilly cabin, she stared straight ahead, faded curtains hiding the passing scenery of the freezing night.

Every turn of the wheels will take me further from Isaac and all I left behind—not that any of it was ever really mine in the first place.

Her throat burned with harshly supressed tears, but she kept her expression as blank as a sheet of paper. There were two other passengers aside from the snoring man—a couple of twittering ladies whom apparently even the lateness of the hour couldn't silence—and she refused to draw their attention any more than she had already. Their eyes had swivelled in her direction at once as she boarded the coach, taking in every detail of her face beneath her drab bonnet with the kind of curiosity she'd been forced to endure all her life. Probably she appeared cold and unfriendly huddled in her corner, but social niceties seemed so irrelevant now her heart felt as though it was carved from ice.

I was never stared at like that at Marlow Manor. Indeed, I almost forgot what it was to have people transfixed by something so entirely unimportant as the colour of my skin. Isaac certainly never gave me cause to think it mattered.

She felt another tendril of grief snake upwards and took a deep breath to steel herself against it. The last time she'd travelled by stagecoach had been with him, when the hours they'd been forced to spend together had begun to soften her resolve to guard against the damage she feared he might do. She hadn't a clue then as to what was to come, no way of knowing that same handsome man was just as dangerous as she thought and that he would take an axe to the fledgling vine of her future hopes.

The acceptance she'd thought she'd found, the chance of a family to love and be loved in re-

turn, had all been a lie. Little Christopher was
Frank's child, born to a girl Honora had grown
to care for and yet would now never see again.
She'd thought herself almost a mother figure for
both Charlotte and her baby—but had Isaac truly
wanted that? Had he really intended to complete
his family, or had he simply kept Honora close to
prevent her from exposing his ward to scandal?

*The only thing I know for sure is that he never
loved me. How could he have lied to me otherwise, knowing how much Frank hurt me doing
the same thing?*

With a shuddering sigh in place of the cry she
wanted to utter, Honora closed her eyes, blocking
out the inquisitive looks her fellow passengers
levelled at her from beneath their lashes. She
wanted more than anything for this cursed journey to end, leaving Isaac miles behind her like
dust shaken from a traveller's boots. The memory of him wouldn't be so easy to escape, however, she knew for certain—and nobody could
ever replace him. He was her husband, but more
than that. For a short, sweet time she'd allowed
herself to believe he loved her and the warmth of
that feeling would follow her the rest of her life.
It would haunt her, both bitter and wonderful at
the same time, and the only way she would ever

forget that cherished smile was when her heart finally ceased to beat.

'Are you travelling far?'

Honora opened her eyes to find one of the talkative ladies leaning towards her. Apparently her bleak expression wasn't enough to save her from banal conversation and she struggled to find a civil reply.

'To Somerset. I've still some miles to go.'

'Still some miles?' The older woman tutted in what might have been a passable show of sympathy had there not been such a gleam of sharp curiosity in her eye. 'Why, we've hardly left Northampton. What a long journey for you to undertake all alone!'

The second woman seemed equally delighted at the chance to be dismayed, like her friend murmuring how great a shame it was Honora found herself in such a predicament. Honora said nothing, allowing their voices to wash over her as inconsequential noise. Nothing mattered but the dagger in her chest that delved deeper with every moment, the prospect of a life lived without Isaac twisting the blade with brutal malice.

'No wonder you look so downcast. But never mind. At least this road is a good deal safer than it used to be. When I was your age there were highwaymen at every crossing. Don't you recall those dark days, Mrs Croft?'

'I certainly do.' Mrs Croft nodded gravely. 'One never knew when they might strike—the very memory of it makes my blood run cold. I was robbed once, you know, so I know more about these things than most.'

Honora inclined her head, but didn't respond. She hadn't the least intention of picking up her unwanted companion's heavy hint to ask for the story, no doubt embellished until it bore little resemblance to the truth. What she wanted was to be left *alone*, damn it, to try to find some consolation in silence and the jolting rhythm of the cabin's swaying progress through the night. Certainly she had no interest in this Mrs Croft's tale, although it seemed her lack of answer posed no obstacle to the lady's willingness to tell it.

'It was a coach very like this one. Post, with a guard sitting on top to protect us poor travellers. Not that it did any good.' The woman paused to give Honora a tragic glance that set her teeth on edge. 'The first we knew of it was when we heard shouting and a great pounding on the side of the carriage. Our driver tried to shake them, but he was compelled to stop the horses and then those brigands pilfered us all! I was lucky to escape with my life. A gentleman challenged them and they knocked him to the ground quite viciously. Of course I feared they might do the same to me, so I handed over my purse without delay. It would have been a mistake to upset them. I might not have survived.'

Once again Honora nodded reluctantly, although in her current mood of hopeless unhappiness she might almost have *welcomed* such an attack. It would serve to take her mind off Isaac, even if for only a moment, and she would gladly take *anything* that might help erase the haunting memory of his face.

'I'll never forget that evening and how those brutes' voices echoed in the darkness before we even saw them. Until my dying day I'll remember—what was that?' Mrs Croft sat suddenly upright, clutching her friend's arm with bony fingers.

'Mrs C? What is it?'

'Can't you hear…?'

'Hear what?'

'There! There it is again!'

Still huddled in her corner, Honora watched as her companions craned their necks in unison, heads held to one side as they strained to listen to something outside. Above the trundle of the wheels, snores of the sleeping man in the opposite corner and hollow clop of the horses' hooves, there was nothing Honora could make out and with a small shake of her head she was about to dismiss their alarm—until a faint sound made her pause.

'There! Shouting, following the coach!'

Mrs Croft's mouth sagged and even in the gloom of the carriage Honora could see she'd gone pale. Her own pulse skipped a fraction faster at the sight and faster still when she heard another indistinct cry roll across the fields hidden by the tatty curtain.

'It can't be. In this day and age?'

'You think—?'

'Don't you? On a darkened road, with nowhere to stop for miles around? Shouting for us to halt? What other explanation can there be? Oh, heaven save us!' The two older women clung to each other, some trace of their infectious fear beginning to creep in Honora's gut.

'What is it? What do you suspect is happening?'

Still clasping her friend's arm, the first woman leaned forward dramatically. 'The very worst, of course. Bandits, just as we described! Thieves! Men who would chase down a coach and pounce upon all inside!'

Mrs Croft gave a strangled gasp. 'I couldn't bear it, Mrs Norris! I'm sure my heart would give out if forced to suffer such indignity again and I can't spare a single guinea from my purse. Whatever will we do?'

Honora sat for a moment, thinking fast. The voice was definitely getting louder and as it grew clearer there was no mistaking its intent.

'He's telling the driver to stop the coach!' Mrs Norris's eyes were round and afraid, although it was Mrs Croft who seemed to suffer the most. She had a hand pressed to her mouth and stifled breaths came from behind it, loud but not enough to cover the new sound of a rapidly approaching horse.

'Hooves now! He's getting closer!'

All the commotion finally woke the lone male passenger. He sat up abruptly, rubbing his eyes, and looked around him with clear bewilderment.

'What's happening? Is something amiss?'

'Amiss? Amiss?' Mrs Croft seemed on the brink of hysteria, holding on to her friend with a vice-like grip. 'We are to be murdered where we sit, sir! Even now a highwayman is closing in on us, intent on who knows what harm—what are we to do?' The woman spoke wildly, all cold nosiness evaporated in her panic. 'I was half killed as a girl in this very situation…or might as well have been, so afraid was I for my life. Must we submit now like lambs to the slaughter?'

Still thinking, Honora glanced down at her own hand luggage, her mind coming to rest on a plan. For all Mrs Croft's shrilling she might just be right. The motives of the man who chased their coach were unlikely to be pure, the heavy hooves of his horse now sounding nearer than ever in the stillness of the night. How long until he drew alongside, forcing the driver to stop and then flinging open the door to threaten the passengers within? A swift glance around the cabin showed expressions of fear and confusion and from somewhere deep inside her Honora's courage rose.

'No,' she answered grimly. 'We won't be submitting to anyone. Not while I've breath in my body.'

She saw Mrs Norris's mouth open as if to reply, but before anyone could speak there came an almighty *thump* on the side of the coach—the unmistakable sound of a hand slapping against wood, making all four passengers jump. The deep voice came again from outside and Honora heard the driver call back, although the next moment the jingle of the coach horses' tack seemed to be slowing to a halt.

'Is he *stopping*?' The gentleman traveller cast about him incredulously, his eyes darting from one face to another. Probably he feared he would be expected to protect the ladies, Honora thought, a daunting task for a man who looked as though a stiff breeze might carry him off. 'Does he want us all to be taken by this madman?'

'Nobody will be taken tonight.' With steady hands Honora took up her reticule and reached inside, drawing out her flintlock with quiet purpose. Mrs Croft's jaw looked as though it might touch the floor as she watched Honora check the barrel and settle it comfortably in her palm, just as the coach shuddered to a final halt and for a moment there was silence, a taut window in which it seemed nobody dared to breathe—

And then came footsteps from outside.

Honora was on her feet before the door even opened, bursting through it just as the handle began to turn. The man on the other side stumbled back as she came barrelling out, holding the pistol in front of her and with one fluid, automatic motion bringing it round to point at his chest.

'Stop right where you—'

She broke off as she recognised the face gazing down at her from beneath an expensive hat, pale in the moonlight, but more familiar than any other.

'Isaac?'

Her heart ceased the frantic rhythm it had

been drumming against the bodice of her gown. For some measureless time it stood still, hanging immobile within the cage of her ribs, before springing back into life so sharply she might have winced.

'This is the second time you've pointed that thing at me. I'd rather it didn't become a habit.'

Honora simply stared up at him, not returning his uncertain smile. Her face had frozen into a rigid mask and her arms likewise, the flintlock still aimed at his fine black coat with no hope of her being able to lower it.

Her mind raced against itself behind the blank slate of her expression. Why had he chased after her carriage, scaring those within half to death— and then stand so calmly before her as though it were the most natural thing in the world, when only hours ago she'd sworn she would never look upon him ever again?

'Don't make jokes.' It was difficult to make her dry lips move, so stubbornly had the muscles tensed. 'What are you doing here?'

At her back she sensed the burning curiosity of more than one gaze, but she couldn't turn away from Isaac, the power of his dark eyes pinning her in place. A breathless mixture of joy and anger roiled inside her, each fighting for supremacy. Was she happy to see him, or bitter he hadn't allowed her a clean break? His face was the one she had ached for with every turn of the coach's wheels, but that didn't change the facts. He'd lied to her, taken her for a fool, and she'd meant it when she demanded he let her go.

'I'm not making jokes. My business here is deadly serious.' Carefully, Isaac reached out a hand and gently moved the barrel of the pistol aside. It gleamed mercilessly in the moonlight, silver and deadly, and at last Honora lowered it, placing the flintlock on a fencepost leaning to her left.

'And what business is that?'

Honora tried to keep her tone flat, but the quaver in her voice betrayed her. The very last thing she wanted was for Isaac to see his effect on her—pulse leaping, palms clammy, stomach alive with butterflies—when it was all in vain, her idea of what had once been between them now shattered beyond repair. 'What business can take you so far from home, running after a woman who has no desire to be caught?'

She thought she saw him grimace as though with a spasm of pain and equal shares of satisfaction and dismay flitted through her. He deserved to feel some measure of the agony he had caused her, yet she didn't want him to suffer, her damnably foolish love for him overcoming any wish for vengeance.

Isaac hesitated, throwing a glance over her head in the direction of the carriage. With one long stride he was beside the open door and with brisk finality closed it firmly in the rapt faces of the watching passengers inside.

'It's business that is between you and me, and you and me alone. I don't think it requires an audience.'

Honora didn't move. She felt him come closer, caught the faintest whisper of his unique, clean scent drifting on the night breeze to assail her once again and, once again, she was helpless. She ought to turn away and climb back into the carriage, to carry on her journey in search of refuge from Isaac's allure—but she couldn't. Until she knew why he was there, what he had come to say, she could no more flee from him than she could have walked all the way back to Somerset on foot.

'So?' She cast him a look out of the corner of her eye, refusing to meet his open gaze. 'What is it you have to tell me? What could be so important you would come all this way?'

Isaac made no answer. For a half-second she wasn't sure if he'd heard her, until he spoke in a voice that made her every nerve spring to life.

'I've come to beg forgiveness and, more than that, I've come to bring you home. Back to Marlow Manor where you belong, with the husband that loves you with a passion he can feel in his bones.'

Looking down at the scant form of his wife, Isaac could hardly tell what overcame him more: relief to be in her presence once again or admiration for that reckless courage he'd marvelled at since the day they met. Who *wouldn't* feel a gleam of wonder for a woman who leapt into the unknown, charging from the coach with no idea of what stood outside, but willing to face it regardless?

I must bring her back with me. There can be no meaning in life if I'm forced to live it without her.

She hadn't moved. Honora stood bathed in moonlight, her bonnet slightly askew and its shadow half concealing the planes of her face. Isaac had no way of knowing what thoughts lay beneath, or whether she had even listened to the declaration that had welled up from his soul— until she slowly shook her head.

'I don't believe you.'

With four short words she threw cold water over the glowing embers of Isaac's hopes and he braced himself against the instinct to let them smoulder to ash. Once he might have accepted that rejection—but that was before Charlotte's wisdom, far beyond her years, had finally shown him the right path.

Fight for her. I know the feelings we had between us were real, but I need to convince Honora, too.

'I know you don't. And I deserve every ounce of your suspicion and mistrust.' Isaac spoke baldly, giving himself nowhere to hide from the uncomfortable truth. 'I misled you and kept secrets from you that I never should have concealed. Every accusation, every thought of yours that I'm not worthy of your time—I'm guilty of them all. I have no defence.'

He shrugged, the empty-handed gesture of a man with nothing more to lose. What could ever hurt him more than knowing he had caused the woman he loved such pain? If he had to admit his flaws before a jury, he would. His foolish pride was worthless and he would list his faults if it meant Honora might pause, if only for a moment, to think twice on her resolve to leave.

'At first my aim was to protect Charlotte. Once I saw you would never harm her I resolved to tell you everything. A confession was on the very tip of my tongue until I realised you might despise me for my friendship with Frank, built on the very same vices you loathed in him. I couldn't bear to lose your good opinion, destroying along with it the family we had made—I thought to spare you pain, although now I see my silence caused it anyway. Since Charlotte was trespassed upon I resolved to cast off my former misdeeds and become a better person, both for her sake and my own, helped by your example.'

From somewhere in the darkness Isaac's horse gave a soft snort and he saw Honora's eyes flit across to it. She didn't look at him, however, and he could only wait with his blood roaring in his ears for her to find a reply.

'You still profess to love me, I suppose?' Her question was quiet, the doubt in it real and raw and enough to make him want to take her in his arms. 'And yet where was your love for me when you lied about Frank? You ought to have told me of your past behaviour, let me decide for myself whether you deserved a fresh start rather than conceal your similarities. I would have understood.'

She lifted her head, for the first time meeting his eye without flinching. There was some glimmer of the old fire, the dauntless nerve she'd shown him that first night in her rundown parlour, but alongside something else: sadness, disappointment—and the barest flicker of hope Isaac hardly dared believe he glimpsed before it was hidden away once again.

That tiny hint gave him all the bravery he needed to proceed. 'You're right. My friendship with Frank soured the moment I discovered he was the father of Charlotte's child and I was forced to recognise myself in his reflection. In truth, I wanted to kill him myself and may even have stooped so low if fate hadn't intervened on my behalf. I suppose I'll never know now how far I would have gone.'

He scuffed the frozen ground beneath his boots. Airing one's soul was a difficult business and the unwavering stare of his wife did nothing to make it any easier. The carriage still stood tall behind her and now the coachman was confident nobody was going to be shot he peered down questioningly at Honora.

'Are you boarding again, ma'am? Only I've places to be and this isn't one of them.'

For a long minute there was only the sound of a cold breeze through bare branches and the gentle snuffling of horses, and Isaac held his breath. Would Honora hold true to her word and flee from him again? Or maybe, just maybe, was there the smallest chance she might stay to hear him in full?

'No. I'd be grateful if you'd throw down my bag. I shan't go with you any further.'

A wave of relief swept over Isaac from head to toe as the coachman obliged, then another as with a click of his tongue the horses were set on their way. The carriage moved off into the gloom, growing more and more indistinct until only Isaac and Honora were left, standing at the side of the road like aimless ghosts.

'I wasn't sure you'd stay.'

'Neither was I.'

'I'm glad you did.'

Honora sighed deeply, as though it came from somewhere inside that never saw the light. 'More fool me, but for some reason I can't seem to tear myself away. How is it the only man I've ever truly loved is one I can hardly trust? I fear it, the workings of my own mind. I hardly know what to think.'

Isaac shook his head. That one word—*loved*—sent a pulse through him, a signal to every sinew to strain and want to cry out loud. If Honora still felt for him what she had before, wasn't there still the chance she might allow him back into her heart?

If you work for it. It would be a miracle, but even sinners can be granted a second chance.

'I understand and I have asked myself a similar question more than once. How is it the only woman *I've* ever loved is one who threatens me with a pistol whenever I make her angry? Not that I didn't deserve it this time. Under the circumstances I think you were quite restrained.'

Honora shot him a dark glance. 'My mercy only extends so far. Perhaps you ought to go on with your apology before I change my mind.'

She pulled her worn pelisse closer about her as the wind tugged at their clothes. Even in the faint light of the moon Isaac could see her face was set with cold and, screwing all his courage, he took a step closer.

'You're freezing.'

Her hands were bare, he'd noticed. She must have left her gloves on the coach. And with the sensation of taking a risky gamble he reached out to touch. Carefully, as gingerly as one might approach a wild bird, he took one small hand in his and chafed it, never taking his eyes from Honora's. He steeled himself for the moment she pulled away, trying to lessen its sting—but to his everlasting wonder it never came. She stood, gazing up into his downturned face, and the bleak chill of the night disappeared in a blaze of fire that snaked from that little hand to wrap around his heart.

'Honora.' Isaac's voice was low, hope and

yearning and hesitation stealing all its strength. 'At first my thoughts were only to preserve Charlotte's reputation, but for a long time since I realised the goodness of your spirit my desire was to save you pain. I wanted to tell you—tried to, in fact—but I couldn't bear to destroy the safe haven you thought you'd found. Further than that... I couldn't face the fact you might scorn me. Your good opinion is all I want, will ever want.' He swallowed, hard and painful, but the words choking him now with their bitter truth. 'Can I ask...is there even the smallest chance I might earn it back? If you returned with me to Marlow Manor, might you allow me the honour of trying each day to show myself worthy of your trust once more?'

He felt himself breathing, the uncanny awareness of even the smallest function of his own body. It was like being in a dream, within reality and yet separate from it, and so it was as if through a fog he watched Honora's gaze slide away from his own.

'You hurt me, Isaac.' She fixed her attention on their hands, fingers entwined now and Isaac never wanting to let go. 'Nothing can turn back time.'

'I know that. I'll never be able to erase what I did. But I promise you this: there will never be another secret between us. From this day, my thoughts are yours. Every concern, every desire, you'll know them all. I swear it.'

Honora turned her face away, but in the glimpse of her profile Isaac could have sworn he saw the most reluctant of tiny smiles. 'Know your every thought? That sounds more a punishment than a privilege. Am I never to have a moment's peace?'

'If you want it. You'll have plenty of time to consider your own on the ship to the Americas. I understand it's a long journey.'

She looked back at him sharply. 'What do you mean?'

'Don't you want to see your parents again? Heal the rift that Frank created between you? If I've learned anything, it's the importance of the people you love. Such a gift should be cherished.' Still holding her cold fingers, Isaac gently drew her nearer and with only the briefest of hesitations Honora came to him, her body close to his and the earth's axis tilting as Isaac felt crystal-pure relief pour over him like a stream. She was almost in his arms, a mere whisper away, and the urge to pull her into them shouted in his ear. 'I love you, Honora. What makes you happy makes me happy. For you to see your home again and repair the bonds you thought broken is my dearest wish—as well as to meet the people who sent such light into my life. I've everything to thank your parents for and I can think of no better way than face to face.'

The feeling of Honora's cheek coming to rest against his chest was one Isaac would never forget. The warmth of that simple touch flooded through linen and silk, swept aside wool and brocade, and lit the space beneath his ribs like sunshine after a storm. She was with him, her ear against the rapid thrum of his heart, and when his arms came up to seize her Honora did nothing to resist.

She held herself against him with her back straight and proud, not swooning or drooping beneath his kiss as many others might. Honora's lips met his and held their ground, giving no quarter even when his assault on them made her bite back a gasp. Her hand tore free of his grasp and moved to his neck, deft fingers stroking the short hair at his nape to stir feelings Isaac didn't know he could feel. It was a kiss, but more than that: it was a promise of sorts, using their bodies instead of words, a binding agreement that neither would abandon the other until their very last day.

In their embrace he was clay and she was the sculptor. She made him what he was and in the passion of their kiss neither one of them could spare a thought for what had gone before. Only the future seemed to matter, the path they would tread together, although as their breathing became short Honora smiled against Isaac's flushed lips.

'I never thought we'd do that again.'

'Didn't you?' Isaac ran a hand through his hair. Somewhere between the beginning of that kiss—that abandoned, wonderful, life-changing kiss—and the end he appeared to have lost his hat, but with Honora still trapped in his arms and his other hand firmly planted on the delightful curve of her hip it seemed an irrelevant detail. 'Not disappointed, I hope?'

'I'm not sure.' Honora reached up to trace the outline of Isaac's lips and he felt himself curve against her, his longing for her needing no speech to make it plain. 'Perhaps we ought to try again to make sure.'

'Do you think you could stand it?'

'Possibly.' She smiled and it was the most beautiful thing Isaac had ever seen, the answer to every question he might ever have. 'We've a lifetime to decide, just as you've a lifetime to prove yourself worth my while. I'm sure between us Charlotte and I can mould you into the perfect man.'

Isaac's mouth curved. 'That's a daunting prospect, but one I humbly accept I deserve. When will this moulding commence, do you think?'

'Why, at once, of course. Shall we go home and begin?'

* * * * *

MILLS & BOON

Coming next month

CHRISTMAS WITH THE EARL
Sophia James

She liked talking to Christopher Northwell more than she had ever enjoyed talking to anyone. He was quick and interesting and solid.

Solid?

A strange word to use for a person, but it was what he *was*. The Earl of Norwich wasn't shallow or small-minded or petty. He was a man who could be depended on—a man who had backed her up in difficult circumstances and had not expected anything at all in return.

The kiss they had shared came to mind, and she wished he might simply lean forward and take her into his arms again, as he had yesterday. The small jolt of a thrill seared through her and she looked at him, hoping he would not recognise in her face what she felt all over her body. God, she had always been so frigid, so stand-offish, so reluctant to endure touch—and yet here she was, burning like a candle with sheer and utter want.

The star in her hand was warming…a small gift perfectly given. She would hang it above her bed tonight and watch to see how the moonlight altered each prism.

The glass star…the Christmas bouquet. Her chamber would be turning into an altar of worship for the season and she was welcoming it. Just as she was welcoming Christopher Northwell—although today he gave no impression of wanting anything more than just talk, and his stance was decidedly formal.

'My father may not at first be…easy company, but if you would allow him the time to adjust and get used to your ways I am sure he will relax.'

'My aunt once knew your mother, so perhaps that might help?'

'It might.'

He gave the words back as if he felt it would be the exact opposite, and such uncertainty resulted in a rare silence between them.

He was not telling her everything—she was sure of it. She had heard gossip in Society which stressed that the Duke and his only offspring did not get along. She had heard it said too that Christopher Northwell was wild and undisciplined. And yet she had never seen one glimpse of that side of him. If anything he seemed always in control, and he was indisputably logical.

Nothing quite added up.

Continue reading
CHRISTMAS WITH THE EARL
Sophia James

Available next month
www.millsandboon.co.uk

COMING SOON!

We really hope you enjoyed reading this book.
If you're looking for more romance, be sure to
head to the shops when new books are
available on

Thursday 29th October

To see which titles are coming soon, please visit
millsandboon.co.uk/nextmonth